a Lucky Strike for GOD
AND OTHER STORIES

~Karen Pietkiewicz~

a Lucky Strike for GOD
AND OTHER STORIES

~Karen Pietkiewicz ~

Mosaic Press
Oakville, On. - Buffalo, N.Y.

Canadian Cataloguing in Publication Data

Pietkiewicz, Karen, 1938-
  A lucky strike for God and other stories

ISBN   0-88962-588-3

I. Title.

PS8581.I47L8 1995   C813'.54   C95-931465-2
PR9199.3.P54L8   1995

No part of this book may be reproduced or transmitted in any form, by any means, electronic or mechanical, including photocopying and recording information storage and retrieval systems, without permission in writing from the publisher, except by a reviewer who may quote brief passages in a review.

Published by MOSAIC PRESS, P.O. Box 1032, Oakville, Ontario, L6J 5E9, Canada. Offices and warehouse at 1252 Speers Road, Units #1&2, Oakville, Ontario, L6L 5N9, Canada and Mosaic Press, 85 River Rock Drive, Suite 202, Buffalo, N.Y., 14207, USA.

Mosaic Press acknowledges the assistance of the Canada Council, the Ontario Arts Council, the Ontario Ministry of Culture, Tourism and Recreation and the Dept. of Canadian Heritage, Government of Canada, for their support of our publishing programme.

Copyright © Karen Pietkiewicz, 1995

Cover and book design by Susan Parker
Printed and bound in Canada
ISBN   0-88962-588-3

In Canada:
MOSAIC PRESS, 1252 Speers Road, Units #1&2, Oakville, Ontario, L6L 5N9, Canada. P.O. Box 1032, Oakville, Ontario, L6J 5E9
In the United States:
MOSAIC PRESs, 85 River Rock Drive, Suite 202, Buffalo, N.Y., 14207
In the UK and Western Europe:
DRAKE INTERNATIONAL SEVICES, Market House, Market Place, Deddington, Oxford. OX15 OSF

Table of Contents

The Chicken Dinner 1
A Lucky Strike for God 13
The Cricket 89
Rachel and the Night Child 97
The System 105
The Conversion of Terrence McPhee 141
Maudie 149
The Boy Who Wished to be God 157
The Book House 163
Mr. Brown's Legacy 181
Counting to Ten: Michael 195

The Chicken Dinner

Carl was late again. It was happening with increasing frequency these days; Brenda had begun to notice this in August. Either it was the ball team, or a beer, or the used car he bought to fix up. He seemed to be spending vast amounts of time on his car, always with the excuse that he wanted it on the road 'before the snow flies'.

He didn't call as often as he used to either. Sometimes during her lunch hour the phone didn't ring at all. Lately she had taken to waiting until just before one, and if he hadn't called her, she would call him before he started working again. But lately Carl was never there on his lunch hours.

It was getting to be like with Tim before the final break-up; Brenda had begun to feel the familiar fingers of anxiety creeping down her throat, tightening her chest and squeezing her heart like a crushed bird caught in some cold, inescapable grip. But all Tim wanted was sex: Carl is different. Having thus reassured herself, Brenda returned to the preparation of her meal.

The phone rang. Brenda jumped, and raced across the room.

He wasn't coming.

KAREN PIETKIEWICZ

Now Brenda hung up the phone, placing it carefully in its black cradle. Suddenly drained, she dropped limply on a kitchen chair. The pots perked and bubbled happily on the range; the timer on the oven signaled that the roast was finished. She rose, turned off the oven and turned down the bubbling pots. She had made enough food for a week.

Leftovers.
Brenda stared at the primly sealed Tupperware, bulging with condensation from the hot, contained food. Potatoes, beef roast, buttered carrots: leftovers. She felt again the tightening in her chest: pictured her heart, still beating, sealed in pink Tupperware. Quickly she put the warm food in the refrigerator and closed the door.

It was a long, dull evening. Brenda watched 'Three's Company'. She felt tears in her eyes when Jack rejected the fat brunette in favor of the stacked blonde. After all, the brunette had a nicer personality, even if she was fat. She was glad Jack felt guilty. He should. She felt vindicated when Jack accepted his blind date, and disregarded the fat, even if it were only for an evening. You never could tell, thought Brenda. He could really get to like her.
Now, as Brenda watched the sitcom couple enjoying their romantic dinner for two, she remembered her own once hot dinner chilling in the fridge. Abruptly she shut off the set and sat staring at her barren table.

Tuesday morning the office was hectic. Most of the orders had come in late; letters of explanation had to be typed and sent out. The fluorescent room was sullen with the sound of angry keyboards. Time dragged. Finally, it was noon.
Brenda took her small lunch and went out to the employees' area. She chose a quiet corner, out of the way, and didn't look up when the pool girls came in. This way they didn't join her, and she was glad. She took out the magazine with the chicken on the front.

THE CHICKEN DINNER

"Chicken Supreme", it read. There sat the chicken, glazed and shining and surrounded by small sugared grapes still on the stems. The drumsticks had paper fringes; the vegetables were awash in melting hunks of butter and the dinner rolls steamed from under the crisp linen wrapper.

She would make "Chicken Supreme" for Carl. He had always liked chicken. She would tell him how special it would be, and he would come. He always came for chicken. She could never recall his having missed a chicken dinner.

Brenda finished her lunch and headed back to her desk. The rest of the girls were still eating and she had the office to herself. She would call Carl. Usually she didn't dare call during his work hours. But he wouldn't mind when he heard about the dinner. A meal like that takes special preparation. It was necessary she know for sure in advance.

The phone rattled at the other end of the line.

"Systems International."

"Carl?"

"Oh. Hi." It was Brenda of course. He knew he should have called.

"Did you eat your lunch yet?"

Brenda seemed to be preoccupied with food lately. Carl felt aloof, hostile, and guilty all at the same time.

"Yeah. Yeah, I just finished," he replied, trying to sound like his old, interested self.

"So, how was your evening?", Brenda asked, predictably.

"Okay. It was okay. We got everything finished. We finished about eight." The minute he said it he knew it was a mistake.

"You should have called me. I could have warmed up the food."

Brenda began as he knew she would, the irritating whine beginning to seep into her voice.

"I couldn't call. Bob was only in overnight; I didn't want to just walk out on him. So we went out for a bite after." Carl shot that one in quickly.

"You could have brought him here," Brenda began, launching the attack. "You could have both come over to eat, then we could have watched a movie. There was plenty; you know I always make plenty." Her voice trailed off, and Carl could feel the old guilt creeping in. On it would go. Carl hated these conversations; hated the feeling he was feeling, the wanting to hang up the phone, to get in the car, to just get out, out of range of the begging, whining voice whose pathetic logic about missed meals and forgotten phone calls he could never seem to placate.

"I guess I could have. I will the next time. For sure." That should help, he thought. He waited.

"So did you go out after?"

She was back again. Back with the questions, back with her way of always peeling off the lid where Carl kept hidden what he knew to be true: that he was bored with Brenda, bored of her voice, her ever hopeful face, her now familiar, soft, shapeless body and her neverending meals. He felt like he was being buried up with food.

"We went to the late show." That would fix her.

"Oh."

Carl recognized the familiar silence he knew was coming, waited for it to end.

"What did you see?" Brenda began again. She never quit. She just never quit.

"You wouldn't have liked it."

"I may have. What did you see?" Her voice was bright.

"Porn. It was porn." Carl listened to himself lie as though he were eavesdropping on a stranger.

"Oh."

More silence.

Carl broke. "How's about I drop by tomorrow. I'll bring a pizza." He couldn't stand the silences. They were worse than the whine.

"Oh. Well, actually, that's what I was calling about, about Wednesday." Brenda's voice escalated. "I thought I would take the afternoon off and make a really special meal for you, to make up for the one you missed."

More food. Carl began to feel it all again.

"Yeah. Sure," he rang out enthusiastically, hating himself.

THE CHICKEN DINNER

"Want to know what I'm making?"

Here it comes. The Big Whammer, Carl thought, waiting.

"Chicken Supreme", Brenda announced over the phone like it was the second coming of Christ.

"Great. I like chicken." It was all he could say. He could feel himself drifting away, floating off in space while his hand, still holding the phone to his ear, twitched convulsively. He could see himself seated at the desk still talking and nodding while he watched safely from the furthest corner of the ceiling.

"So I'll see you Wednesday, okay? Don't be late!"

Carl fell into himself with a thunk, just in time to answer, "Right. See ya Wednesday."

The phone clicked off, and it was over.

Carl sat staring at the phone. Then he plunged into the stack of papers on his desk with a fury. The next time he looked up it was four. He left early; at the station the smoke shop was out of papers. This was a first for four o'clock. Carl flowed onto the train and settled into his seat. A girl with good legs sat across from him. Carl stared at the legs absently until the girl gave him a look and shifted the other way around.

She had nice tits, too. Too much make-up, but nice tits. Carl stole a glance at the front of the girl's blouse while she was reading to see if he could see where the nipples were. They weren't there. Probably she had those flat kind, the spread-out kind he didn't like. Redheads had flat nipples most of the time. He avoided redheads for that reason.

Carl thought of Brenda's nipples. They weren't bad. At first they were great.

Thinking of Brenda's nipples brought the phone call flooding back. Suddenly the subway seemed unbearable. Carl exited at the next stop. On the street, in the fresh air, the crowds were thinning. A few stragglers scurried down the steps to the waiting trains below.

Carl went into Chatters and ordered a beer. He thought about the evening before. The show had been Bob's idea, not his. Bob was a Bo Derek fan. "Now there's a set of tits," he'd said, and on the way home he'd asked Carl half a dozen times, "Wouldn't you like to get into That!", or, "Wouldn't you like to crack that package!" and, "Jesus! What an ass!" and, "Did you see that stomach!" and on and on; how he'd lick the honey off her any old day, and how they were really going at it right on the screen, and, "God Damn!" What do you think it'd be like to be a cameraman with *that* goin' on right in front of you! You wouldn't walk straight for a week!", he'd said, and the next thing Carl knew they were at the hotel where Bob disappeared up the steps two at a time, waved and was gone, and Carl was alone.

Carl sipped at his beer. Bob was like that, Carl thought, he'd fuck a snake if he could hold it still.

Carl thought of Bo Derek fucking. Nothing. She didn't do a thing for him. He tried to recall the fuck scene, how she hung on to the guy, her blonde hair trailing, her vacant blue eyes staring into space like a doll. All he could think of was how stupid she looked, her head hanging over the edge of the bed like some third rate porn flick with her long throat stretched out. He examined himself thoroughly, even probing into the deepest part of his secrets where he searched to see if maybe he was just acknowledging what he knew to be true: that she wouldn't look twice at him, not even once would she look. But he didn't give a damn. She was an airhead. Who wants to fuck an airhead? Except Bob.

Now the other one was different; the dark haired one with the smile, and the happy eyes. She'd be a fun fuck. Carl thought about the cute brunette with the dimples and sexy accent. He tried to think of how her body had been in the film, but he couldn't remember. All he could remember was her happy face and how happy the guy from Scotland looked when he was getting ready to fuck her. They looked like they were going to have a great time. A real fun fuck. And that's what he wanted, Carl suddenly realized, a fuck that was fun.

But it wasn't going to be with Brenda. Brenda was definitely not fun to fuck.

The girl came by and Carl ordered another Light. She was nothing , Carl thought as she moved off with the tray. And she had the same fake smile Brenda had stuck on her

THE CHICKEN DINNER

face lately. "Okay here?", she had said, with the bright fake smile, as if she really cared whether or not he ordered anything or even dropped dead on the table before her eyes.

Carl slumped back in the booth, feeling dully the beer that was beginning to seep into his limbs. His eyes followed the waitress from table to table, but his thoughts were stuck on Brenda. He thought of how it had been at first, when he had been eager to be with her; when he went over right after work; when he didn't even think of his friends and his car sat in pieces in the back yard, waiting. He thought of how it had been then with her: how she had been shy; bashful almost, and how flattered he'd felt by it all, showing her the ropes. She'd been trusting: loving and vulnerable. Carl felt as though she had been waiting just for him. It had been heady stuff; all through late winter and into spring they were together. They'd ski, and afterwards she'd fix something to eat at her place, and after that, they would watch the late show then go to bed and screw half the night. Sometimes he didn't get home until four, but he still made it to work on time, and he felt great. Carl could remember how he'd sit at his desk and think up things to do in bed and how he'd try and get Brenda to come round to it.

By then he'd discovered that Brenda wasn't much for innovation. Basically, she was the classic nice girl. Carl remembered times when he felt guilty after he'd done a few things she didn't really like. That's when he'd first noticed the hopeful look on her face. The look he'd grown to hate, he suddenly realized, as he upended the second beer.

Brenda spent Tuesday evening baking. She made the sweet rolls and the pie crust in advance. She cut up the bread for the stuffing. She practiced sugaring grapes. Later, she curled up on the couch with the new Cosmo and ate the grapes she had practiced on. She read the Starscope: it looked good. Then she read the Agony column.

Things were starting to swing back the other way now. She could tell by the questions. And there were a few on herpes. People weren't so heavy into sex and technique anymore. She was glad. There was even an article entitled, 'How to Win Your Man the Old Fashioned Way', and she settled in to read it. About ten she began to get restless. She recognized that she was hoping Carl would call. When he hadn't called by 11:00 she could feel herself wanting to call him. But she didn't call him. Instead, she forced herself to go to bed. She was glad to have read the article. It gave her strength. Calling him was one of the things you just don't do.

Wednesday was the day. Brenda got up early and set the table. This was in case Carl came by directly after work. One of the things a man likes to see is a set table. It makes him feel like he won't have to wait long to eat. It also would make her look efficient and in control. The article had a lot of good points.

Brenda brought the recipe to work. She showed the girls the Chicken and explained how to do the grapes. Joanne had asked, "So are you getting your ring for Christmas?", and Brenda had wiggled the fingers of her left hand, and said, "Could be, you never know!", and they had all cheered. Barb had said, "Go for the gold!", and all the girls laughed. Brenda felt good all morning. At noon she dashed home, put the chicken in the oven on cook control. It was still early, so she went out shopping. She pulled in and parked in front of the Dream Shoppe.

Everything was on sale; probably they were clearing stock to make way for Christmas. Brenda sifted through a bin of bikini underwear, but decided against them. They weren't all that comfortable and no one ever really got to see them, except taking them off and putting them on, which was hardly worth the price. She turned to the rack of Bedtime Treats. They had some black, and many more white lace things with red trim: little G-strings with patches in strategic places, some hearts, and some with playboy bunnies complete with ears. They had a His 'n Hers set. The man's thing was like a pouch with an embroidered bunny face and white satin ears lined in red. Actually, it looked ridiculous. She couldn't imagine any man wearing it, much less Carl. They had bra things with

THE CHICKEN DINNER

holes in the end for the nipples to stick out, and crotchless panties. But it was all too obvious. She settled on a beautiful pink nightgown with a matching peignoir, trimmed in marabou. It cost a fortune. As the clerk was wrapping it up Brenda thought: this will be for 'dessert'; she could feel her face flush at the thought of it.

On the way back to the car she stopped in the jewelry shop and bought two beautiful crystal wine glasses from the display beside the rings.

Carl worked through his lunch so he could leave again at four. He'd been doing this often lately; it kept some of the weight off. He had considered joining a health club and stopped in for a trial session, but it was staffed with young studs complete with bulging biceps and bronzed, gleaming bodies. He felt completely out of place.

Lately he had begun to wonder just where the hell his life was going to, and the trip to the health club hadn't helped any. Everywhere it seemed he saw gorgeous women on the arms of really in control types of guys carrying racquet ball racquets: or couples screaming by on bikes, real power machines, and always the girl was clad in black leather that stretched maddeningly over a tight, trim ass, while her arms encircled the driver's waist, hands clasped below the belt. He'd begun to notice every woman around, and wonder what it would be like with them, and whether they'd like it. At times like this, he never thought of Brenda at all.

Actually, it was only when he was getting ready to go over that he could bear to think of her, or when she called, which she did more and more frequently as of late, so when he got home the first thing he did was to take the phone off the hook.

He took his clothes off and threw them over the chair. If Brenda were here she'd hang them up. First with the Look, of course. He looked at his pants draped over the chair with a perverse sense of satisfaction, and lay down on the unmade bed. The clock read 5:15. He should be showering. Instead he lay there thinking of Brenda. He knew: she wanted to get married. He'd thought about it; at first he'd thought about it all the time. It was nice having someone who cared. It was nice having his meals cooked, and a regular oil change instead of cruising the bars. He'd liked it all, at first. She was the kind of girl you should marry. It wasn't that he liked anyone else that way. He just didn't like Brenda that way. Not any more.

He wanted out.

Carl lay on the bed staring at the ceiling. He felt ugly, and guilty. He could see Brenda's face break, the tears begin. He could see her shoulders hunch together, and shake, like they did when she turned her back and cried. He hated it, hated when she cried like that; and he hated himself worse when he gave in and took her back in his arms. Her arms would reach up around his neck and she would sob and shake in his arms, and cry on the front of his shirt and leave make-up stains. At times like that he almost wanted to kill her; to run out of the apartment and never come back, but always he just stood there holding her, saying it'd be okay, things would be okay. And then they were always okay for awhile, and that was what was so wrong: that's all it was anymore. Okay.

He'd just have to tell her outright. He wanted out. And if she started to cry, let her cry. He wasn't getting sucked in by that again. He would tell her tonight. After dinner. That was the whole trouble. Carl thought, as he headed into the bathroom and turned on the shower. He wasn't going to dinner, he was the dinner. But not after tonight. Tonight was the last chicken dinner.

Brenda listened for the bell. As an afterthought she raced out of the bedroom and took the safety chain off the door so Carl could use his key. She pulled the curlers out of her hair and threw them into the bottom drawer and pulled the brush through the rolls of bobbing hair. Then she grabbed her dress off the bed and threw it over her head, but not before she put a Kleenex between her lips. That was an old trick she remembered from her mother, back in the old lipstick days. Now all that was back. Even the earrings were getting bigger. Brenda gingerly pushed the posts of her ear-

THE CHICKEN DINNER

rings through her ears. The bigger earrings had been making her ears tender and sore from the weight.

Not bad. Brenda looked in the mirror. She dabbed on perfume behind each ear and on each wrist. Not too much for dinner. Then she took the pink gown out of the box and lay it enticingly over the bed just as the bell rang.

"Carl?"

"Yeah. It's me."

Brenda kicked the empty box under the bed and raced to open the door.

Three weeks later, Carl Ferris hunched over the pay phone outside of his office.

"Sylvia?" he asked, a bright lilt to his voice. "It's me, Carl. Is everything still on for tonight?" Sylvia had been the shy type; he had had to work on her for the past two weeks to get her to go out, and he was still afraid that she might pull out at the last minute.

"Sure," said, the soft voice on the line. "I'm looking forward to it."

She was going. Carl felt his chest fill.

"So I'll pick you up about six-thirty," he said softly into the receiver pressed between his shoulder and his ear, "Bye-bye."

He hung up the phone.

"Whew!" said Carl, right out loud. Then he pulled out his sunglasses and slid them over his ears. "She's a real sweetie," he said to himself as he stepped briskly off the curb. "Nice tits, too."

He could hardly wait to show her all the ropes.

* * *

A Lucky Strike For God

"Run on down to Crandall's and get your daddy a pack of Lucky's, now, will you, eh?" The man folded a one dollar bill into a tight square and placed it in the palm of his daughter's small hand. "That's thirty-two cents. You ask old Mrs. Crandall to make you one of your daddy's special ice creams, and then get your old daddy a sack of those pink mints that he likes. Now, have you got that?" He looked over his dime store glasses and down into the child's eyes.

"Now go on. Run!"

The small girl turned and skipped out the door, letting the screen slam behind her.

Virgil Mallon lit up his last cigarette and drew from it.

He unrolled a blueprint of some sort, adjusted his glasses, and began to work on the cluttered kitchen table.

"Aris?" A woman's shrill voice came in through the screened door. "Aris? Are you in there? It's me, Madge..."

The man continued to work. After a minute, footsteps gritched in the cinder drive, faded, and disappeared.

The morning wore on tediously; the man bent over the still curling scroll, a hard lead pencil in his right hand. He reached for the cigarette package on the far end of the table and tapped it twice. It was empty.

"Jesus Christ," said Virgil Mallon, and returned to work.

The girl finally came home.

"Where the hell've you *been*?" the man queried gently, while making a silly face at his small daughter, "to Spain and back?"

The girl carefully took the cigarettes out of the small brown paper sack and handed them to her father.

"I thought you'd died and gone to heaven," the man added, wiggling his eyebrows up and down as he removed the cellophane wrapper and peeled back the tinfoiled top of the pack. "Your daddy almost had a nicotine fit!"

The girl watched as her father lit the cigarette, drew in, and exhaled the spume of smoke.

"Now let me tell you something, sweetie," the man said, leaning close to the little girl, "don't you ever do what your daddy's doing. These here are coffin nails. Your daddy's tried to quit a hundred times, and he can't do it."

The man was smoking steadily now, pencil on the table, the work pushed to one side.

"My father was a boxer, that's what he was," Mallon began. "That would be your granddaddy. Did you know that?"

The girl stood listening to her father, watching him puff away.

"He was a bare-fist boxer," Virgil Mallon pronounced, "He never smoked in his life."

The girl poured four hard round pink mints out on the table and began to line them up like hockey pucks along the metal edge of the table.

"My father told me if I made it to twenty-one I would never smoke," said her father, starting up again. "but I got hooked in Rochester, working construction. That was before I met your mother."

Now Virgil Mallon stared out straight ahead, no longer looking at the child. "She doesn't like smoke."

Abruptly, he stubbed out the remnants of the cigarette, leaving only a smear of ash.

A LUCKY STRIKE FOR GOD

The girl took the mints from the table one by one and dropped them in her shirt pocket, then turned and went outside.

It was late morning. A car pulled into the driveway and a woman got out. She was carrying a paper sack filled with groceries from Mingey's grocery, and was heading toward the house next door. An older, grey haired woman appeared on the back porch, descended, took the sack in one of her arms. Pulling herself back up the weathered steps by means of a lead pipe railing affixed to the side of the house, the older woman took the groceries inside. The younger woman returned to the car, grabbed more groceries, and followed, a filled sack in each arm. When she came back out, she was followed by the older woman, who held a child in her sagging arms.

"What time do you want her?" Aris Mallon's mother untangled the child's fist from her hair.

"If you could keep her until about noon, it'd be better. I was sick today."

"Whatever you like, Aris." The older woman turned and went back inside, while her daughter closed the car door and moved toward the smaller house that shared the common drive.

Virgil heard the back door open, and slam shut again. He looked up.

"Is that you, Dearie?" he reached out to his wife in a careful, sing-song voice. The man had stopped working as the dark haired woman appeared before him.

"Did you bring us something for supper?" There was no reply. The woman had begun to empty the paper sacks on the cluttered bake unit. "What'd ya get for us, dearie?" Mallon began again. "Something more than chicken this time? You can only eat so many chickens." He was looking up, a hopeful, good-natured smile on his face.

KAREN PIETKIEWICZ

Virgil Mallon was older than his wife, and there were three long creases slowly deepening in his forehead. As he spoke to Aris, his glasses hung off the end of his nose, and he peered over them in an exaggerated manner.

"Did'ja get me some turnips, Dearie?" he tendered again, as though a conversation were actually taking place. "Did'ja remember to get your old lover some turnips?"

"I got your turnips," the woman said, emphasizing the "got".

Aris Mallon now folded the empty grocery sacks, pushing the accumulation on the counter back toward the wall to make room. She began to move about in the L-shaped kitchen add-on, opening doors and shoving things into the disordered, bulging cupboards.

Although she was substantially overweight, Aris Mallon was attractive in a compelling sort of way. Her skin was strong and her lipstick complimented the high color in her cheeks. Her brunette hair, rich and thick, was permed and becomingly waved around her face. She wore a cotton flowered housedress, piped along the neckline and down the front to where the rose-colored buttons pulled the fabric taut over her stomach. The sleeves of the dress, short and cuffed, capped her upper arms, which tapered somewhat disproportionately to a smaller forearm, and even smaller hands. She wore wedge-heeled shoes, wedgies, as they were then called, and thin, white ankle-socks, rolled down at the cuff.

But it was not Aris Mallon's shape, or even her clothing that defined her. Rather, she seemed to have a certain repressed and smoldering temperament that flicked in and out of her eyes at unguarded moments. Her arms, as her legs, were marked with dark spots where the mosquitoes had often fed, and she had a habit of holding her hands, fists clenched, across the front of her stomach when she stood. On the occasion when she perched on the chrome kitchen stool, or sat with her legs crossed, she had a way of twitching her right toe up and down, up and down.

Now, as if in anticipation of some familiar scene, she seemed keyed to record each subtle nuance that she perceived to be passing between her husband and herself. To this attention the man instinctively responded, sending out more verbal feelers. For Aris Mallon was capable of instant and devastating reactions. Thus Virgil proffered and withdrew, proffered and withdrew, waiting to see which side of his wife would present itself to him this time. His queries, carefully framed in lighthearted little volleys of attempted humour or exaggerated terms of endearment, were designed to elicit some satisfactory response to which he could attach himself. Sometimes when Virgil's cautious but hopeful little forays were rejected, as they usually were, he would resort to awkward displays of physical affection, as though, perhaps, Aris could not hear.

Now he rose and moved toward where his wife stood packing the Saltines onto an already overstuffed shelf. Jocularly, he put his hands on her hips, and bent to kiss her neck.

"Haveya got a little kiss for your ol' Virgil, haveya?", he suggested, adopting a loosened grammar as he reached about her waist.

The woman quickly twisted and withdrew, hissing an uncomfortable comment about the open door.

Her husband, stung, returned to the table, his mood visibly changed.

2.

Virgil Mallon now lit up and drew deeply, staring out over the room. His elbow rested on the coffee-splotched table, the cigarette in his hand. His fingers were deeply stained with nicotine, the nails chewed to permanent stubs; his glasses hung inappropriately from his face like some comic charade.

But it had not always been like this, for when Virgil Mallon was a young man his eyes were clear and steady. His hair, now beginning to grey, had been richly black, and, except for two uncontrollably stray locks, was worn swept back from his brow. He was well groomed, and careful in his appearance. Occasionally flamboyant in dress, he was handsome in a powerful, energetic way. He was a natural storyteller, possessed an ebullient nature and a gifted tongue, and often, his own laughter rang out the loudest and the longest at the tales he himself told. Yet there was inside him a hidden core that could only now and then be seen: a wrinkle of expression between the brows, a distant vision hidden in his blue eyes.

When Virgil Mallon spoke it was often of the early days in Widham. There, in the small village of Southern Ontario, he was called *Fitter*, an aberration from the *Fisher* of his youth, for he was a wonderful swimmer and diver. He would climb to the top of the limestone cliffs near his home, on which hung the spectacular nests of the great fisher birds. There, he would watch as they plunged from their tightening gyres, claws outreached for the unsuspecting fish. And so it was with Virgil. Climbing again and again to his aerie high above the Gagawong River, he, too, would execute consecutively perfect dives throughout the long, hot summer afternoons, cutting the water with a single slice, leaving a single spreading circle. Often he would disappear completely in the swiftly flowing water, to surface beneath the overhang of some far bank. He became a trout, finning in place, nose to the current. From there, he watched his friends on the other side gather to search the surface, hands shielding their squinting eyes from the unyielding sun. At other times he would let the current take him beneath the bridge, where, pulling himself up on the girders, he would climb to the arching top and quietly wait while they looked for him.

On one such hot summer day Virgil had challenged a passing young man, a local trumpeter known for his strong lungs. Together they dove from the overhanging cliffs; the young man surfaced, but Virgil did not. And when the worried youths spotted him at last upon the silver span of the bridge downstream, he laughed and took flight once more, arms outspread, skin glittering in the sun. The metamorphosis complete, he compacted himself into a single point above the water, disappeared, and swam upstream, to surface at the very feet of his concerned friends.

A LUCKY STRIKE FOR GOD

"Fitter, you're a bastard, you know that, don't you?" said the most courageous of the worried young men on the shore. "One of these days you're going to break your neck."

"Howson," said Fitter Mallon, "you only have to know two things: how to go down, and when to come up. That's all there is to it."

And Fitter knew how to go down. He was twenty-one years old when the Depression came crashing over his head. Out the window went his youthful dreams of building the beautiful summer homes that had been springing up like mushrooms on the hundreds of islands in Georgian Bay, and off went Virgil Mallon, thumb outstretched, heading for Syracuse.

For the next four years Virgil picked up what he could working sawmills and doing rough carpentry. A single man, he required less; a Canadian working in the States, he took cash, and less than his due in return for the work offered. Finally, he landed a stretch in a finishing mill where he learned to operate every machine in the place. When the mill work finally ran out, he hopped a freight to Rochester, where he pounded the streets for odd jobs: a roof to be done, a sagging porch to be reinforced. He found work because he was a hard worker, capable, and fast. His jovial good nature and vivid imagination were embellished by stories he picked up riding the boxcars, or sleeping beneath thestars; these stories he related with flourish to the men who hired him. Accordingly, he was often a dinner guest in the very homes where he worked. In four years he was never out of a job for more than a day at a time.

On those days of freedom, Fitter Mallon took his fly rod in hand, shouldered his wicker creel and headed for the branching streams that tumbled through the wooded, low-lying hills. By this time he had managed to buy an older Ford pick-up; upon reaching the chosen stream, he would open the small door of the glove compartment where he kept a vice, a pair of scissors, and a paper sack filled with rooster hackles, marabou feathers, and assorted threads and twines. He would clamp the vice on the springy door, and tie his own flies, to be spun through the air, reel clicking, thumb controlling the line.

Then up the stream he would move, wading the holes, sometimes skirting along the brushed path on the bank, walking the narrow trace of the other fishermen before him. After each strike, he would gut the responsive but unfortunate fish, wiping his blade on the damp green grass. Lining the creel with cool, fresh, grass, he would carefully set the fish inside, and continue up the stream until he had seven trout. The magic number reached, he was back in town, offering the succulent repast to his latest employer and like as not joining the feast.

In the fall of his twenty-sixth year Virgil Mallon headed West. Crossing the border at Niagara, he hauled his truck up the two lane roads toward Sudbury and turned left on Queen's Highway 17.

It was late afternoon when Virgil pulled into a small settlement just East of Sault Ste. Marie. There was a roadside diner off to his left. It was of log construction surrounded by some maples, a stand of yellowing aspen, and several large spruce trees. The diner was set back off the main highway, and there was a gravel road beside it that led down to the water. The place appealed to Virgil and he pulled in for his supper. After, the sun still warm, he backed down the rough, boulder-strewn road to the edge of Lake George.

There, he slid the gear shift into neutral, pulled the handbrake, shut off the motor and stepped out of the truck. The air was clean and crisp, heavy with the rich scent of evergreens, and the living smell of water. A small wave rolled in and splashed against the few scattered boulders at the water's edge, while a wash of smaller ripples lapped at the sand shore. Virgil tugged at the crotch seam of his pants, kicked out with each leg, and stretched. He walked to the cooling water, cupped both his hands together, and scooped up double handfuls which he splashed over his face and down his neck, scrubbing his skin with his hands. He shook his head, ran his wet hands through his hair, pulled it back into place.

A LUCKY STRIKE FOR GOD

He went over to the side view mirror of his truck, bent down, jutted out his chin and inspected the lightly emerging shadow on his face and neck. Satisfied for the time being, he stood for a minute and looked at the water. Then he reached in and brought out a guitar that had been wedged between the seat and the dash. Moving around to the back of the truck, he clambered up into the box, balanced his suitcase on the jumble of his tools and possessions, and sat where he could face the breaking waves. The instrument spread out his knees, Virgil Mallon began to play.

For music was bred in his bone. Virgil had spent years listening through a closed door to his father, who stood before the east facing window of the upstairs bedroom where he alone slept and played strange, haunting music on his worn violin. Once when Virgil had risen very early to fish in the predawn light, he had looked back and seen his father standing in that very window. The silhouetted form of the distant old man was imprisoned by a narrow, gothic arch of tapered sandstone window blocks that were set in the facade of the small brick house. His father had stood behind the lace curtains and played and played, an ethereal pattern of light and dark puzzling his face and limbs. The next day and for many other days after that, Virgil had crept up the narrow, polished stairwell and peered through the keyhole at the man that was his father. The horsehair bow frayed and flailing, the old man's body keened and davened with each impassioned note.

When Virgil Mallon was old enough to work, he saved what little money he could and bought a used guitar. Soon dissatisfied with merely strumming chords, he took to playing with finger picks and a steel bar, Hawaiian-style, as it was then called. Interspersed between the plucked strings and the clear tenor of Virgil's fine voice, the descant of high wailing notes reflected the tremolo of his father's strings, the adagio of his poised and trembling wrist.

Now, alone in his old truck, Virgil Mallon played and played. A light breeze trifled with the calm lake as the sun began its descent to the shimmering rim. His song drifted and settled in the small, open spaces in the woods behind him as the evening mist began to gather in the soft pockets of moss beneath the now swaying evergreens.

A man and his wife emerged from the cafe back on the road Virgil had driven down. They stopped, listened, turned toward the water.

> *"Marie Elana, you're the answer*
> *to a prayer;*
> *Marie Elana can't you see*
> *how much I care;"*

sang a young man somewhere close by. The dowdy couple stood in their places and listened.

> *"To me your voice is like*
> *the echo of a cry;*
> *and when you're near my heart*
> *can't speak above a sigh",*

sang Virgil, unaware of his audience, his voice now interspersed by the accompaniment of his instrument.

"I wonder where he is?" asked the woman.

"The poor fool's in love, that's where he is," said her husband, opening the car door for himself while his wife climbed in the opposite side. As the couple drove off, Virgil Mallon continued to sing, lost completely in his music.

> *Marie Elana say that we will never part,*

he sang out, his voice rising;

> *Maria Elana take me to your heart,*

he pleaded to the invisible woman, his face tilted upward, eyes searching. As the sun dipped into the far distant water, a great swelling tremolo rose from within him, and he promised:

> *A love like mine is great enough for two;*
> *to share this love is really all I wish to do.*

A LUCKY STRIKE FOR GOD

3.

Aris Mackintosh Mitchell reached the corner of Dakota and Seventh shortly before six p.m. At six ten, a blue 1934 Ford pulled slowly around the corner and crept over to where she stood. The door opened and Aris slid into the front seat. As the car moved away from the curb, an arm reached for her, pulled at her shoulder, drew her toward the wheel.

Rolland Mills was a farmer's son. He was as wise to the ways of the sexual instinct as he was wealthy because of it, for his father bred cattle, and prospered greatly. The young man had many times watched, his eyes narrowed to two slits, his groin full, as the great lumbering bull would mount cow after cow, and Mills would stand and listen to the great bellowing cries. On such days he would often masturbate in an obscure place in the barn, conjuring up in his memory the figure of some unwitting girl to service himself with her image.

Aris Mitchell was just such a girl. Sidetracked from school and wearied from day after day at her boring, puerile job, it was her habit to catch a ride to Beach Lake each weekend. Often she went with a girlfriend or two; on such occasions she would pool her change with that of her friends and together they would stop off at an unpainted wooden house on Cote Street. There she would wait, hunched down in the back seat of the car while one of the older girls made a swift transaction with the local bootlegger. The flat, stubby bottle secured in a brown paper sack, the girls would make for the lake, spread their beach blankets, and giggling, nip at the burning hootch throughout the afternoon.

Beach Lake was enticingly convenient to the Stewart Mills' farm; in August, when haying was in progress, young Rolland would daily drive over to the cooling water, plunge in, and dry himself by sitting on the high banks to bask and eat his lunch. On Sundays he would often spend the entire day at the lake watching for girls. On one such Sunday his eager, impatient eyes fixed upon Aris Mitchell.

KAREN PIETKIEWICZ

Aris was different sort of beauty. Dark and slender, with strong bones and inscrutable, deep set eyes, she wore her hair in a straight, defiantly short bob. The eldest of nine children, to her lot had fallen the never-ending demands of the rail of siblings who were thrust in her arms to be diapered and changed, or pinned in the wooden high chair to be fed. Daily, the infants were harnessed in the old wicker buggy, to which were attached those who could toddle or walk, demanding their daily accustomed promenade. Finally, Aris quit high school and went to work.

Now, her aborted education behind her, the dreary dimestore days of her latest job stretched out ahead of her endlessly. Her singular escape was enveloped in the privacy of her forty minute lunch. A *Movieland* magazine rolled and thrust in with a sandwich, an orange, and a hard boiled egg, she daily purchased a Coke from the lunch counter and ensconced herself in the employee's booth where she spent the mid-day minutes that were her own. When the working day was at last over, she would walk wearily home. Late in the evenings when the tide had been bathed and bedded down, Aris Mitchell would finally slide into the dimly lighted parlor with her growing record collection, slip one from its paper envelope and set the stubby needle in the groove. There, her arms wrapped about herself, she would spin, a dervish caught in the sticky threads of her own imagination while the music played and played.

Now, on this particularly hot Sunday afternoon, far from the cool safety of her mother's front parlor, Aris Mitchell lolled before the undiscovered eyes of Rolland Mills. He examined her where she lay, peered at her as she stood to dive, waited to see her pull herself from the lake, watched to see her breasts flatten against the dock. He observed her trim buttocks, thinly suited, poised. She became a tasty dessert to his bagged lunch. The swelling feeling in his groin would begin, and he would open his legs, set his feet further apart, allow his knees to splay. His scrotum would spill, sideways and deliberately, from the narrow crotch of his swimsuit, while all the while he pretended not to notice.

A LUCKY STRIKE FOR GOD

Aris, now drying on the dock, did not see Rolland Mills as he sprawled on the upper bank until she heard the boys' snickering remarks. "Get a load of Slab up there toasting his nuts!", they would joke, but in their hearts they feared the nerve of the confident boy and his cunning, boldfaced designs.

By this time Aris Mitchell had noticed the brazen young man. Intrigued by the comments of the youths, and hidden beneath the crook of her elbow, she had furtively looked up to see what she had never seen before.

It was done.

From that day forward, Aris Mitchell watched for each sunny Sunday, and on those Sundays she watched for Rolland Mills. Obsessed with gaining him for herself, his form had enlarged precipitously to become the sole beacon in Aris's sea of boredom, the promise of a cozened future that beckoned to be hers. Enervated by the growing electricity of her own burning desire and mesmerized by the sway of her imagination, Aris began to descend the dank staircase to where Rolland Mills now appeared, lounging lasciviously in the inner chamber of her mind. She smiled carefully, and to herself.

But the very much aware, and fully experienced Mills had ideas of his own. He now began a rain of slick attentions upon the labile young woman. Intent upon his own desires, and unwittingly assisted by Aris herself, he ensnared her within her own web. Swept along in the current that sparked between herself and the burning young man, Aris was soon assured that Mills would be hers. To this ancient tune, the calculating and inexorable Mills smilingly danced, eyes alight with the knowledge of his impending conquest. A confident smirk on his face when among his abashed and jealous friends, he knew that Aris Mitchell was certainly, inevitably, his.

As Aris's dreams filled with days of endless happiness, Rolland Mills dedicated himself to the excitement of the coming nights. Emboldened with the success of his chase, he would, on selected evenings during the long week, glean the car from his father by fabricating a plausible excuse. He would hang around the house for an appropriate amount of time, leave by the back door, so as not to call attention to himself, and head for town. As Stewart Mills watched his only son back the car down the long drive and head for Bullard, he would sit smiling quietly to himself behind the evening paper, before turning back to his reading.

It was a short drive in to Bullard. Once there, Rolland would slowly cruise Dakota Street looking for Aris, and as often as she could escape from the house, Aris would be there. They would then drive several miles out of town where they turned onto the now familiar side roads, There, they would creep along beneath the canopy of overhanging maples; as the leaves trailed along the car roof, the couple would exchange sips from the bottle of Canadian whiskey Rolland had usually purloined from his father. In this furtive manner the couple would drive and sip until, the stars popping from the darkening sky, they pulled into Beach Lake.

There Rolland Mills would begin again the slow and systematic seduction of Aris Mitchell. With a patience bred of wealth, an acquiescent family, and the security of a devoted, duty-bound mother, Rolland Mills, fat with a sizeable dollop of his father's money in his wallet, had nothing but time.

Inevitably, inexorably, the day had come. Armed with his usual bottle, a three-pack of tightly rolled and banded Sheiks waiting deep in his pocket in the puncture-proof tin box, Mills finally descended upon Aris. By the time the last Sheik was extracted from its paper band, the foolishly inebriated girl was feeling quite sick. No sooner had the sated young man withdrawn from her than she rolled to her side and vomited in his father's new car. Furious, Rolland Mills drove Aris to the corner a block from her home where he dropped her off, pausing only long enough to record her in his rear view mirror as she retched by the side of the road.

Two months later Aris stood on Lisle Street in Bullard, Michigan on a warm but fading fall evening. It was the night of the 1935 Homecoming game. Not inclined to sports, Aris had

A LUCKY STRIKE FOR GOD

followed the townsfolk to the Friday evening game only to watch the parade and evaluate the dewy-eyed, white gloved pastel confections perched on the open polished cars. Alone on the sidewalk across from the open gate of the Athletic Field, there was a defiant bitterness about the line of her jaw, a pressed-closed narrow thinness on her lips. The pin-curled fluff of the waving beauties obviously behind her, she watched with an ill-concealed scorn as the fanciful young girls, cradling roses in one arm, smiled and waved with the other. "That'll soon change," pronounced Aris to no one who could hear.

As the last of the shining cars disappeared into the gaping gates of the stadium, Aris started for home. Reaching into the Woolworth's sack she carried as she walked, she pulled out the record she had purchased earlier in the day, and slipped it from its sleeve. She looked at the record. It was one of the new, transparent plastic discs, between whose grooved sides was sandwiched a glossy print depicting a strutting, full-breasted and behatted black woman in a tight yellow dress. Bending toward the black woman, his hat in one hand and a shiny trumpet in the other, a nattily dressed Negro in a navy pin striped suite grinned and dipped his bowler hat. Scrolled across the disc was the label: *Sugar Blues*.
"Do dah doot n dah; do dah dah; dah ba dah, dah dum da, dah; dah; dat n da dah," Aris Mitchell ground out, as she thrust out first one hip, and then the other. Continuing toward home, she anticipated the possibility of turning the volume up full blast. The thought quickened her step. She had a new disc to spin on her whirling player.

4.

Virgil Mallon crossed the international border on a small, white, car-carrying ferry on that very same day, and headed straight for a telephone.

"What number please?" whined the operator.

The young man stretched a wrinkled scrap of paper out on the polished counter between two fingers of his left hand, as he held the receiver in his right.

"Seven-two-three-two," he replied, and waited for the sound of the ring.

"Hel-lo o ?" An older woman's voice answered.

"Ma!"

"Virgil? Is that you, there?"

"Yup, it is, Ma. I'm right here in town. I'm on the main street by the Monkey Ward store.

"Do you know how to get here, now, Virgil?" asked his Mother, happy to hear at last the voice of her youngest son.

"Yup. I can find the place, all right. I've got the directions right here in my hand," announced Virgil.

Inquiring after the aging aunt whom his mother had come North to nurse, Virgil asked, "How is Aunt Vimmi?"

"Vimmy's not too well, but your Uncle Robert , now there's a man in good health," his mother's voice pronounced over the telephone.

"Well, that's good for him," Virgil replied, the crinkled, hand-penned map in his left hand, his stomach beginning to anticipate one of his mother's wonderful meals. "So I'll be there shortly, Ma," he said, carefully interrupting his mother.

He hung up the telephone, raced out, and jumped in his truck.

5.

After the stinging rebuke Aris directed at her husband, the uncomfortable, familiar silence between Virgil Mallon and his wife Aris had returned. Virgil sat at the table, his coffee grown cold, his eyes, distant.

Now, deep within Mallon's soul powerful figures arose and began to speak, as if to fill the air with something in lieu of the nothing that was there.

A LUCKY STRIKE FOR GOD

"You want to be careful with the Catholic girls, Virgil," his mother had said carefully, as she prepared a departing breakfast of eggs and toasted bread for her youngest son. "If you marry one, your life won't be your own. Find yourself a girl who doesn't belong to the priests, and who knows what to do about wifely matters."

"See that you take after yourself," said his father, who had appeared at the foot of Conrad Street on the day Virgil planned to leave town. "No one else is going to do it for you." His father had said not another word.

"If you marry that girl, be prepared to have twelve children" said his sister Threasa, after the unexpected confrontation in her home.

The voices withdrew, leaving Virgil to fill in the empty silence.

Virgil Mallon now began to speak to his wife. "Do you know what's the matter here, dear?" he inquired of Aris, and as quickly answered himself. "It's that God-damned Church." With that said, he reached for his cigarettes, withdrew one, and began tapping the end on the tabletop. "You spend too much time in that God-damned Church."

There was still no answer from his wife.

At times like these border-line encounters with Aris, Virgil Mallon would disappear. He would fix his eyes on some distant point beyond the flesh colored rims of his glasses and stare out of the window beside the table where he sat. Only his right arm would move, bringing the cigarette to his lips and back again, to rest, and burn between the yellowed fingers of his right hand.

The door rattled, creaked, slammed. The girl had come in to eat.

Little Murial Mallon walked cautiously through the cluttered back hallway and stood for a moment in the far kitchen door. Sniffing the now familiar tension in the air, she girded herself visibly, shifting her small weight forward while her thin shoulders rose, and drew tight. Then she moved nonchalantly past the stove where her mother had begun to cook, and on into the modest front room while her father sat smoking and staring.

"Aris!" A voice rang through the window.

Aris Mallon suddenly stirred and came to life. She moved to the open window beside which her husband sat, to wave gaily with one arm. The other arm she kept pressed tight across her lower ribs, her left hand clenched in a fist.

"Come on in, Madge," she called out in a nervous, too bright, voice. Aris disappeared toward the sound of the opening back door.

In a moment the visitor was seated at the end of the table yammering away.

"What would you like, Madge, one or two?" Aris reached for the lumpy, coffee encrusted sugar bowl and moved back toward the stove to retrieve the steaming pot. "Virgil, move your stuff aside so Madge can have room for her cup," she called out, her voice too high and bright.

"Just sweep it on the floor, my dear," the man said, with a grand gesture of his arm. Blueprints, pencils, cigarette pack tumbled to the floor between the table and the window, along with a peanut-butter encrusted knife and some opened bills.

Aris Mallon, standing at the stove, solidified, then moved puppet-like toward the pin-curled guest, a brimming cup of coffee in her hand.

"Don't mind Virgil. You know how *he* is," she countered to the bug-eyed Madge, emphasizing the "he". She set the cup before her guest and poured one for herself.

"Ya wanna stay for dinner, Madge? Aris's making chicken."

The man spoke again, still staring far away, and still smoking.

"No; no, thank-you Virgil, I've got dinner in the oven." Madge Brumwell swallowed several quick gulps of her coffee, looking increasingly uncomfortable. "My God, Aris! Look at that time!", the woman suddenly said. She rose with her cup, drained, it, and set it carefully down. "I have to go home. Jim will be in soon." Her voice was an octave higher than usual, her artificial grate amplified as she quickly backed out of the kitchen and left.

Virgil Mallon now spoke.

"I don't like that woman, Aris. She doesn't know when not to come, and she doesn't know when to leave. She spends all her time on her God-damned knees or in someone else's house eating their food instead of looking after her own business."

Aris spun in her place. "You don't have to be rude! You don't know how to behave with civilized people! I can't even have friends over."

"You don't need friends like Madge, Aris. She doesn't sleep with her husband in the same bed. She doesn't even sleep in the same room, for Jesus Christ's sake! That poor fool Brumwell sneaks down to the Chicken Shack once a month while his wife is following the priest around over there like he was the Second Coming. She cuts all those God-damned flowers of hers and runs them over to the Church every day while her husband sits home waiting to eat after he works for her all day. You don't need friends like her around."

"Well it's none of your business!", snapped his wife. "You've got your own friends; leave me to mine!"

"Mine don't come between a man and his wife at mealtime. They know enough to stay home for dinner. She eats here, and she eats there, and she eats everywhere, just so she doesn't have to go home and be with her own husband."

"That's not true!" his wife now flared, her eyes burning, and slammed about the small kitchen, angrier than before.

"You don't know anything about people, Aris, that's your problem. You don't know a God-damned thing about what goes on in real life."

Now the woman set the table in stony silence, opened a can of Green Giant peas, poured them in a pan on the stove.

"Murial, come and eat!" Aris Mallon called to her daughter. She began to mash the pot of potatoes with a hand masher, heaped them in a bowl, set them on the table. The girl began to dish up her own plate, while her mother prepared a pan of gravy from the drippings.

KAREN PIETKIEWICZ

"Yawanna leg, do ya?" Virgil Mallon leaned toward his daughter. He forked a chicken leg and dropped it on the child's plate. "Yawanna wing too?"

"I don't like wings." Murial pulled her plate back and the dangling wing disappeared.

"How about some of these?" Virgil heaped a huge pile of lumpy potatoes on the girl's plate beside the chicken leg, and then spooned on some peas. He began to fill his own plate, pouring the brown gravy heavily over the white mounded heap.

The woman sat coiled, dishing her plate sparsely and picking at the food while the small girl watched from deep beneath her lashed eyes.

As Virgil Mallon began to eat, he looked at his wife, tense and angry and perched in her place like a wooden doll. There was something about the woman he could not understand, something pitiful, and very small. With this thought, Virgil felt an upwelling of shame, and a deep sadness for the woman across the table from him. He felt he had said too much; after all, what was her Church to him? He didn't have to go. A flood of feeling swelled his heart and he spoke.

"Aris, come on, let's go to the movies tonight. Willya come with me? We'll take little Murial, here, in to your mother's to sleep. I don't care about your Church. If you want to go, you can go. I won't stand in your way. Come out with me tonight. We'll go see a show together."

"I don't want to go to the show! I don't want to go anywhere with you!" His wife exploded from her place wailing, and ran out of the room, catching the kitchen chair with the pocket of her dress, and tumbling it to the floor as she rushed by. The girl heard the bedroom door slam closed.

Virgil looked heavily after her. Turning to the girl, he heaved a sigh, and pulled back from his place. "She doesn't want to go with me, Murial," he sighed. "She never wants to go." He leaned back in his chair, withdrew his package of cigarettes and placed one between his lips. He struck a wooden match from the small box beside his plate, lit up, stared out the window again.

A LUCKY STRIKE FOR GOD

The girl finished eating and stood up in her place, looking at the floor. The man observed the child, standing there.

"You run along next door and ask for some cookies, now. You stay in your grammy's for awhile. Your daddy has to talk to your mother."

The girl stood up, picked up the rest of the chicken leg and walked out.

6.

The bedroom door was still locked.

"Aris, come on now, open the door. Come on and we'll go for an ice cream. Come on now." Behind the door, he could hear his wife's muffled sobs. He tried the knob, but it would not turn. Reaching into his pocket, he withdrew a finishing nail from the handful he had been carrying at work, and inserted it into the lock. The doorknob moved and the brass tongue clicked; he turned the knob, which now opened the door.

His wife Aris sat red-eyed on the bed, a wadded handkerchief pressed to her face.

"Get out of here! Get out!" She screamed up at him, her face blotched and red, her eyes streaming.

"Now Aris, don't do like that," Virgil began, and moved to the edge of the bed as his wife pulled away. He moved again to sit down beside her. Reaching out his arm, he put it around her shaking shoulders and tried to draw her to him, but she hunched away from him, crying and rigid, and did not move.

"Aris, sweetie, you can't let the priests run your life. You can go to church on Sunday however much you like, but you gotta keep the priests out of our bedroom. It's not normal, a man with no wife telling married people how to live. They don't know anything about love between a man and a woman."

The woman began to sob again, her shoulders shaking violently, her head bent in her hands.

"Jesus, Aris, don't do that! I hate when you do that!"

The man jumped up. "What's the matter with my Aris now? What's the matter now?" He sat down hard on the bed again, beside his sobbing wife.

Now he tried to turn her toward him, but still she would not move.

"Come on now, Arie, what's the matter?" The man spoke softly to her, leaning close to her face. "You been going on like this for days. Tell me what's the matter."

"I'm pregnant!" The woman wailed, and threw herself face down on the bed, sobbing and shaking violently.

"Jesus H. Christ." The man rose to his feet, hands dangling at his sides. "Jesus H. Christ," he said again, and stood staring.

The woman continued to wail.

"Jesus, Jesus, Jesus, Aris! Didn't your mother show you anything to do? Most women know these things. Didn't you ever learn what to do?" The 'do' hung in the air twice.

His wife turned, her eyes filled with hatred. "I told you it was the wrong time," she hissed at Virgil. "It just must have been the wrong time!" Her eyes were red and swollen, and she rubbed at them more with her balled fists.

"God damned priests! God damned church!" The man dropped to the bed, his head buried in his hands.

"Don't say those awful things!" the woman screamed, and began to wail again.

"Jesus Christ Almighty, Aris, we've got to use something. A married couple can't live and not make love, it's not normal. That's what married life is for! It's not just for babies. Can't you understand that?"

"It's not right!" The woman began to wail again.

"God damn that Church; God damn it, I say!" The "damn" burst out between clenched teeth as Virgil Mallon sprung to his feet. His arm reached out; in one swift instant, he grabbed the plaster statue of the Virgin Mary from the window sill and smashed it on the floor. With a backhanded sweep of the same arm, he cleared the cluttered top of his wife's dressing table, sending the perfume atomizer he had given her on their anniversary flying across the room. Now he reached to the top of the mirror, ripped the dusty, braided palm frond from where it was wedged and flung it across the room while his wife sobbed on.

"That's three, for Jesus Christ's sake! Three! The Lord said to go and populate the earth, Aris, but he didn't mean just me!" Virgil Mallon was pounding his three middle fingers into the center of his chest. The "me" hung in the air like a knife.

The wailing had begun again, but Virgil walked out of the room. Then he turned and walked back in. In an upswelling of despair, he seated himself beside the sobbing woman, and patted her arm piteously, rubbing his work worn hand over her shoulders, and stroking awkwardly at her turned back.

"It's O.K. Aris. It's O.K. Your old Virgil will take care of you. Come on, now, stop crying. I'll push that rear dormer up through the roof next spring and we'll put Murial up there like she's been asking. Come on now, stop your crying."

But the woman wailed on until he left the room.

7.

The next day was Sunday. Aris Mallon had recovered sufficiently to ready herself for Church. After showering in the small bathroom that opened off the kitchen, she wrapped herself, dripping, in her chenille robe. Moving to the mirror over the kitchen sink, she began to apply her makeup while her husband sat at the table, his eggs grown cold on the plate.

"The toilet is leaking again," said his wife, as she dabbed behind her ears from a bottle of Blue Waltz perfume. "You better fix it today because it's ruining the tiles." There was nothing at all in her voice.

The man pushed his plate away and left the room. He went down the basement stairs and began rumbling around in his tools, then came back up the stairs, heavy footed, and carrying the battered box of plumbing supplies which he set on the floor outside the bathroom door. In a few minutes he had begun to work.

"Aris! Are you ready?" The back door opened and Madge Brumwell walked right in to the kitchen.

"I'm coming; I just have to put on my lipstick and slip into my dress," said Aris. She bent over the kitchen sink and strained toward the narrow, wall-hung strip of mirrored glass while Madge moved to the bathroom door, to stand staring at the bent back of Virgil Mallon. She leaned over, hands on her hips.

"*What* are you doing, Virgil?" she demanded, like a school teacher.

"What's the matter, haven't you got eyes?" The man had risen and pushed by her to retrieve a tool from the box.

"Yes, I've got eyes, Virgil, and what I see is that you're working on Sunday!"

"I'm surprised you could figure that one out, Madge," said Virgil Mallon, and bent his back toward her again.

"Virgil, just because you aren't Catholic is no excuse. Everyone knows better than to work on Sunday. It's the Lord's Day. You should know that."

"Well, I'll tell you what, Madge: since you're so good at talking to the Lord, you just tell him to come over here and fix my toilet, and I'll be glad to go sit in his Church."

"Virgil! You are going to end up straight in Hell with a mouth like that! You should know better." The woman was aghast.

Virgil Mallon stood up slowly, and turned to face the spluttering woman. Then, moving up close to her bulging eyes, he bent and put his nose up to within an inch of her face and said in a wicked whisper, "I'll see you there, Madge!"

"Jesus, Mary, and Joseph! Did you hear what he said? Aris! Did you hear what your husband said to me just now?" Madge Brumwell had stepped back from the bathroom door with both veined hands at her throat. Aris turned, lipstick still in hand, and faced her babbling friend for a long minute. Then, spinning on her feet, she pushed by Madge, and made a beeline for the bedroom door, slamming it shut behind her with the now familiar explosion, leaving her friend and her husband in the shattered silence.

A LUCKY STRIKE FOR GOD

The man now moved toward Madge with slow, deliberate steps. The woman's eyes widened, and she backed up.

"You can keep right on backing, Madge, and you can back yourself right out of this house before I stick your head in this here toilet that I just got working, and hold it there for good.

And I don't want to see your painted face in my house again. Do you understand that?" Virgil Mallon spoke slowly, quietly, and precisely.

"You're crazy, Virgil," the woman hissed, backing further over the red asphalt tiles toward the door. "Everyone knows you're crazy! You don't know how to behave like a civilized man!"

With that she turned, and ran out of the house, slamming the door on its hinges. She trotted away down the back alley, the sounds of her staccato feet fading fast behind her.

Virgil Mallon returned his tools carefully to the box and headed back down to the basement. He set each wrench in the proper bin, cleaned the tip of his soldering gun, replaced the coil of solder. He went back up the stairs. Filling a bucket with water from the shower stall, he began to wipe the fixtures. He continued upwards, wiping the walls of the small room which were dingily smudged with fingerprints, working carefully and steadily until he came to the border he had placed mid-way up the wall.

Virgil's border consisted of a sequence of black silhouette decals in the form of slender, beautiful women. Each lovely black form held a great white ball over her head between delicate upstretched arms. Around these decals Virgil worked carefully, wiping gently so as not to wet and remove the decorative trim. After this, he turned to the small shower, scrubbing it from top to bottom until it shined. At last, he cleaned the tile floor, scrubbing and rinsing until the room was immaculate. He emptied the water, wrung the rag, took the bucket and disappeared back down the basement stairs again to his workshop.

As he did, he heard his wife's quick footfall as she hurried out the back door to Church.

8.

After two weeks of lonely, chilling silence, Virgil Mallon called the priest. At seven o'clock Monday evening Father John O'Connell arrived, stepped inside, and took a seat on the worn wine and grey striped sofa across from Virgil Mallon.

"Well, I guess you got me." Mallon pronounced, as he sat stiffly on the matching chair, the wrinkles on his forehead more, and deeper, his work-scarred hands by his side. He was wearing khaki pants and a new shirt he had saved in his top drawer since Christmas. "She's in there." He motioned toward the bedroom door behind his right shoulder. "She's been in there for two weeks."

"So what seems to be the matter?" asked the priest, pulling a pack of Chesterfield's from his pocket. "By the way, do you mind if I smoke?"

"I thought priests weren't allowed to smoke."

"We're not, in public. In private, I smoke about a pack a week. I picked it up in the Navy." The priest bent his head over the cigarette, lit it, raised his head and exhaled.

"I was in the Navy," said Virgil.

"Is that so?" said the priest, tipping his head to one side and exhaling the smoke from his cigarette.

"I was a C.P.O. in the Seabees," said Virgil.

"I was in the Islands before the hit, playing trumpet in the Navy bands," said the Reverend O'Connell. We used to do all the gigs for the brass. It was a good life while it lasted."

"Is that right?"

The smoke from the two men drifted upward, to hang in the corners of the small room.

"Your guitar?" The priest motioned to the instrument that sat on a metal stand nearby.

"Steel guitar. I used to have an old Gibson acoustic but my wife kicked the sides in," said Virgil, matter-of-factly.

"Really?" remarked the priest, pausing to look at the man seated before him.

"She kicked it before we even got married. If that doesn't tell you something, nothing will."

A LUCKY STRIKE FOR GOD

"That's too bad," said the priest.

"I bought her a piano but she never played it. She thinks she needs lessons. I told her to take lessons but she never gets around to it."

The priest shifted back on the sofa, after butting his cigarette. "So what seems to be the problem here?"

"She doesn't like me. Ever since little Cerise was born, she sleeps in her bedroom."

"Well, it does sound like you have a problem here," said O'Connell. Leaning back on the sofa, the priest crossed his left arm over his chest, and folded the other toward his cheek, where he rubbed his hand over the side of his face as if examining for some errant stubble.

"Tell me, Virgil - that is if you don't object - are you a man who is faithful to his wife?"

Virgil Mallon's face set almost in affront. "I don't hold with a man who runs out on his wife," said Virgil Mallon.

"I thought that was the case," said the priest. "So tell me, if you can, how all this got started?"

"I don't know how it got started; it got started with your Church, that's where it got started," said Virgil. "I don't mean any offence to you personally, but I never wanted to have anything to do with your Church and here I am living with it, day in and day out."

"You knew your wife was Catholic before you married her," said the priest.

"That's a whole other story," said Virgil Mallon, his voice evasive, a curtain dropped in his eyes. He sat for a moment, body still, eyes distant.

The priest waited.

"I want to know what you tell women like her on Sundays," Mallon began again, "and what I'm asking you is, what do you think you even know about women?" His voice had begun to escalate as the words tumbled from his mouth. "A fellow like you, not even married! It's God-damned unnatural! You ought to at least get married so you'd know what the hell your talking about before you go around poking your nose into married folks' bedrooms!"

KAREN PIETKIEWICZ

John O'Connell, S.J. looked at Virgil Mallon, and then he rubbed his hand over his face and mouth once again. He reached behind his neck and massaged it in a kneading, circular motion.

"Well, that's getting it all out on the table," the priest announced, bringing his chin to rest on his thumb. His bent index finger seemed to seal his lips and a burning spark of interest began to grow within him as he observed the distraught and angry man before him.

"*That's* the problem, O'Donnell - O'Connell - or whatever you call yourself," said Mallon, with utter finality. He then leaned back as if to widen the gap between himself and the priest.

"A man doesn't have to be married to recognize a problem like this," the priest began.

"I'm not talking about recognizing a problem, I'm talking about fixing a problem!" Mallon blurted out. He suddenly dropped his head in his hands, and after a few seconds, he looked up and across at John O'Connell, his brow furrowed, his blue eyes clouded with pain. "What the hell can you do about it anyhow," he said in a quiet voice. "What would you know about wanting a woman?"

"I know about wanting women." said John O'Connell, S. J.

Virgil Mallon looked with incredulity at the priest. "Well I'll be damned!" he said. He could think of nothing else to say.

"So I guess that's getting the rest of it out on the table," said O'Connell, a tight, sardonic smile on his thin lips.

Virgil Mallon could not understand his wife. Now he could not understand the priest. "What do you mean, you know about wanting women," he shot out, "and what are you still doing in that get-up if you do?" With a wave of his hand Mallon indicated the black suit of the seated priest.

"I don't really know," said O'Connell, withdrawing another cigarette and striking a match to it.

"Well, you went to school to be a priest, didn't you?" said Mallon.

A LUCKY STRIKE FOR GOD

"I went to school for music," the priest said suddenly. "I had a year in before the Navy but I ran out of money. When I was doing music I never seriously thought about women."

"Is that right?" said Mallon, now listening intently.

"That's the God's truth. I never thought of the women except for their voices. I already had my share of women. One was never enough. It seemed like it always had to be more, and different. Never any end to it, and it never went away." The priest snorted. "Of course, when you finally got into one, she never seemed to go away either."

"Well, I know about that," said Virgil.

"Women were an endless hassle, not like music. The music stayed with me. Anyhow, that's what I thought at the time. You know, for a while back then, I was on an everlasting high. No woman ever did that for me for long."

"I studied harmony," said Virgil, who had for the first time in two weeks completely forgotten about his wife. "With the Oahu Correspondence School of Music."

"That's O.K.!" said the priest, interested.

"Thirteen books of theory and harmony. It took me three years."

"That's alright," said the priest, nodding his head. "I couldn't afford to go anywhere for awhile after the war, so my cousin's a priest, and he told me the order would put me through school. At the time I thought I had everything all figured out."

"I thought we were supposed to be talking about *my* problems," Virgil now volleyed, his focus suddenly returned.

The priest looked him dead in the eye.

"We are. But I don't know anything about women, Mallon. If I did I probably would have married one of them. I don't. I had them, but I never understood them. I can only talk about music, and I'm not sure I even understand that anymore."

"Then, what the hell are you doing in my house?" said Virgil Mallon, his black mood suddenly returned, his shoulders fallen once again. "You've got my wife spending half her time on her knees in your church instead of in bed with me and you can't tell me a thing? What the hell good are you, anyhow?"

41

"Not much, I guess." The priest now leaned back and looked straight across at the worried man. "You know, Mallon, I don't have any answers for you. I guess some of my compadres think they do, and for some people, maybe they do; it takes all kinds. But from what I can see, your trouble, Mallon, is, that you actually take your marriage seriously. You actually love your wife. And that's your problem, because from what I've seen most men don't love their wives, and for that matter, most wives don't love their husbands. From what I've seen, and I see a lot of this, they just go on from day to day, doing what they did the day before, and the day before that. They have kids, raise them, and get old. Most men never think of things like love and music, and after awhile they never even think of women. They just do, and then they die."

Virgil Mallon looked puzzled and uncomfortable. The lateral wrinkles in his forehead were deepened and his blue eyes darkened.

"John - what's your name there? I don't call priests 'father'."

"John's fine," the priest said, comfortably.

"Well, since you don't know anything about this, let me tell you. It looks to me like you just took a free ride on your Church to get at the music, that's what you did."

"I suppose that's one way too look at it," affirmed the priest, raising his eyebrows, and reaching to butt the ash from his cigarette in the standing metal ashtray.

The two men sat facing each other, silent. Mallon began to feel uncomfortable. The priest across from him wasn't at all what he'd expected.

"Well, I'll say this much for you, you could do worse than play music." Mallon felt he should soften up.

"That's true," said O'Connell.

"Why don't you try to play something a little more cheerful once in a while," Virgil spontaneously decided to advise. "You could get something happening in there to bring people up. You could play stuff people like to hear, like the black folks do. All that music I hear over there is about death. Jesus Christ dying, and men dying and everyone suffering and dying.

A LUCKY STRIKE FOR GOD

Who the hell wants to listen to that? And look at that miserable sight hanging up there!" Mallon seemed to be on a roll, as he gestured toward the crucifix he had nailed to the wall at his wife's behest. "Isn't that the damnedest thing you ever set eyes on? No wonder you've got to have an Easter! It's so the poor fellow can come back and have another go at it."

John O'Connell, S.J., opened his eyes wide, and suddenly began to smile. Then he began to laugh. In another minute he was laughing until the tears rolled down his face while Virgil Mallon sat transfixed. "Mallon, you don't need me here to talk to," the priest sputtered across the room, wiping his eyes with the back of his hand, and starting to laugh again.

Virgil stared at the priest.

"Sta-bat Ma-ter Do-lo-ro-sa.," the priest began to chant, stopping to howl again with laughter, and choking on the dregs of his cigarette. "Women, Mallon. We'll never escape them!"

Virgil Mallon began to feel a great burden floating upwards from his shoulders. Completely at a loss for words in the presence of this supposed man of God, and as a means to fill the air, he now proffered, "Say, there, John: would you like a small glass of wine?"

"Sure, I'll have a glass of wine," said the priest, who began to howl again.

Virgil Mallon went out to the corner china cabinet he had built and reached for two of the better glasses. From beneath the sink he withdrew a dusty partial bottle of sweet red wine, which he rinsed beneath the faucet and uncorked awkwardly. He poured a little into each of the two glasses which he had rinsed and polished with a dingy checkered towel. From the living room he could hear the Reverend John O'Connell still laughing.

"'Tis the month of Our Mother, the blessed and beautiful May," O'Connell bellowed once again, between spasms of laughter and the occasional choking cough. "Oh, God," said the priest, "I haven't had a laugh like this in fifteen years!"

KAREN PIETKIEWICZ

Mallon sat down, staring in bewilderment at the peculiar priest who was now splayed in relief against the back of the sofa, knees apart, toes pointing at either wall.

Father John O'Connell then sat up, head in his hands, and heaved a great sigh, as he reached for the small glass of wine.

"Strange Fruit," he said, his face now fallen.

"What's that?", said Mallon, his mind searching to place the remotely familiar phrase.

"What I mean is, " said O'Connell, "did you ever hear Billie Holiday sing that number? Because I heard her sing it live, in some hole-in-the-wall out East. I never heard a woman sing like that. I've been afraid of women ever since."

"I knew a black woman once," Virgil offered. "She carried a razor in her purse. I saw her slash a man right in the face. That was in upper New York State. He had it coming."

"That's not what I mean," said the priest, his face puzzled. He drained his glass. "It's the hole in women, Mallon. You can fall into a woman and never climb back out."

Virgil Mallon looked sadly at the priest who sat across from him. "The problem's not the hole, O'Connell, it's the fear," he said quietly, and began to speak. "Falling into a woman is like diving into a river where you know there might not even be a bottom. A man has to know how to go down and when to come up. You have to go down that hole to get to know a woman. Sometimes it feels like you're blind, and I've figured out that's because we are blind." Mallon leaned back and looked at John O'Connell. "Now I don't know anything about your priest business, John, but the way I see things there are two species on this earth and that must mean something, and I don't care who put them here. The way I see it, a woman is the other half of a man, and together, they're the other half of whatever put them here. It's the only sensible way. Now when that man and woman come together, that's as close as you're going to get to God." Mallon paused for a minute, his eyes suddenly blear. "And if that doesn't work for you, you could find yourself facing the Devil itself," he suddenly pronounced, "And it's not just women. A man can meet the devil in himself quicker than any other way

A LUCKY STRIKE FOR GOD

when he gets with a woman, and you don't know from one day to the next which way she's going to take you. Life and Death is all part of it. The point is, O'Connell, a man's got to know the parts before he can know the whole. And you can't know a woman any more than you can know God if you're not willing to meet all the parts of her. And this is where we start," said Virgil Mallon, "right here," - his arm was rising up and plummeting toward the floor, - "right in this house," - he was now punching a work-worn index finger out toward the room - "and right in that there bed," he finished, swinging his arm around and pointing straight at the bedroom door that adjoined the small living room.

With that, he fell back in his chair.

The two men now sat in strained silence. Mallon felt suddenly embarrassed, as though he had been caught in the grip of some passing spell. O'Connell smoked slowly, exhaled the smoke in a soft stream, and spoke.

"I guess some of us don't have the guts for it," the priest said in a quiet voice. He looked tired, and beaten, arms between his legs, eyes fixed on the worn rattan rug on the Mallon's hardwood floor.

9.

Murial Mallon climbed the twenty-six steps of the choir loft behind her Aunt Carol and wound her way through the shuffling women. She was the youngest member of the choir.

And she loved to sing. She loved to hear the voices all sounding together: the high, wavering ladies' voices, the low, rolling men's voices, and hers, like her Aunt's, right in the middle. There were only four altos in the choir. These took a place closest to the organ, and she could hear the thump-wheeze of the bellows as the organist strained against the pedals with her legs and feet.

Murial was at last close enough to the front row to see over the loft railing, where for several years before, she could not. Those were the years when she was too young, too small, and had to sit quietly to one side while the rest of them sang. Thus she learned the hymns from constant repetitions. One day, singing her way to church with her Aunt, she was inveigled to sing for the choir mistress. She was given her own hymnal the next week, the youngest ever member of the choir.

But now the joy was gone. Her voice came out when it was supposed to come out, and sang the words it was supposed to sing in the time it was supposed to keep. For Murial Mallon's heart had fallen inside her. It lay in some deep crevice behind where it was meant to have been. Like a small clock bumped from the shelf, only its ticking within her told her it was there at all. From such a deep, lost place, she could no longer call it up, not even for the hymns. She sang like a rewound gramophone, her eyes stuck fast to the words.

Her father wasn't there.

Now when Murial sang, she recalled her father's black suit, the shirt with the too-tight collar, the tie with small trout stamped diagonally across it. He had worn the tiny, gold plated fishing rod with the silver line, on his tie; Murial had saved the pennies and nickels of her allowance and all the money given to her by her grandmother for doing small chores, to give it to him for Christmas. Murial recalled the few months when her father agreed to go to Church. She had only been able to see the back of his head as he stood and sat and knelt beside her mother in the wooden pew, but she knew that her fishing rod was there on his tie.

After several Sundays of her father's restless fidgeting through the ceremony, Murial noticed that he would ease out of the pew just as the Consecration was about to begin, slip through the side door of the Church, and disappear. Once, Murial had seen a stab of darting anger follow him from the sharp angle of her mother's face. Later in the mass, when streams of communicants were shuffling back and forth from the altar rail to their pews, her father would return, slip back inside, and take his place as though he had never left. On one such occasion Virgil Mallon raised his eyes to the choir loft just as his daughter's eyes fixed upon him.

The following Sunday, the dry, unleavened wafer of a communion host sticking to the roof of her mouth, the cool

A LUCKY STRIKE FOR GOD

morning air moving in from the opened doors, Murial smelled cigarette smoke. As she returned from the Communion rail, she saw her father outside the front entrance way, smoking on the sidewalk. As it always was with them, Virgil Mallon turned toward his daughter the minute he felt her glance. His hand dropped to his side. Murial walked straight through the Church vestibule and right out the door, scraping furiously with the tip of her tongue at the particles of sticky host and swallowing at the pieces to clear her throat.

"You're not supposed to be out here, daddy," Murial said to her father, in a semi-whisper. "You're not supposed to smoke here either," she continued, worried that her father would been seen, worried even more about the unknown something that she felt closing in as though it might descend upon them at any minute.

"Now don't be criticizing what you don't know," said her father, cautioning his daughter with the upraised index finger of his right hand. Stepping to the side of the walk, he glanced up so as to be out of sight of the opened church doors. "Let me tell you something, Murial. When I was your age, I lived way outside town. I played with little Indian boys. Their fathers, and the medicine man, and the Chief, and all those Indians smoked tobacco in long pipes like you saw in that movie we went to last week. Now those Indians believe that the puffs of smoke carry their prayers up to God. That's how those Indians pray. Lots of times they smoked right outside where the prayers wouldn't get stuck in the rafters, like they might in that place in there," said Virgil Mallon. He was bent earnestly toward his daughter's face, a wave of his hand indicating the frame church.

"The Indians in the movie were inside a roundhouse," Murial countered.

"Sometimes they were; sometimes they weren't," said her father. Anywhere was fine for those Indians. But in your mother's Church, the only ones who can make smoke are the priests. Besides, a person's better off to be in a roundhouse," concluded Virgil Mallon, a familiar twinkle starting up in his eye, "at least the Devil can't corner you there!" He began to laugh his silly, familiar laugh, reaching out to pull Murial's flowered straw hat down over her eyes. "See there? Your daddy's just going to just stand out here for a minute and smoke a Lucky Strike for God."

Suddenly Virgil Mallon bent close to his daughter's face, a serious look replacing the suddenly vanished humour. "Now you get back in there before the whole mob comes after us," he said. Murial turned and ran inside.

That was the last time her father had gone to Church.

Now Murial Mallon worried and worried and worried. For the year before, while attending released-time religious instruction in the same Church where she so enthusiastically sung, she had learned the terrible truth. "Heaven is like a huge hockey arena," the black robed nun announced. "The Catholics will have the best seats - right on the Blue Line. The Anglicans will be just behind the Catholics, and then the Methodists, and the Lutherans and the Baptists." The black robed nun advanced droning down the religions, as she seated the denominations in their heavenly places in order of their relative affinity with her Church. After the Christians, she reluctantly seated the Hindus, the Moslems, the Buddhists. At the far end came the Pagans and finally the Jews.

Murial Mallon had begun to cry. There before the child's stricken eyes were homes being wretched apart by religious denomination. A great wail sounded out across the stadium as fathers, mothers, children, grandparents, aunts and uncles, cousins, nieces and nephews - the mistaken ones, the ones who did not convert - reached piteously toward the turned backs of their former families.

Where would her father be when he was dead? Would he not be there waiting for her in Heaven so they could be together again? He would not. And even if he were, he would not be with her. He would be in the very back row. He would have to sit alone forever and forever and forever. The heaven to which Murial Mallon had so fervently aspired dissolved before her eyes. With tears streaming down her face, she resolved to sit with her Dad.

A LUCKY STRIKE FOR GOD

10.

The day after her eleventh birthday, Murial awoke in the night to the sound of raised voices and cupboard doors slamming. Her parents were arguing. She took her pillow from her bed and placed it in the air vent that ran past her room and out into the main part of the house. There she lay, her head resting in the hole, straining to hear, her heart pounding, her limbs stiff and tense.

"A man can't work on a meal of bacon and ice cream, Aris! What about some vegetables, once in a while? Do you think you could make me some fresh vegetables now and again instead of just opening a can?"

Murial could hear her father's pleading voice.

"What do you do all day long when you're home here?", her father's voice continued. "I give you all the money and you don't even wash and mend my work clothes. How am I supposed to work when there's nothing to wear?"

"Why don't you get a regular job instead of working in that shitty shop of yours and getting glue and sawdust all over your clothes!" Aris Mallon snapped, "And why don't you make your own damned vegetables if you don't like what I serve," she spat, her voice ricochetting down the air vent to where her daughter lay chilled to the bone. "You don't get weekly checks like other men! I never know how much money I'm going to have to spend!" hissed her mother, through the dark vent.

"Well, God dammit." said Virgil Mallon. "God dammit to Hell! I build homes, Aris. That's my trade. I'm not cut out to sit behind a desk. What I need is for you to set up a budget and follow it, if you're bent on handling the money. If you paid more attention to how you spent it we wouldn't have bills stacked up everywhere to pay."

"You're crazy! Everyone has bills!" screamed Aris Mallon.

"Well, not like ours." retorted her husband. "You waste money, Aris. Look at this!" The weary Virgil Mallon reached to the streaked and fingerprinted refrigerator door, yanked it open and exposed the chaos within. Shelf after shelf was crammed full to the edge with wilting vegetables and fruits in varying stages of decay, bowls of food long dried completely out, leftovers tinged with green mould. "There are three separate heads of lettuce here, Aris! Look at this!" Reaching inside, he flung the cellophane parcels out on the cabinet beside the refrigerator one by one. "Look at this! This lettuce has been in here for a month! Not even the birds would eat it! I've never even see it on the table. What are you waiting for, Christmas?" Virgil Mallon took up a wilting handful of green leaves. "Look at this! Gone to brown from cutting it with a knife, and now you've bought another one! Don't you ever look in here before you spend? And what about that breadbox over there. A full loaf, unopened and molding, and that one on top, dried out like a bone. Aris, we can't afford waste like that!"

"I'm getting out of here. I don't have to listen to this," screamed his wife, thoroughly enraged, her voice now ringing through the metal shaft to vibrate in Murial's ear.

Curled on the chill floor, her head still pillowed in the return air vent beneath the wall, Murial now heard the cluck cluck cluck of her mother's wedgies, followed by a kick at the back door. The door closed with a reverberating slam. An engine started up in the drive and Murial looked up from her hole long enough to see the lights of a car flash over the ceiling of her room and disappear.

11.

Virgil Mallon sat alone at the kitchen table smoking his hated cigarettes. He was hooked to cigarettes, just as he knew he was hooked to Aris. How had this come to be? But he knew. He was lonely, she was attractive, and she was more than that: Aris was daring, and she wanted better than she had. He could not help but admire her for that.

Yet she was hooked worse than he was. She was hooked on the Church. Or was she? Virgil knew a number of Catholics by now; some of them must have some sense because they didn't all have kid after kid. Maybe it was the gin, Virgil now thought. Aris had always liked her gin.

"Buy me a gin fizz," she had said long ago, when they had gone to the after hours joint on Portage Street. "That way, no one can tell what I have in my glass."

But Virgil could tell, just as he could tell now when she drank, and he knew she drank too much. Still, Virgil knew people who drank much more than Aris drank, and managed to hold up their end of things.

Maybe she didn't care.

But she must care; look how piteously she cried when things went wrong. Maybe poor Aris was too soft-hearted. Maybe that was what was wrong. Maybe she was too soft.

Round and round Virgil Mallon went in his head, but he got absolutely nowhere.

As he sat there smoking, the image of his mother rose before him in his mind.

Virgil Mallon's mother, Malka, had been orphaned at the age of six. Taken in by a neighbor according to the order of the day, she had been consigned to work for her benefactors in return for room and board. At fifteen years old she married Jacob Mallon, twelve years her senior, against the advice of his own sisters. Jacob was a handsome, temperamental man whose recommendations were his intelligence, his love of music, his ability to box, and his outstanding skill at metalwork. However, once married, Malka found herself left to her own devices while her husband minioned with his friends, obsessed himself with his music, or boxed for wager. Only occasionally did Jacob Mallon apply himself to his trade, and on those occasions he would usually invent brilliant but outrageous devices he could not sell. When the babies began to come, Jacob's sisters, unable to look upon the travails of their brother's growing family, gave Malka the use of a chilly old brick house, with a small garden, and secured her a position as laundress for a local Doctor.

KAREN PIETKIEWICZ

Thus, while her husband Jacob explored the limits of his own self, Malka Mallon worked long hours in the homes of the wealthy, as cook, cleaner, and laundress. Her reputation as a caterer soon placed her in demand. But unwilling to forsake those who had helped her and still depended upon her skills, and in addition to her catering, she continued to launder and clean for those special families who were good to her. For this she was given her wage and more: platters of unused food, sacks of wonderful, leftover baked goods, and worn but serviceable clothing and linens.

But Malka was not satisfied with food and dress alone. She brought to her children the manners, refinements, and disciplines of the cultivated people for whom she worked. After long days of polishing and scrubbing, she would polish and scrub again; her clothes brush in one hand, the waisted bar of harsh yellow soap in the other, Virgil's mother knew no difference between washing the clothes her children wore or the skin they carried on their backs. All fell beneath her energetic arm. At the table, proper manners were expected, and if they failed to surface, they were extracted by some force. On Sundays, and again on Wednesdays, her children's souls were laved by the sermons of whomever rose to the pulpit in the non-denominational summer church. Baptist, Methodist, Presbyterian, it did not matter: all were a force to bear upon the rough stone beginnings of her offspring if she were to polish them into the gemstones of God.

Virgil Mallon, the youngest, and closest to his mother, found himself ever beneath the shadow of his mother's backbreaking work. He knew the warmth of her heart, felt her loneliness, burned at the inequity of her laborious life, and when he looked at his father, it was with disdain. He vowed to do better for his own.

But what did Aris vow?

While Virgil Mallon paced the kitchen floor, his wife finally came home. She marched into the bedroom, slammed the door, and locked it.

A LUCKY STRIKE FOR GOD

12.

A light snow fell during the night. Murial Mallon stared at her mother's footprints, drifted over by an early morning snow. After a few minutes out of doors, Murial's hands were cold, and she pulled at the back door of the house and went inside, licking flakes of snow from the sleeve of her wool coat.

"Now what!" snapped Aris Mallon from where she sat in her robe, quickly closing her magazine on the cluttered table, and covering it with her arm.

"I need my mitts."

"Well take them and get out of here. I'm eating."

Murial walked gingerly across the kitchen, her boots squeaking on the linoleum, and edged between the chair and the sink cabinet behind where her mother sat. A lettuce and mustard sandwich, half eaten, sat on a white luncheon plate on the table, a glass of Seven Up fizzling beside it. Murial went into her bedroom and retrieved the new mitts from the drawer where they lay. She returned the way she had come while her mother tapped her foot impatiently.

Murial looked at the glass filled with ice cubes.

"I need a drink," she said, staring at the now familiar glass.

"Well, get one and get out," said her mother.

Murial went to the sink. She stood on her toes, reached for the glass, drew water, and drank, all in a series of carefully executed movements. Then she went back outside.

That evening her grandmother had come to make supper. Sometimes Grandmother Mitchell came to make suppers every night for a week. "Your mother is sick, Murial," her grandma would say, each time the meal was over. "You can help me with the dishes." Murial would help her grandmother until the dishes were all done, because the dishes were always done when her grandmother came. And when her mother was sick, her father would take her to the movies. He would buy her a Hershey bar with almonds in it, and a box of candy corns. After the cartoon, he would hurry out again and buy her a Coca-Cola. They went to many movies because her mother was often sick.

    Murial Mallon did not like to think of her sick mother, for when she did her mind darkened with the memory of an earlier time. It had been before the war, and she had been little. Her father had carefully dressed her in her green velvet church dress, the one with taffeta ruffles around the pocket, and they had gone to the show. But while they were there, Murial had put a square of Hershey's bar in the pocket and forgotten about it. It had melted, even though it was wrapped in paper-foil, and her church dress was ruined. Murial had never forgotten that long ago night, but not only because of the dress. For at 8:17 P.M. Eastern Standard Time, on December 7, 1941, the movie Virgil Mallon and his daughter were watching suddenly whined to a stop. Before the crowd could raise a murmur of complaint, the lights came up in the theater and the velvet curtain closed over the screen. As the crowd blinked its surprise, Mr. DeCorsi, in his neat grey suit and silvery tie, had stepped out from the wings and onto the narrow staging before the wine curtain.
    "Ladies and Gentlemen. I regret to tell you that we have just received word from Washington. The Japanese have attacked Pearl Harbor. America is at war."
    One by one, the audience began to rise, until all were on their feet. One by one they filed from the Palace Theater and out into the dark, chill night.

    The next day all the fathers came out of their doors with bags thrown over their shoulders, or suitcases carried in their hands. Down the long street they went, going away to the war. When they were almost out of sight, one by one, they would turn and wave, then they would disappear.
    Murial Mallon's father had gone from her while she stood on the curb and cried.

    But tonight, they would go to the movies again. They would walk down Bishop Street to the corner, and turn left.

A LUCKY STRIKE FOR GOD

Then they would walk down Spring four blocks, and turn right. Then they would cross the busy, slippery street and head for the alley behind Raeburn's Furniture Store to watch the rats run out.

13.

Virgil Mallon stood, his breath frosty in the growing dusk. Hand in hand, father and daughter looked upwards at the railed balcony that hung over the back lane before the furniture store.

"Now you watch, Murial. Watch right there by that center post, and I'll throw a snowball right at that garbage can up there. Are you watching? You watch for that big fat rat to jump out. It'll run right down that post to the ground. Are you ready?"

It was her favorite time, this time before the shows. Murial watched intently as her father dropped her hand, bent, and scooped up some snow.

"Here goes," whispered Virgil Mallon, and flung the snowball with deadly accuracy at the overflowing trash can that sat tipsily on the sagging overhead veranda.

Whang! The icy missile hit the metal and splattered through the slatted rail to the ground below. Sure enough, out jumped a huge rat and pelted down the supporting post to the top of the cement support below, where it jumped to the snow covered ground. Once safely down, the creature paused as if thinking itself escaped. After a few minutes, growing confident, the rat began to creep blatantly around the base of the post where it emerged on the other side. "Throw another one," Murial whispered urgently. As quickly as the rat heard her voice, it crouched ominously, small eyes glittering.

Murial froze in place. Suddenly, the dark creature stood erect on its hind feet and the girl bolted toward her father, grasping at his jacket as if to pull herself up by the handfuls. But the rat did not approach. Instead, it looked straight at Virgil Mallon, threw its small, arrogant head back, sniffed the air, and waddled confidently away.

KAREN PIETKIEWICZ

14.

On the twelfth of April, 1942, C.P.O. Mallon sat in a small glass cubicle overlooking the long turquoise swimming pool on the U. S. Navy base in Norfolk, Virginia. He was not interested in the things of war, nor was he in the games of men. It had always been that way for him. Once, cajoled into a hunt, he had reluctantly gone into the woods after a deer. A marksman, he had shot a buck as it leapt. It crumbled to the ground, pawing desperately with its black hooves at the moss covered soil. Its sides heaving, its pink tongue hanging from the foam flecked mouth, Virgil had watched the heraldic creature die, seen the lights blinkout in the frightened eyes, and then: nothing. He left his empty gun on the dead animal and walked all the way home.

Virgil Mallon was a stranger in this indifferent, lonely place. He longed for the day when he would be free of the great machine that fed man after man into its gaping maw, just as the men were now being fed into the waiting ships, to be spewed out on the shores of Europe, so very far away. As he trained the young pilots to escape from their planes, he thought of each of them in turn. Where were their homes? Who might their parents be? And when the training was complete, he watched as one after the other, his young boys walked up the long gangplank into the waiting leviathan that tugged at its moorings, belching grey smoke. The too-bright faces of the soon-to-be men crowded over the railings, arms waving white hats in the blinding sun, while on the docks, crying women pressed against the great high fence. Some held babies in the air while small hands stuck through diamonds of wire, waving and waving good-by. At the rear of the crowd, a few older, grey-headed women, handkerchiefs pressed to their eyes, seemed unable to push their way forward. As the great ships pulled away from the docks with their load after load of fodder, Virgil Mallon grieved in his heart for the men who would never return. Now and then there would be a lucky one, an older fellow who didn't pass

A LUCKY STRIKE FOR GOD

the physical, a nervous youth who broke and was sent home. There were religious objectors, shunned, and spat upon. Virgil Mallon felt relieved that these, too, might escape the looming maw of death.

To Virgil's mind, young Gerald Wheatley was one of the lucky ones. A shy boy, but smart and good with figures, Gerald had been kept Stateside in a clerk's job, but it was not so with his brother, Frank. For Frank was an idealist. Confident in his vision of the perfect order, he was eager to join the fray, to do his part to right the cosmic wrong. Hot for combat, he had rapidly escalated himself into the Naval Air Corps. The best of the home town boys, he had presented himself to his former neighbor, Mallon, by grinning and waving from the edge of the training pool at the Naval Air Center. Primed, Frank Wheatley climbed eagerly into the mock fighter at the top of the slide and swaged himself into the seat. At the ready while the mate secured his harness, the youth gave his own thumb's up signal as the crew moved aside. Down the track and into the deep pool he plummeted in the wingless cockpit, to rest, caged, at the bottom of the pool.

Now the seconds ticked by as the readied divers watched their bent wrists, but Frank did not appear. On signal, the divers leaped into the water and retrieved the gasping, panicked, would-be pilot as he scratched and clawed at the still buckled belt.

Faced with this unacceptable failure, the foolish young man's ego overwhelmed his abilities. Down he went again until, on the last try, he emerged from the trainer triumphant, and crawled, spitting and swaggering, out of the pool. But Virgil Mallon knew what the foolish youth had done. In the split second as the trainer plummeted by, C.P.O. Mallon had seen Wheatley struggling prematurely to free himself from his belt, and thus from the anticipated degradation of the corp. When the trainer hit the water he had only to clamber out, the massive bruises from the unbelted impact as yet unmanifest, and later, kept hidden beneath the uniform he was required to wear, the cap he would not remove.

Five weeks later, Frank Wheatley shipped out, and within six days he was dead. Overshooting the carrier on which he was to land, he floated in his aircraft for many long minutes, while the crew peered helpless from above. His panicked struggles recorded by a hundred sets of eyes, the unfortunate boy was seen to look up, bewildered, just as the plane plowed forward and disappeared beneath the waves. He was never seen again.

How to go down, and when to come up, thought Virgil Mallon, as he boarded a crowded train for home a week after the hearing about the death of Frank Wheatley. He was weary of war and the talk of war, and longed to be back home. But there would be no peace there either. This he knew.

15.

As the train West ticked off the miles that stretched between Virgil and his wife, he began, painfully, slowly, to move back through the years until he came to his last day in Widham. There he had sat on the docks with Sarah Elizabeth Williamson. The second daughter of a prominent and wealthy Kingston lawyer, the Williamson family summered in Widham, and it was there, over a period of three years, that a bond had begun to grow between the two. It was the last time Virgil Mallon had been truly happy.

It was the time of the final summer dance. Virgil could still remember the hundreds of stars of every different size and arrangement that had exploded in the heavens on that long ago night. It seemed to him as he sat on the dock with Sarah, that every star reflected the infinite, wondrous possibilities of his life. But he had not been able to bring himself to speak of his dreams to Sarah, or of his love for her. He had no money, and Sarah Williamson did.

Now Virgil thought of Sarah again, and how it had been when they first met.

He had been carrying clean laundry for his mother; all day, back and forth to the dock, he would lug the freshly ironed clothes and linens, neatly pressed and folded, and

A LUCKY STRIKE FOR GOD

wrapped in brown paper. Summer residents came in and left; others returned, outboards roaring over the water. Smaller dinghies pulled up on the sand, while the sleek varnished wooden yachts, spewing great rooster-tails, slid sideways into the docks. Heaving lines, the sun-tanned, full-toothed young men who lived in the summer homes scattered about on the many islands laughed and bantered, securing knots, and helping the girls step ashore. The huge engines of their expensive boats thrummed and growled beneath tightly fitted brass hinged hatches, or from deep within the slickly varnished sterns.

Sarah Williamson had been one of those girls, and as Virgil walked toward her, his arms loaded, he felt embarrassed, and lesser than the girl who stood looking about on the dock. But so radiant was her smile, so genuine the light in her bright eyes that he forgot everything but the vision who stood before him.

"You're Malka's son, aren't you?" said the wonderful, bright eyed girl, with an interested, open smile. "My mother sent me in for the laundry; is that ours?"

"If you're from the Williamson's, then I guess it is," said Virgil, heisting the packs higher in one arm, and approaching the girl. "I'm Virgil Mallon," he said, extending his hand, for his mother had taught him their ways. At first taken aback by the unexpected gesture, she was then obviously pleased. She quickly moved forward, grasped, and shook the hand.

"I'm Sarah Williamson," she said, blushing, "you can just set those things in the boat.

Virgil was suddenly glad for the manners his mother had taught him, although he knew, as well, he would not admit it to anyone. But then, with his mother, such words had not often been necessary. For there flowed between the two of them a silent river of love. It was now, as it had always been, and Virgil Mallon knew that it was so.

So Virgil had placed the bundles of laundry carefully on the leather seat of the Williamson's launch, and left, but not before the brightness of Sarah burned permanently into the retina of his eye. From that sunny summer day on, Sarah

KAREN PIETKIEWICZ

Williamson walked handin hand with him during the day, and returned to him night after wonderful night. She shone, ethereal, through the celluloid of his memory, where he developed her a hundred different ways in more than hundred different dreams. When she was eighteen and went away to school, the letters flew between them. Daily, weekly, she wrote to him, and he wrote back to her. When Virgil had finally left town, her letters followed him from boarding house to boarding house; his replies were posted from a dozen different towns.

But he had left her, and now it was too late.
Where had he gone wrong?

16.

Aris Mallon sat curled in the easy chair she adopted when her husband went away. Beside her was a tall floor lamp over which she had draped a remnant of black cloth in deference to the instructions for the black-out. On the table beneath the lamp rested her usual lettuce sandwich, but now the brown crusts were neatly trimmed from the white bread. Beside the sandwich sat the bubbling drink, and on the arm of the chair, a Hit Parade Magazine. The lamplight filtered, the window blinds tightly shut and sealed on every side, Aris Mallon felt comfortable in her little house. Alone except for the sleeping children, she was content to withdraw from a world that interfered with her goals.

But now her brows were gathered tightly together, making two deep commas on her forehead between her eyes. In her hand she held a small, neatly printed letter in dark blue ink on cream colored paper.

Her husband was on his way home.

As Aris Mallon sat staring at the letter she held before her she felt as though a gate had somehow slammed irrevocably shut. A fathomless tide of rage began to rise in her chest,

A LUCKY STRIKE FOR GOD

seeking a sluice through which to pour. Burning indelibly in her mind was the figure of her husband, Virgil Mallon, tie askew, hair disarrayed, racing across the front room.

It had been a terrible fight.

Now Aris plummeted back through the months to when her husband had first come home on leave. Framed in the front door of the small house, roses in one hand and a paper parcel in the other, she had seen the gold entwined anchor that was her husband's Navy insignia shining through the small window of the front door before he ever opened it.

For the first few days everything had been wonderful; Virgil had come bearing gifts. In the parcel were two stuffed animals. In his duffle bag was a seashell doll for Aris's dresser, pieces of gold military jewelry, a smart looking dress for herself. There were postcards and photographs, medals from sharpshooting which he hung in his den, perfume to be given to Aris, more toys for his children, and a box of seafoam candies in pastel colors, packed daintily in a great round box.

But after the initial greetings had been exchanged and the gifts distributed about, and while her husband was eating his breakfast on the second day of his leave, the black telephone began to ring. Aris Mallon raced for the receiver just as Virgil removed it from the hook. A Donald Duck voice quacked over the line, followed by a click.

Virgil Mallon, his face ashen, hung up the receiver and dropped onto the kitchen chair before his plate of congealing eggs. Slowly he raised his eyes to where his wife stood, her arms at her sides, her fists in two clenched balls.

"Aris, what in hell have you done?" he asked his wife, disbelief quivering in his eyes.

"Who was that on the telephone?" asked Aris, a brittle edge to her voice.

"It was Edward Mingey, from the grocery store, that's who it was, Aris. What have you done while I was away?" The man's voice was ragged and weary.

"I didn't do anything, that's what!" snapped his wife.

"Aris, he says I owe him two thousand dollars."

"Well, he's wrong, that's what he is! I don't owe him that much money."

Virgil Mallon's shoulders slumped, his head tipped back and to one side. He eyed the woman before him, his adam's apple obtusely protruding from his exposed neck.

"How much money do you owe him, Aris?" he asked, slowly. "How can anyone run up that much money in grocery bills?"

"I told you, it's not that much," snarled Aris. "Besides, what does it matter? I make my payments."

Her husband slowly rose from the chair.

"What did you spend it on this time, Aris?" he asked, walking wearily toward the front room. "Was it clothes? Did you buy more clothes when the God damned world is falling apart? Is that what you bought?" He walked across the living room and opened the bedroom door. Turning on the light with his left hand, he walked around the bed and opened the small closet door. "Is this what you spent it on, Aris?" he hollered from the bedroom. "More God dammed clothes?" With that, Virgil Mallon reached into the closet and grabbed a great armload of his wife's clothes and came staggering out of the room, his arms filled to overflowing. "Don't you have enough clothes," he bellowed, his voice gravel, and rising. He flung the clothing down at his wife's feet. "Or maybe you bought some more coats? Is that what it was? Two or three more coats?" He now moved toward the coat closet he had built in the front hall.

"You leave my things alone!" screamed Aris, and raced by her husband to barricade the front hall closet door.

Virgil stopped in his tracks. A silly, artificial grin suddenly stretched across his face. His eyes, straining, unfocused, struggled to fix on his militant wife.

"Oh. So that's what it is, Aris. A new coat. Is it maybe ten new coats, Aris?" Reaching straight through the battering arms of his now flailing wife, he slid the pine closet door back on its metal rail with a bang.

There it hung.

A LUCKY STRIKE FOR GOD

Shimmering slickly on a padded hanger was Aris Mallon's new fur coat. Above it, perched on the narrow shelf, was a matching fur hat.

Virgil Mallon came apart at the seams. Snatching the coat in one arm, the matching hat in the other, he wretched them from the closet and sped across the room to where a cast iron wood stove burned in the corner.

"I hope they burn well, Aris, 'cause we haven't got a God damned cent for coal!" said the wild-eyed Mallon, struggling with the overload of fur in his left arm. His right hand reached for the coiled wire handle that was stuck in the lid of the stove.

"Leave my coat alone!" screamed Aris, beating at her husband and yanking at the coat until it slipped from his arms. But Virgil had the hat tight in his hand and there was no stopping him. Before his temper had run its course, he had thrown the hat into the stove. Bright yellow flames leapt hungrily from the open lid.

"I hate you! I hate you! I hate you!" screamed Aris, and fled sobbing through the bedroom door.

Only then did Virgil notice his daughter Murial standing in the middle of the room.

17.

And now they're sending him home for good, thought Aris Mallon, as she stared at the letter in her hands. And sick to boot. They're discharging him and the war isn't even over. What would he be like now?

Aris stared at two of the words in the middle of the page. 'Nervous breakdown.' What was that supposed to mean? Was he crazy? He was always like that, thought Aris, of her imminently returning spouse. He was high strung. Everyone said so. Not one other man in the neighborhood was like her husband was, except maybe Leo Goetz. But Leo was only like that when he drank, and at least Leo went to Church. He was even an usher.

Yes, thought Aris Mallon, with growing conviction, her husband was crazy just like his sister. Their whole family was crazy. Everyone knew that Threasa had stuck a fork in her husband's hand once when he slapped her in the face. Imagine sticking a fork in someone. She probably deserved to get slapped anyhow. No wonder they got divorced. She was just like Virgil.

18.

Virgil Mallon came home, seabag in hand. His once sharply pressed uniform was creased from the long hours of travel, the tight, high knot of his tie was loosed from his throat, and his blue eyes were filled with shame. For fraught with distress about his philanthropist wife, and exhausted with concern about his family, his home and his dissolving business, the man had arrived at a point where he was utterly unable to concentrate on his duty. After an almost accident which he could not seem to address, he was honorably discharged and sent home. There, it was suggested, he might organize and implement the Civil Defense in his small Community. After several days of exhausted sleep, and more of long, painful talks, he rose, took his sawdust covered work clothes from the nail upon which they still hung, and began again.

Once Virgil arrived back in town, his elder sister Threasa was deeply concerned about her brother. A registered bookkeeper with substantial working experience, Threasa came up with a plan. With full confidence in her brother's abilities, and in an attempt to help him get back on his feet, she proposed that she would invest some of her capital into a joint business with Virgil. Together they would hire two men and he and his sister would purchase older, run down homes to renovate. They would then re-sell the homes at a substantial profit. It was a time when big money could be made; the housing market was brisk and the demand high for those who had a mind to work at it, and both Virgil and Threasa did. The first house was purchased at auction, the required men hired, and work commenced.

A LUCKY STRIKE FOR GOD

But in no time, Aris Mallon intruded upon the happy plans, beside herself with rage.

"I don't want your sister involved in our business!" she screamed at Virgil, when the idea first came about. "Everyone in town will know what we make! I won't stand for her doling out our paychecks like I was a two year old!" Aris raged. On and on it went. Day after day, week after week she sulked and cried, slamming cupboard doors and flinging the plates with a clatter upon the table with neither cloth nor napkin to be seen. Red eyed and furious, she sped from room to room, avoiding her husband relentlessly, while battering at his sanity with the cockles of her all consuming greed. Nevertheless, while the battle wore on in the Mallon home, the small business gained steam. In no time, the shrewd and tightfisted Threasa, at one with her chosen career, managed to accumulate a sizeable reserve toward the purchase of two more homes.

But it could not last. On one dark day, the sky overcast, work delayed in view of the impending storm, Threasa and Virgil huddled across the kitchen table in the Mallon home, deep in debate over the allocation of their hard earned funds. Suddenly, a furiousAris Mallon pounced upon them both. Storming out of the bedroom, she planted herself, hands on hips, before her husband's sister. "You can just quit right now, Threasa," said Aris, the words burning through her tight lips, "because there isn't going to be any business where you're involved or I'm getting a divorce! I'm the wife in this family, and it's my place to be involved in the finances, not yours!" With that, Aris marched out the door.

Day after day, Aris contrived to rail at her husband; hour after hour she sequestered herself behind the locked bedroom door until at last Virgil relented. Faced with what he perceived to be the dissolution of his home and family, and wearied by his wife's tirades, Virgil Mallon had not the strength, or the perception, to resist.

"Alright, Aris, you win. If you take the bookkeeping course, you can handle the books," he had finally said to his still defiant wife, and gave in. Threasa closed up the books, gave up her apartment, packed up her clothes and left. Within one month she had secured a well paying Civil Service job and been posted to the East Coast, while Aris Mallon went back to school.

Now the weeks went by. Aris seemed to be satisfied at last. Out the door she went twice a week, notebooks in hand, while her husband toiled day and night.

So immensely relieved was Virgil at the cease-fire in his home that the folly he sensed as closing in upon him began to subside. Little by little, the naive and trusting man laundered the stubborn clots of doubt that had stuck to him, and struggled to patch over the hole he sensed was there with bits and pieces of his remaining hope. Gathering up the scattered remnants of his onetime dream, Virgil rebuilt in his mind the business he would thrive at, and the home he would provide for his family. And Aris, purring contentedly at her new job, and hovering protectively over the chequebook, gave every appearance of having at last found her niche. Lulled more by the lack of obvious distress than by any real progress, Virgil succeeded in tearing out the faulty timbers, the worm-bored wood, the cracked foundations of his marriage, until he believed it had been renewed. If Aris has a hand in the business, he reasoned, it could be the very thing she needs. Daily he assured himself, his dialogue proceeding smoothly. Yes, now that Aris is personally involved in the money, she will appreciate the value of it, he concluded, thinking of his own stumbling journey through the rocks and pitfalls of finance. Slowly, he began to believe that the thing could come to pass. Aris will learn, he soon convinced himself, and with the growing demand, the business could not fail to prosper.

Thus Virgil Mallon created a tenuous scaffold upon which to balance as he worked, a construction of the mind to bridge the gap between that which he sensed and feared, and that which he hoped and dreamed and longed for. Refusing to look at that which he did not want to see, he returned to work, renovating the home he had acquired at great risk, for that purpose.

A LUCKY STRIKE FOR GOD

Soon, green ledger books in varying sizes were everywhere in the Mallon home: on the coffee table, the bookcase, the floor beside the bed. Statements came and went, pay cheques were issued, jobs began to roll in. Little by little Virgil chipped away at Aris's grocery debt, the remains of which still hung over his head. For sixteen months he labored at the small business that had somehow survived the dissolution of the partnership with his sister and the near-devastating loss of her investment. Slowly but steadily he staggered to his feet.

But now, cigar boxes of assorted bills began to line the bottom of Aris Mallon's clothes closet, along with the rubber stamps, ink pads, envelopes, staples, and rolls of postal stamps. There sat, as well, in one of the pasteboard cigar boxes, a stack of quarterly withholding checks made out to the Internal Revenue Service, both for the business, and for each of the men that Virgil Mallon had hired. Unmailed and thus uncashed, the supporting funds from the sidelined checks began to find their way into the coffers of various shops in town, while Aris, an inveterate dibbler, told herself each time that she would replenish the funds the following week. But the months went by, and Aris fell further and further behind, her eye fixed on the bauble before her, and not on the path behind. In the end, the money dispatched irretrievably throughout the city's happy merchants as though she were their sole supporting means, the Internal Revenue Service fell upon Virgil Mallon with a vengeance. The merciless deadline dangled over his now greying head like the proverbial sword of Damocles. Mallon was forced to reduce by almost half the payments for the work that he had done in order to bargain for an advance payout. Only thus could he secure the delinquent sum for the outstretched hand of the taxman.

In the weeks that followed the devastating blow, Virgil Mallon approached door after door, knocked, and spoke in an embarrassed whisper. If successful, he left with a handful of cash, or a handwritten check, carefully folded into his jacket pocket. If not, he returned the next day, and the next. Finally, having accumulated but little more than half of the money he owed, he had gone, cap in hand, to the local bank and borrowed the rest. Added to his unpaid balance, it was an enormous sum. The bank required, as collateral, a mortgage upon the small house he had built and painfully paid for, and upon the shop from which he made his living.

Now Virgil recalled, in tired retrospect, the voice of his older sister, Threasa, before she left town.

"Marriage and business do not mix, Virgil. You had better listen to what I'm telling you because I'm telling you this for your own good. If you think Aris Mitchell can handle your books for you, you're dumber than I ever thought possible. Look around you. That woman can't manage the money in her pocketbook, let alone a business."

He was ruined.

19.

Virgil Mallon drove the six miles to Bill Malhouski's small cottage on the Raber River road. He had hoped to speak with Bill, ask him to put off cashing his paycheck until Monday afternoon. But Bill was not at home. Virgil dropped the white envelope through the mail slot in the Malhouski's front door and climbed back into his truck, but he did not go home. Instead, he drove further down the road. After several miles he came to a narrow bridge where he turned left onto a bumpy two lane dirt road that wound along beside the Raber River. As he drove, he thought of how it had been: how he had loved a girl and left her, how he had come up North when he did, how he had met, and married, Aris, and how things were between Aris and him now. All these things flowed through his mind just as the turgid, slick surfaced river beside him wound through the thickening wood. Finally, he stopped and leaned back against the worn seat of his old truck, his arms limp at his sides. There was no twine in the glove compartment, no hooks or feathers, no leader, no sinkers, no line; there was nothing to fish with at all. There was only an accumulation of nails, screws, wood plugs, bits of molding ends, a dried up bottle of glue. In the back, there were scraps of gyprock and lumber, Celotex, and half filled cement sacks, on top of which were piled two sawhorses, the tops scarred from many cuttings, the sides dripped with rivulets of hardened glue, and many different colors of old paint.

What a fool he had been with his life. He should have listened to his sister Threasa years ago, the night he met Aris at the football field. It had begun to rain so he had taken Aris over to Threasa's but she was not home. Because Virgil had a key, they went in anyhow, and ended up making love on the living room sofa. Threasa had walked in on them, spun on her heels and walked right out again. The next day she said to Virgil, "You are asking for trouble, boy. That girl doesn't know from Adam, and you are going to end up married to her."

And so he had. For three weeks Aris cried piteously: her period had not come. That next weekend, Virgil Mallon and Aris Mitchell eloped. The following week, in a small hotel room in Becksford, Illinois, one day after Virgil found a job, her period began.

20.

Now the bottom of Aris Mallon's clothes closet was cleaned out, and her husband was gone. He had taken all the boxes of bills and papers, all the new elastic bands, the stapler, the account books, a handful of his clothing, and left. She knew where he was because it was a very small town: he was at Herman Boychuck's home, on the point. Mary Boychuck had called Aris, exacting her not to tell. Of course Aris did tell, but she did not tell anyone the truth, because she did not have to tell the truth. In his humiliation, her husband had said only what was necessary: he had incurred an unexpected debt. Thus while Virgil Mallon staggered from door to door under the weight of the assessment, attempting to salvage what he could to sustain his family, Aris, in hushed whispers to her neighbors, and confidences to her friends, told all who would listen that the problem was Virgil's. He had had a spell of illness. After all, didn't the paper from the Navy say he was sick? Didn't the Navy all but say he was crazy? One by one, she showed them all the paper. And look what else he had done! He had burned her hat. He had thrown her clothing on the floor. He had even cried in front of Herman; Mary had told her so. Imagine a grown man, crying!

Everyone believed her. Why shouldn't they? It was true.

But in her heart Aris Mallon was stiff with fear. She had not counted on this. She had not counted on his falling apart; she had not counted on the size of the debt, and above all, she had not counted on a Virgil Mallon unable or unwilling to work.

She would have to fix it somehow.

From that moment, she turned a new face. She rose industriously and cleaned the house. She emptied the refrigerator of the molded food. She washed the mounds of mildewed laundry that had lain on the floor for weeks.

Above all, she accepted all the willing hands that rushed to her aid, the extra food dropped by the house, the bundles of vegetables from her neighbors' gardens. She bathed, groomed, perfumed, powdered, and made well of herself. She wore her best housedress, and her best night dress and waited night after night for her husband to return, but Virgil Mallon did not return.

Finally, she called Mary Boychuck over for coffee and they talked all afternoon.

21.

Murial Mallon sat in the top of the tallest of three evergreens behind her grandfather's garage, her hands sticky with the sweet scent of balsam pitch. There was a light wind; it swayed the topmost branches of the tree and Murial leaned back into the flattened, needley arms. Looking up at the sky, she would inscribe the arc of her small movement against the drifting clouds. From the cradling branches she could see the waist high, overgrown field below, where wound, permanently bent into the tall grass, the foot path to her father's shop.

A LUCKY STRIKE FOR GOD

Now Murial thought of her father's cat, the great grey multi-toed mouser who lived in the shop. "Who will feed Muffy?" she asked of a wrinkled grandmother face that had appeared in a drifting cloud, but the grandmother face withdrew, and did not answer. She shifted her position, now uncomfortable in the knotty branches. Accidentally, she placed her hand on a great gob of pitch, which she tried without success to wipe off on her jeans. It would not come off. "Who's going to sweep the shop?" she asked her hand, as she picked at the bits of needle, and grey-green mossy specks that had affixed themselves to the pitch on her palm. Murial thought of the mountains of sweet smelling shavings she had many times rolled in, the mounds of sawdust she had often pushed before her on the big broom, the treats her father always bought for her when the work was done.

The wind began to pick up, and the air to chill. Murial lay back again upon the pliant branches and waited. No matter how strong it blew, Murial knew that she would not fall from the tree because the many thick branches would not let her. When the wind finally came, it pushed before it a great sailing ship, the bow thrust out, the many white sails flying as it plowed the cloudy billows. Murial looked carefully at the great ship. If she squinted her eyes tightly, she could see Muffy; her mother was there with Cerise and Rosetta. Pulling herself upright, her hands gripping the prickly trunk, her feet splayed on two smaller branches, Murial stood watch until the ship began to dissolve, but no where could she see her father. Soon nothing was left but a ragged wisp of onetime sail, a cloudy flotsam in the sea of blue.

She climbed down the Balsam trunk and went home.

When Murial arrived at her home, no one was there. She went quickly into her mother's bedroom, fell on her knees, and bent to look beneath her parents' bed. A square tin sat close against the forward wall; she withdrew the box and opened the flowered lid. Inside were several squares of her mother's fudge, quite dry, an old sack of hoarhound drops, opened, with a red elastic band around the top, and several pink mints. Murial took two pieces of the dried fudge, set them on the bedcover, pushed the box back up against the wall, and stood up to listen. Then she went out to the kitchen and tore off two squares of waxed paper. In one she wrapped the pieces of fudge, in the other, some scraps of fat and gristle from the uncovered roast on the kitchen stove. Both she stuffed in her pocket; grabbing her sweater, she slipped out the back door, ran behind the garage and plunged through the grassy path in the field.

    The shop was locked when Murial arrived. As she had seen he father do many times, she bent down and lifted the scrap of board from where it lay over a cement block. Reaching into the oval hole in the block, she withdrew a small, round, cardboard container and unscrewed the perforated metal lid. She dumped the key in her hand, opened the door of the shop and went inside. For the next two hours, Murial worked furiously. She sorted small, random boards into piles. She put end cuttings and splintered strips into the scrap barrel. She swept up great mountains of shavings, which she situated in strategic spots to be burned. Finally finished, and sticky with the dusty work, she placed the wrapped parcel containing the two pieces of fudge on her father's swept-clean table saw. She put the scraps in Muffy's bowl on the outside step and immediately the cat appeared from the thick bush. Locking the shop door, she replaced the key and headed for home.

    That evening Virgil Mallon came in over the pot-holed drive to his shop. He retrieved the key, ruffled the head of his great grey cat, stepped inside the shop and stood in amazement. The shop was wonderfully clean, and there on his saw lay the small waxpaper parcel, a twist in either end. He untwisted the ends of the waxed paper, wherein lay the two pieces of fudge.

    "Could it really be?" thought Virgil Mallon, thinking now of the fudge his wife would make for him when things were going well. Could she have come to the shop and left the candy for him? She had a key of her own. Could she have swept up his shop, even? Mary Boychuck had told him Aris

A LUCKY STRIKE FOR GOD

had greatly changed. Could it be true? Perhaps he should think things over.

22.

When Virgil Mallon came to talk, Aris was ready. She admitted her mistakes. She offered to go back to school again. She would even get a part time job to help out. During these talks, sometimes her husband would begin to relax a bit; sometimes he would even smile. One evening, he brought pink mints for himself, and butter mints for her.

Every day now, Aris worked industriously. The house had never looked better. She prepared several good meals. Slowly, Virgil began to come around. Finally, finally he took her to bed. After that she waited for him to return, as she knew he would return.

In two months she was pregnant again with her fourth child.

Exactly two years later, Aris gave birth to her fifth child.

23.

It was a cold February morning. Virgil Mallon sat before the dregs of his cooling coffee and waited for his daughter Murial to clothe herself against the bitter cold. Outside, the icicles glittered like imprisoning bars over the small kitchen windows, and the February chill seeped through the kitchen wall. On this morning, Virgil had not gone to the shop, had not stoked and stirred the dwindling bed of coals in the huge, potbellied iron stove that heated the building, had not built the accustomed fire to warm his work for the day. Instead, he got in his truck, dropped Murial at the front door of the high school and drove to his new job. The drydock was down by the river; ice had formed along the shore, and in places it reached across to the far side, leaving only a few gaps where the moving water could still be seen. As he drove, slumped in the front seat of his truck, cigarette after cigarette accumulated in the ashtray that now overflowed beneath the dash.

"You could still have your shop, Virgil" Aris had beamed brightly at him, as he sat staring at the job application before him. "You'll have a regular job, and you can have your shop work too!" Virgil slowly placed the application in the prepared envelope before him and sealed it in. "I'll mail it first thing in the morning," said Aris, excitedly. "Better still, I'll drop it off for you, on my way downtown!"

24.

Three years later, Virgil Mallon and his brother John stood by the side of their father's grave. The seconded minister shook both their hands, offered his condolences and left. Behind the stand of spruce trees, two men stood leaning on long handled shovels, waiting.

No one else was there.

It had been sixteen years since Virgil had seen his father, back when John's first wife had died. Now, Virgil could barely find his way around Widham, so much had changed. For after his mother left her husband to move north, there was little reason for him to return. He had not been close to his father, and Jacob Mallon had not been a man to write letters. The old man had chosen to live his last years alone in the donated house, where he had finally died.

After the brief service, Virgil drove back to the old house, a key to the door in his pocket. His father had closed off the upper floors years ago; his meager belongings lay strewn about by the high walnut bed he had reassembled downstairs in a curtained side room. Virgil ruffled through some scattered papers, looked in the old desk drawers, and set aside that which was meaningful to him from that which was not. There were several photographs which his sister had asked for, and some items of old furniture to be disposed of or sold, which he left in the care of his brother. Other than that, there was nothing in the house that called to Virgil in any way at all. Still, he felt compelled to look: to crawl down into the cellar, to mount the creaking stairs to the locked door of the room outside of which he listened to his father play so many years ago.

There, on the highest shelf in the closet lay his father's violin. Virgil reached into his pocket and withdrew the smallest key from the handful of keys he had found in the old desk drawer. He inserted it in the rusty lock and the violin case opened. The instrument was wrapped tightly in an ancient linen cloth. Lifting it from its place, he unwound the cloth, stepped into the shadow of the arched window, and brought the violin to his chin. With the frayed horsehair bow raised in his arched right hand, he attempted a single, wavering note. Then he placed the violin back in its case, grasped the worn handle, and drove back into town.

On the corner of MacKenzie Street and Queen stood Sarah Williamson Fresch.

25.

Virgil stood before the post-office in Oswego, New York, a pastel letter in his hand. His heart was heavy in his chest, for he had never been unfaithful to his wife. It was 1962 and he had been married to Aris Mitchell for twenty-eight years. He walked slowly down the street, turned into a restaurant, and sat down. He picked up the menu and ordered his meal.

Virgil Mallon had been working in and out of town the last two years, and on this particular trip he had done well. His expenses had been low; there had been several good meals at the homes of various salesmen, and, to make things more pleasant, he had accepted an offer to stay on an acquaintance's new boat. In the warm fall evenings, he had taken to sitting up on the bow, where he would look out over the water toward the place he had been born, and to where Sarah Williamson Fresch had now returned.

His lunch arrived but he was deep in thought.

There had been letters from Sarah again, ever since they met that day in Widham. Each letter had been carefully read, each carefully answered, folded, and returned to its envelope, each placed securely under Virgil's shirts on the left side of his bag.

As his lunch cooled on the plate, Virgil thought of Sarah and the letters. But more than these, he thought of the shambles he had made of his life. His shop was gone, the property too, and with it all his dreams. What woodwork he was able to do he turned out from a small corner of the new basement. As for Aris, regardless of the regular job, the renovations to the house she had longed for next, and promised to keep up, nothing really changed. Slowly she backslid, and now the structure itself had fallen into disrepair because Virgil was always on the road.

And at month's end when Virgil went home he would feel the tension tighten about his chest from day to day. For after the shop had been sold, the begged for expansions completed, his wife had turned completely cold. With the unexpected bonus of her husband's travel, Aris had free rein. Except for the check that came every other Tuesday, which she hung out the door and took from the postman's hand, she had no interest in her husband. She did not want him there at all, and simply tolerated him, waiting for the day he would, again, leave.

In regard to his children, Virgil was fraught with remorse. Murial had married a false and cozening young man in a bewildering affair her father had never understood. Cerise, always close to her mother, was sullen and hostile. Rosetta, the middle child, brought into the world in the warp of her parent's separation, had been shelved between her parents' fights ever since, and had grown to be a defensive, touchy girl. Virgil realized sadly that he hardly knew her at all.

And as for the younger two, he was rapidly losing touch. Daniel, always a nervous child, was obsequious, irresponsible, and detached. Only his youngest child, Nola, welcomed him at all, and even that was questionable; she tore through his bags for the treat she knew was there for her, and scrambled for the change he would fling across the worn kitchen floor. It was a pitiful ritual Virgil had fallen into of late.

"Here you go; here's my money!" Virgil would announce when arrived home, dramatically emptying both pockets. Tak-

A LUCKY STRIKE FOR GOD

ing his wallet, he would upend it over the kitchen table and loose the bills from their place.

"Come on, Rosetta, Nola, - you too, Cerise," he would say to his married daughter, who was usually there, "Come on; come and get it. That's all your old father is good for," he would say, and flip the coins and bills across the floor as though he were feeding the ducks. Nola enjoyed the game; she would scramble, laugh, tease, and try to pull the bills from her father's hand ahead of time, whereupon Virgil would hold them just out of reach before dropping them into her palm. Cerise would move sullenly forward like a chess player. When she bent to take what she could it was usually with a snide remark.

"I'll take the money; why not?" Cerise would say, her words designed to relieve her of the import of her act. Her husband, when there, would laugh. But Virgil's son Daniel would simply shake his head and leave the room.

"You might as well get down there too, Aris; you've got the rest of it," Virgil would then sing out to his wife, in a mock falsetto voice. At times like this if Aris was around, she would simply smirk, and say nothing.

Thus Virgil Mallon had come to dread the invasion he made in his own home. He felt the antipathy as though he were a intruder his family was forced to accept.

As for himself, the only thing he could say was that he was finally stashing a little money away for his retirement, a small savings automatically deducted, and a few thousand dollars, safe in his own name. He intended it for a little place to fish from. It was the sole financial concession he made to himself in all the years he had been married.

Now Virgil opened Sarah Williamson's fourth letter and began to read. As he turned the pages with his scarred, oversized fingers, they began to tremble in his hands.

> *How have you managed to stay so completely the same after all these years, Virgil?*

Sarah asked.

> *How did you keep that same bright blue in your eye?*

KAREN PIETKIEWICZ

When we met I felt like we had never ever even been apart.
Virgil carefully folded the fourth letter.
He ate his lunch and made a single call.

He drove back to the boat, packed a change of clothes and two shirts, and drove to Tobermory.

When Sarah Fresch stepped off the ferry he folded her in his arms and wept.

26.

On Friday morning, Aris Mitchell stepped up to the teller and began to unload her purse. At the bottom was a small account book in a plastic folder, quite new.
"I'd like to withdraw some money for my husband," she announced to the young girl behind the wicket.
"Hello, Mrs. Mallon; how are you today?" said the young girl. "I saw Cerise and Noel at Woolworth's on my lunch hour."
"Oh, yes," said Aris, "they must have gone shopping for Noel's school clothes. Noel has some money of her own now; she baby-sat all summer."
"That's good," said the girl at the till, taking out four fifties. "I hope fifties are O.K. for you, Mrs. Mallon, or would you rather have two hundreds?"
"Fifties are fine; Virgil just signs the withdrawal slip and sends it to me, and I take out what he needs."
"Men hate banking - that is unless they are businessmen," said the girl, closing the till and counting out the bills. "Fifty, one hundred, fifty, two hundred," she said to Aris, "There you go."
"Thank you, Delores. Say hello to your mother for me."
" I will," said Delores Malhouski. "Bye."

At nine o'clock that night, Aris was finally alone, and she liked it that way. Without her husband to intrude on her

A LUCKY STRIKE FOR GOD

space or her children to bother her, without useless, unwanted company to pick up for, or to have to be polite to, she could do exactly what she wanted.

She took the telephone off the hook.

For Aris had done what she was supposed to have done. She had married and acquired a home. She had had her children and was raising them. Now she wanted to be left alone. She poured the contents of a cellophane potato chip bag into a wicker basket. She opened the chip dip and made herself a wine highball. She turned the knob of her television set until she found the movie that looked good. *Tender is the Night*, the screen soon read, and she curled up on the sofa to watch the show. But no sooner had she settled in than the door opened, and she heard hurried footsteps in the hall.

"Aris? Aris?" It was her mother. The thin, wavering voice called out, "Your phone isn't working, Aris!" The old woman intruded into Aris's living room just as Aris rose from the sofa to face her.

"Your father hasn't come home yet, Aris;" the old woman began. "Do you think he had a late call? Where do you think he could be at this hour, Aris?" Elizabeth Mitchell asked her daughter, her grey head cocked and trembling, her right hand and arm shaking.

Aris Mitchell felt a great irrational rage begin to swell in her chest in the face of the tiresome, aged old woman who was supposed to be her mother. Norman Mitchell had been dead for thirteen years. Would she ever get it into her head?

"Go on back to the house, mom, he'll be home later. Go home and go to bed!" said Aris, her impatience growing by leaps and bounds.

"Well, I might as well do some washing. Give me your washing too, Aris, and I'll throw it in with mine," said the old woman.

The rage now began to expand inside of Aris, to gather in her throat, and in the clenched fists of her hands.

"I don't want to do laundry, mother, and I don't want you to my laundry either. I'm watching a movie."

"Well then, you just watch the movie and I'll take it over myself for you and throw it in. No use to waste hot water," said her mother, and started carefully down Aris's basement stairs. As Aris watched from the top, her mother bent toward the damp cement at the foot of the stairs where the dirty clothes had been thrown down into their mildewed heap. One by one, the old woman turned the soiled garments right side out and dropped them in a wicker basket. Then, hoisting the load before her, encircled in both thin arms, she struggled back up the stairwell. When she got to the top, she set the basket down, turned to flip the basement light, and closed the door.

"Aris, you had better attend to those clothes down there on the wet floor, or they will all be ruined with the damp," her mother said, bending toward her daughter. Consternation was written between her drawn grey brows, and her eyes peered intently into her daughter's angry face.

Suddenly, Aris Mallon slapped her mother full in the side of the head and the old woman let out a wail. A rain of blows now fell from Aris Mallon upon Elizabeth Mitchell; the old woman wailed again and again, raising her trembling arms to shield her head and face.

"I don't care about the damned clothes!" screamed Aris, at her mother's hidden face. "I don't care about any of it. Get out of my house! Get out! Get out!" she screamed, and the old woman fled weeping.

27.

Virgil Mallon reeled in the first good cast he had made in several years, while Sarah Fresch sat sunning herself on a bright pink granite ledge. It was a matter of control, he recalled, as he cast again, carefully tending the line as it fed out over the water. It was strange how things you thought you had lost came back with half a chance. After several bad casts, and one line that had caught and snagged hopelessly in the tag alders behind him, he had found his wrist again, and the feel of the singing line as it spun beneath his thumb throughout the wonderful afternoon.

A LUCKY STRIKE FOR GOD

That evening he sat on Sarah's sofa, after building a small fire on the stone hearth, and he and Sarah talked.

"I don't know what I'm going do, Sarah," Virgil Mallon told the woman who now sat across from him. "All I have is the house, and my pension, and thirteen thousand dollars in the bank. That's it. "

"What do you really need, Virgil?" said Sarah? "What do you really want?"

"I had a mind to get me a small piece of land just this side of Killarney. I was thinking of building myself a small place up on cement piers, maybe even right over a branch of one of those small streams so I could fish right from the door. Build it like a bridge right over the stream, over a hole, and lift a trap door up right in the living room floor and fish right out of the house." As he spoke, his eyes began to brighten, as though some spark rekindled after a long time lost.

Sarah began to laugh softly.

"My God, Virgil, that's what I could never forget about you: you always had the craziest ideas! I think you are the only man I ever met that thinks the way you do. So why don't you go ahead and do it? You can throw up a little place like that for a pittance, and you can always go back to carpentry after you leave the job."

"Do you think so, Sarah?" the man now asked. "Do you think I could make a go of it again?"

"You always made a go of things, Virgil, just like I always knew you would, but you did it for everyone else but yourself. You've got this archaic sense of honour, Virg. That's what I think I've always loved you for. I'm not saying this because I'm looking for something for myself, but maybe it's time you started thinking of you, for a change."

Virgil Mallon lit a cigarette and went out into the screened veranda of Sarah Fresch's small cedar house to smoke it. Sarah rose and followed him, leaning in the doorway between the house and the porch.

"What about us, Sarah? Do you think we could make a go of things at this late age?"

Virgil Mallon had finally asked, putting words to the plea he had been unable to make over forty long years ago. But now there was no fear, no hope, no wonder, no dream. There was only this last evening before he went back home, and Sarah Williamson, here beside him.

"I can't answer that Virgil, any more than I could then," said Sarah softly. "but I loved you then, and I still love you. The rest has to be up to you."

After Virgil Mallon got in his truck to make the long drive home, Sarah Williamson took out a pen, and her flowered stationary. She sat before the paper for many long minutes, and began to write.

Dearest Virgil,

Do you think you were the only one who was afraid? Do you think you are the only one who is afraid now?

Well, it's too late to be afraid anymore, Virg. There isn't enough time left. I love you, and I will be here for you - any way you want me to be.

And she signed it,

Love, Sarah.

But since she did not want to send the letter to his home, she sent to his job at Oswego, to be there when he returned.

28.

Aris Mallon rushed down to the bank at nine o'clock Tuesday morning, her husband's monthly paycheck in her hand.

"I want to deposit this," she announced to the woman behind the till, but it was not Delores Malhouski. "Where is Delores today?" she asked, adopting a bright smile to cover her strangling fear.

"Delores is off sick," said the new girl, turning the paycheck face down. "Where did you want to put this?"

"I'm supposed to put it in Virgil's savings this time," Aris announced, "and I need the balance after, please."

A LUCKY STRIKE FOR GOD

The teller punched in the entry and stamped the back of the check as she slid a deposit slip under the wicket for Aris to sign.

The teller looked squarely at Aris Mallon.

"Mrs. Mallon, are you aware that this account is only in your husband's name?" she asked, concerned. "I really can't give you the balance."

"Oh, it's O.K., Delores always does," Aris said quickly. "My husband works out of town. It's not as if I'm taking anything out; I want to put his whole paycheck in, and he asked me to please get his balance. Wouldn't you be able to do that like Delores always does, until she comes back? My husband is calling me for it, tonight." The words tumbled casually from her lips.

"Well," said the teller, "I suppose it won't hurt this once, but you really should not ask again without a note from your husband."

"Oh, for sure; for sure; " said Aris, "I'll be sure to have him write me a note the next time."

The teller scribbled the number on a slip of blue paper, folded it, and passed it under the wicket. Aris took it and hurried from the bank.

Once safely out of sight in her car, Aris opened the folded blue paper. Seven thousand, seven hundred and thirteen dollars and seventy six cents. She owed him more than five thousand dollars. But as she began to drive, the fear she had at first felt in her throat had begun to congeal.

"Why should I feel bad?" she soon announced to herself in the dashboard mirror. "Half of that money should be mine anyhow." The fear was sinking slowly out of sight. "I never wanted to live in his damn fishing place anyhow." The remaining tentacles of fear now slid into the corners of her heart where they regrouped and coiled in the darkness. "If he really cared about me, he wouldn't think of stashing money away behind my back. He's gone paranoid about it just like his sister Threasa," she now pronounced.

By the time Aris Mallon turned into her drive, she was not in the least afraid. In fact, she had worked herself into a rage.

KAREN PIETKIEWICZ

29.

Virgil Mallon sat at the end of the kitchen table consumed by an overpowering fear. Before him, on the melamine table top lay a sizeable stack of bills, fixed with a red rubber band. Beside the money lay his small grey bankbook, the account closed out.

She's gone and done it again, he told himself, and immediately as he said the words, he plunged into the bottomless pit of his soul.

What kind of woman was his wife, he now asked himself? What kind of man was he? Was he a man? How could he not have seen? Could he even see now? Or was it all some mad nightmare, some insanity that crept upon him from the war? That was what she always said to him, his wife: that he was crazy. That was what she told everybody. That was what she screamed at him when anything went wrong. Maybe he was crazy. Was he crazy? What does it even mean, crazy?

Virgil Mallon spun down the centripetal whorls of his mind like a runaway ice sled shooting through the eroding tunnels and vertical drains of a wasted, frigid hell. Images flashed before him: the burned remnants of his wife's fur hat, his daughter Murial, the old, smashed guitar Aris had hated, Sarah Fresch, waving from the dock. The Ouija board from which his wife and her sister read on the kitchen table in spite of Virgil's protests, came careening at him through the air. Down, down he went, utterly lost, until the last door opened.

There sat his mother, rocking and knitting, the clock behind her chair ticking away. Tick, tock, tick, tock, impassive and serene, the mother waited for the son whom she knew would return to her. Virgil Mallon fell on his knees before her; his arms folded beneath his head, he lay on her lap and wept.

As Aris Mallon walked into the room her husband was still head down, arms folded on the table. But now, Aris had an agenda. For in the mailbox she had found Sarah Fresch's letter, forwarded to the house by the office out of which Virgil had last worked.

A LUCKY STRIKE FOR GOD

Now she flung the opened letter at her husband's head and began to scream. As she screamed out her volumes of hate, blorbles of incoherent rage spilled from within her to flood the chambers of her husband's ears. But there the words stopped. For Virgil Mallon finally stood up. Raising his head, he took the letter in his hands and began to read it as if his wife was not even in the room. As he read, the screaming Aris began to fade from him like a worn out record or a moving picture that suddenly lost its sound. When he had finished reading the letter, he folded it carefully and put it into his shirt pocket.

This time as he stood there, he watched as a man detached, while his wife spewed out the last of the barbs that were within her, the dervish she had become swirling and whirling about the room in a spinning welter of rage. At last, when all had tumbled out, the woman fell to the floor in a heap. There she began to sob, and as she did, Virgil Mallon felt again the familiar tug of his errant heart. But this time he did not move. Instead, he stood quietly and watched as his wife lay sobbing on the floor. When after several minutes Virgil did not move, Aris suddenly lifted her head. Folding her arms beneath her, she pushed, and raised herself up from the floor. Standing before her husband, she fixed her eyes on his and said quietly,

"I'll get you for this." Then she turned and walked out the door.

30.

Utterly alone, Virgil Mallon sat in his chair at the far end of the kitchen table immersed in a stupor of disbelief. In his mind, surrounding him on all sides like denizens he could no longer control gamboled his wife and children, laughing at him sardonically in a circus gone completely awry. As the wallpaper on the kitchen walls peeled even further from the steam of Aris's never attended kettle, Virgil stared at the dozens of pock marks sunk into the new floor from the stilettos of her latest shoes. As he smoked, he watched the ash build on his cigarette, the cigarette diminish with each puff. Behind him, he could hear the forlorn drip of the kitchen faucet, and the water in the toilet, still running.

What was to become of him now?

As he sunk deeper and deeper into the well of his confounded soul, Virgil began to see the figure of his daughter Murial through a haze of blue smoke. Standing before him once again, she asked, " What are you doing to yourself, daddy?", just as she had asked on the day of her unexpected visit to Petosky.

"You're smoking yourself to death; I hope you know that," Murial had said, on the day of the visit, as she moved from window to window of the small motel room of Highway 31 where Virgil had stopped for the night. As the fresh air began to clear the room, Virgil Mallon had stubbed out his cigarette in delight at the unexpected appearance of his oldest daughter.

"Well, how did you manage to find your way here?" he asked, "Your mother told me you weren't coming home until next spring."

"I saw your truck," said Murial.

"Yawana go eat something?" said her father, his eyebrows raised, his lined face still eager, his grey head thrust forward from his chest. Grabbing his old, gold flannel shirt he began buttoning the buttons both ways out, from the middle. "I got this place down the road where the waitress knows me. We'll get something to eat, and then this ice cream. You wanna see the ice cream sundaes she makes me!" said her father, and Murial's eyes filled with tears at the old man her father had suddenly become.

The cafe was small but clean. The waitress, garbed in black taffeta with a crisp, white apron, rustled as she walked. She wore too much eye make-up and too much rouge, but she laughed and laughed as her father told all the old jokes Murial had heard a hundred times before, and soon Murial herself was laughing. After the meal, her father fell serious; the familiar cigarette in his right hand, the smoke rising.

"So, now: what the hell is this I'm hearing about you and Sean. Your mother won't tell me a god-damned thing."

A LUCKY STRIKE FOR GOD

"There is no Sean anymore, daddy," said Murial Mallon, simply.

"What the hell d'ya mean, Murial: 'There is no Sean'?"

"Just what I said, daddy. I left him a year ago, when I came home for the summer. We got divorced.

"He was never right for you." said her father.

"I know that. I thought that was what I was supposed to do."

Then Murial had looked straight at her father and said, "So that's my excuse, Daddy, what's yours?"

31.

Virgil Mallon sat at the kitchen table until his cigarette burned to the end. The ash was longer than the flame and hung tremulously from the burning stubb. Virgil carefully raised the ashtray, flicked off the ash and stubbed out the butt. Taking his keys from the table, he went out to his truck and drove out to his shop. There he loaded his tool boxes and power tools, his ladder, sawhorses, all that he felt he needed to do his work, and returned to the house.

Aris was still not home, and he was relieved.

He went into the house, placed his Hawaiian steel guitar in its case and carried it outside. He went up to the attic, turned the key in the lock, and reached up on the overhanging rafters to where he had placed a large sheet of aspenite. Feeling with his fingertips, he grasped the rounded edge of his father's violin case, drew it carefully down, blew off the dust and went back down the steep steps, locking the attic door behind him. He went back inside the house once more for the books, bills, and papers. Finally, he took his duffle bag from the hook and filled it with his work clothes, topping off the bag with the few dress clothes he ever wore. As he ruffled through the better clothes, he found the small velvet box Murial had given him, opened it, and ran his finger over the golden rod and the delicate the silver line. Snapping the box closed, he threw it in his bag. Then he got in his truck and left.

As Virgil Mallon drove East in the dark night, the dashboard lights glowed with many colors. From the back of the truck, he could hear the tarpaulin flapping, and beneath him he could hear the sound of the tires singing steadily over the road. On the radio, the station was erratic. Virgil turned the knob until he heard a familiar tune. It was one of Aris's favorite songs.

> *I'll be loving you, always;*
> *with a love that's true, always.*

began the tune, but it slowly faded out of range. Virgil fiddled with the knob again, stopping at each snatch of song, trying to find a melody that would stay with him to the end. But when nothing would stay in tune, Virgil himself began to sing.

> *Sweet Lelani, heavenly flo-wer,*
> *Angels fashioned heaven just for you,*
> *We'll walk through paradise together;*
> *You make my dreams come true.*

32.

When Aris Mallon discovered her husband had gone, she gathered her forces about her like a brick wall. For three days she poured out a tale of woe which she did not even have to embellish. The feathers of her flock of friends softening her nest, Aris was showered with considerations, spoken to in whispers, visited with dishes she did not have to cook, and taken to events for which she did not have to pay.

The Friday night after Virgil left, Aris finally found herself alone. She put on her brown jacket and picked up her new bag. She took her car keys from the nail where they hung, and went to the corner store. She bought a large bottle of seven-up and two bags of Old Dutch potato chips and drove back home, where she poured the chips into the bowl, mixed herself a gin fizz, and settled in to watch a movie.

Why not?

She finally had the whole place to herself.

* * *

The Cricket

The girl awakened suddenly. Her eyes probed the dusky silence with a series of piercing glances until they fixed on the outlined shape of her suitcase, opened and overflowing on the luggage stand. She exhaled, hung suspended for a minute, and then breathed deeply once again.

Lying quietly, she moved only her arm, serpentine, from under the blanket until she felt the nightstand. Her fingers flitted silently over the surface and entwined about the watchband. The exquisite, glowing numerals seemed to deny the darkness, and a flicker of impatience crossed her brow. She wound the watch, and slipping it on her wrist, lay motionless once again.

It was half-past two and Raymond wasn't back yet.

The girl now lay awake, consternation written on her shadowed face. Alone in the small, dank cabin, she recalled the lifeless ceremony, the modest refreshments, the jokes, the spilled bottles of beer on the Ryan's side of the dance hall. Amid the customary attempt at celebration, she had watched as one removed, while all around her the appropriate levity was applied as paint on an outhouse door. She had smiled and nodded; nodded and smiled.

KAREN PIETKIEWICZ

And now she was here; here in this room where she had not wanted to be; here in this room where she had never dreamed she would ever be, a surreal alien in someone else's place, completely and totally alone. Behind her, as puppets on the stage from which she had reluctantly withdrawn, jigged and danced the principals of her life: her relieved and smiling mother, the daughter safely wed; her father, appropriating a mien of artificial decorum, a sad bewilderment reflected in his blue eyes; her sister, the bored and blase maid of honor, yawning indiscriminately; her younger brother and sisters racing from table to table with hordes of wedding-dressed cousins.

Now, her father's voice returned to her and began to play over and over in her mind like a gramophone stuck in a groove.

"The boy is not for you," her father had said, many months ago. "He's a party boy, Eleanor."

"You always have to say something ugly!" her mother, flaming up, had flung out, and the war was on.

"I'll have you know that Raymond is an altar boy," she railed; "he's even an Eagle Scout!"

Amidst her mother's heated protestations she heard her father press on.

"I'm telling you, Della, he'll go the way of his folks. He's been raised with a bottle of beer in his hands and he'll likely die with a bottle of beer in his hands and there is nothing you, or I, or young Eleanor, here, can do to change that."

"You're ruining everything," his wife had wailed, and she flew to the bedroom and slammed the door.

But Eleanor knew it was true. Frozen in an obtuse space unknown to both her father and mother, the girl sat silenced by an unspeakable weight that had shackled itself to her heart. Her father, sensing some lost thing in the girl, but unable to put a name to it, turned to face his daughter, with a great, long sigh.

"Eleanor, I do not dislike young Raymond," he began, "but a boy like that who comes from liquor will return to liquor as sure as a crow to the corn crib. He's still wet behind

THE CRICKET

the ears and already he's a beer suck. Now you may not like to hear that, but your daddy's telling you that's what Raymond is and there's not a snowball's chance in hell that he's ever going to change. He'll break your heart, and like as not your head, if you marry him."

The greying man now picked up his pipe in his left hand. With his right hand he reached three work scarred fingers into the open pack of Borkum Riff that lay beside him on the table. Packing it into the worn bowl now cupped in his palm, he lit a wooden match, leaned back in his chair, and drew in.

"This is all your daddy's got to say to you about this. You know your mother won't speak to me for weeks now; I can see that coming as sure as sin. She doesn't understand anything but what the Church tells her, and there's nothing anyone's going to do to change her either."

The man then looked at his daughter where she sat, silent, on the worn kitchen chair. "Now you go on about your business, but you think about what your daddy said." And with that, he withdrew, his eyes fixed on some far distant point, his left arm still, the great sweet smelling puffs of smoke rising and rising and rising.

But it had already been decided. On a dark night, in a dark car the last argument had ensued. "I just want to date around," Eleanor had said to the side of the angry, sullen face beside her. "You and I can still go out." There had been nothing but silence from the furious boy, who had turned on her, inflamed.

"You want to leave me to date Richard; that's what you want. Do you think I don't know? I never even got anything off you. I've been nothing but good, haven't I? Haven't I? Haven't I? Have I ever done anything you didn't want?" The boy was now shouting at her, his rasping face inches from her own, his hands grasping her upper arms like twin vises. He shook her like a rag doll, and as suddenly as he had advanced upon her, he retreated and began to cry. Folding his arms over the steering wheel of the car he sobbed as if he would die.

Eleanor sat motionless with shock and wonder. Her heart began to fill with pity at this person she suddenly barely knew.

KAREN PIETKIEWICZ

"I didn't say I was leaving you, Ramie," she offered carefully so as to appease the sobbing boy. "I still like you; I don't like you any less than I ever did."

"Then prove it!"

In a flash the boy was on her, tearing at her blouse, and ripping at the waistband of her pleated skirt. ""I deserve it! You know I deserve it!"

Now the girl began to cry, clutching at her clothes and pushing at the belligerent stranger she was now confronting. The two struggled on the front seat of the older model car.

The boy was in a rage, and crying again. He twisted at her skirt and tugged at the narrow, confining nylon slip. "I'm not going to do it all the way," he sobbed, while his hands tore at her garments in impotent rage, "I just want to lay up against you! You owe me! You owe me!" The assault began again.

In the face of his piteous fury the girl began to relent. Pushing his chest from hers, and inspired with a last-ditch effort to defend herself from the unwanted assault, she heard herself carefully say, "Alright! Alright, Ramie! But stop forcing me!"

The boy stopped.

"I just want to lean up against you," he began again, his voice soft, and cajoling. "You owe me at least that after three years."

The convoluted logic of his plea, suffused with the surprising outburst of grief and rage seemed to nullify the girl's own instincts, and instead, inappropriately brought forth in their place a blinding pity for the intractable youth. In a stratagem of partial acquiescence, and in an attempt to pacify the now uncontrollable boy, Eleanor partially disrobed in the dark, cold car. Sliding down on the seat, she watched as Raymond, his trousers rumpled on the floor mats, his face a map of intensely focused concentration, struggled with the buttons on his shirt. As he slid overtop of the naively trusting girl, she held a hand out to his chest.

"Remember, Raymond, you promised."

But of course he did not stop. Inflamed at the thought of Richard Bennett in the place where he intended to be, he

THE CRICKET

deflowered the girl in an instant, withdrew, and ejaculated in his soiled, crumpled handkerchief. Opening the car door, he jumped into the dark. Pulling on his clothes with his two hands, he sneered at the girl while the dim light of the dash played over the shocked and speechless form that lay frozen on the cushioned seat.

"Now go to Richard, if he'll have you," Ramie Ryan announced, his eyes as dead and cold as the leaves that lay on the November ground.

But Richard would not have her now, nor would he ever. The virginal vessel she had been instructed to protect, to save for the man she would marry, was shattered forever. She was no longer the waiting Bride of Christ. She belonged to Ramie Ryan, forever and forever and forever.

The pitiful girl returned to her home, her dreams dissolved to nothing.

Now there was this.

Eleanor Rebecca Ryan looked at her watch. It was twenty of three. Thinking back three hours to the enigma of the tastelessly well-planned shivaree, she felt sick. No sooner had she and her now husband, Raymond arrived in the tourist village of Newberry, than the menagerie burst in upon them. Horns blasting, headlights blinking on and off, the besotted hoard had pounded at the door while she fled to the bathroom and cried. In a great glut of macho braggadocio, the erstwhile groom had joined his leering, reeling friends, allowing himself to be bandited into one of the waiting cars on the shoulders of several drunks while he beat, Tarzan style, on his chest. In a cacophony of blaring horns and squealing tires, the reeking mob disappeared into the night with the groom, leaving the officially consummated bride utterly alone.

The silence in the small cabin was now broken by a singular chirp. Eleanor Ryan stiffened as a solitary cricket skittered into a band of moonlight that issued from the window and divided the darkness of the floor. The insect stopped with a soft click, poising and preening in its silvery bath with an infinity of delicate movements. She watched the silent ceremony until, as if offended by her ocular intrusion, the cricket sprang into the silent shadows. The girl lay a long while, and listened to it chirp.

Dawn came hesitatingly, almost reluctantly, pushing gently at the last remaining star until it lost its tenacious grip on the heavens and disappeared into the light. The new Mrs. Ryan watched the heavy breathing of the form now sprawled beside her. A muscular young man, his hands lay open, palms upward, childlike in their relaxation, while a series of imperceptible movements played on his closed lids. The girl averted her gaze; she rested her eyes on the orchid she had never worn, still freshly wrapped and encased in its cellophane shroud. It lay on the dresser like a vegetable.

From beneath the bed the cricket called again.

Now, before her mind's eye, Eleanor Ryan saw the cricket ensconced in a minuscule bamboo cage. She determined to catch the cricket in the morning just like the Oriental girl did in "Teahouse of the August Moon". She would make her own tiny cage for the wedding cricket. Everyone knew that cricket on the hearth brought good luck.

She wondered if it worked without a hearth.

Two hours later, the alarm went off with a shrill ring. The new couple rose together. Eleanor wandered absently to the far side of the small room while the sound of running water announced a new day. She waited kindergarten-like for her turn in the bath.

Finally, a cloud of steam signaled the open door. The girl went in and closed the door behind her, shutting out the now familiar chirp of the ebony insect waiting under the bed. She ran the water, removed her toothbrush from its celluloid container, and brushed her teeth. The brush was new, and the bristles stiff. She held it under the hot water, ineffectually. As she brushed her teeth, she observed the crimson flecked water as it swirled down the drain.

Suddenly, a sickeningly sweet odor reached her nose and she started. She could hear a series of hissing sounds outside the door. Reaching for the knob, she pulled on it and stepped out into the adjoining room.

THE CRICKET

There on the floor crouched Raymond Ryan, the index finger of his left hand prodding the feebly twitching cricket while his righthand enclosed a can of Raid. Rising, he looked quizzically at his new wife's stiffened form.

"Finished?" he asked.

* * *

Rachel and the Night Child

It was a strange and misty day. The sun hung heavily in the sky and tired birds sat on silent branches in the trees.

Rachel started out to school. From the fence the mourning dove called once and flew away. Rachel watched it flutter into the soft daylight. The grey-white clamshells, crushed and dusty, crunched beneath her red shoes. But she liked the clamshells because they brought the ocean to the morning, with wheeling gulls and seaweed chains and sand-dollars waiting to be uncovered.

The old bus was coming down the glimmering asphalt road and Rachel waited quietly as it creaked to a stop. Then she bent down to pick up her lunch pail and as she did, she noticed that there was no shadow when she moved. How strange it was to have no shadow. She climbed aboard the bus and moved to the high back seat from which she could look out at the place where her shadow should have been. She watched the spot as it faded into the distance and finally disappeared.

He was there again. Rachel felt shivery and cold, and goosebumps rose on her small arms. Each morning the nurse brought him in from the old car to the front desk. Rachel looked at the brown boy from the cloakroom where she stood, reluctant to enter. He was reading. She studied him as he sat there. He was very thin. His bones seemed big and lumpy at his wrists and elbows. Rachel felt her arms. It was hard to feel the bones but she knew they were there. It was funny how the bones were. They were white, even under brown skin. Rachel looked again. But now she looked at the brown skin that hung so thinly over the lumpy bones. It seemed a thing apart from her, far, far away and she could not even imagine its substance but only look queerly at its brownness.

It was time for the reading circle. Rachel took her place. Now he sat across from her, there where she could not escape, while his black eyes danced and sparkled as though hundreds of glittering secrets lay just behind them. His eyes were like sunlight on the Gulf, shimmering and changing and never quite still while the rest of him sat stiffly in the small brown chair.

The children began to read. One by one the voices droned in turn. Rachel was restless and uncomfortable and the voices made her very, very tired. Now he began to read. His voice was musical and soft and he read swiftly. Then suddenly he stopped, and looking straight into Rachel's eyes he chanted in a sing-song voice:

"Rachel, Rachel, bright as day, come and watch de night chile play!"

Rachel's heart began to pound and the small reader slipped from her fingers onto the dusty floor. She looked up quickly in the direction of her teacher, and then back again at the brown boy, who sat smiling softly across from her. Her small mind raced in confusion and, reaching down for her book she reopened it and gripped it tightly in both hands, staring fiercely at the black letters as if to absorb them bodily.

The voices began again and the morning wore into noon. Finally the lunch bell rang. The children lined single file

RACHEL AND THE NIGHT CHILD

outside the classroom door before the small table upon which had been set a wire crate filled with half-pints of milk. They each took a carton in turn, then returned chattering to their desks amidst the wrapping and unwrapping of sandwiches from noisy brown paper sacks or tinny metal lunch pails.

Rachel sat silent in her desk, her open lunch pail before her. The sandwiches lay one on top of the other, folded neatly in waxed paper. At the end, also wrapped securely, was an orange, already peeled, and under it two cookies. She looked at the orderly arrangement of her lunch pail. Circles and squares and sharp creased edges: so neat, so orderly. It was beautiful. Suddenly she was no longer hungry. Nothing should disturb the orderly lunch pail.

She closed the box quickly.

Rachel went down the hall slowly. The great doors at the end stood open, revealing the clamour of the playground. The windows on either side of the doorway were dusty and the sun filtered through in indeterminate patterns of the floor. Small specks of dust whirled in the sunbeams, sparkling and glimmering as they floated in the heavy air. Rachel was thirsty. She bent over the white water fountain and pressed the chrome handle. She bent to drink. A great blob of pink gum sat on the circular drain and as she drank she looked at the gum. It was full of small, distinct toothmarks. She wondered if it were his gum.

Outside, the noise of the children playing swirled around her ears. She walked slowly through the playground toward the swings. And then she saw him. He was there, sitting lightly on the swings. And beside him was the only empty seat. Now the noise of the playground became a great swirling thing that had caught her and was sweeping her helplessly down the long tunnel to the vortex where he sat, smiling patiently. Anger began to swell within her, blind anger, and fear. Fear of the waiting boy, fear of the noise and fear of herself, for now she knew that she hated the brown boy with his secret eyes and strange smile because he fascinated her. And precisely because she hated him, and because he fascinated her, she walked deliberately up to the swing and sat down hard on the seat. Then, pushing furiously, she began to swing higher and higher still, until the chains that held her shrieked in protest as she rose and dipped.

As she pumped harder and harder, the brown child became less and less, a blur, a speck of dark in a landscape of light, but he was there, and no matter how hard she tried she could not swing fast enough to make him disappear. Now she began to swing in wild frenzied abandonment. The colors blurred and blended into a delicate prismic bowl capped by the blue midday sky. The brown that was the boy began to fade and blend into the whole until he became only a darker shade of light diffused among the colors that streaked before her eyes, and Rachel was no longer afraid.

The school bell rang. As suddenly as it sounded, the colors disappeared and Rachel scuffed to a stop. She leapt lightly from the seat which continued to inscribe arcs through the air from the force of her movement. She ran swiftly a short distance and then stopped. Turning to the swings, she looked straight at the brown child, who rose slowly and began to walk across the play yard. He looked smaller now, and Rachel noticed that his dancing eyes were quiet; the sparkling secrets were gone and in their place had come a deep and mysterious sadness which seemed to weigh upon his thin frame like an invisible burden, causing him to drag his shuffling feet over the dusty ground.

She waited. And when he was nearly to her she asked,
"Why do you always tease me?"
The boy looked inquiringly at her.
"What you mean by dat, Miss Rachel?"
The girl flushed.
"You know what I mean. In school. You say crazy things." The boy drooped slightly; then, with a patient sadness he answered her simply:
"Miss Rachel, you mus' be mistaken. It ain't me dat's teasin' you."
"Liar!" She screamed at the boy. But he seemed now distant and unaffected; instead, the echo of her voice rang in her own ears and she turned and ran into the school.

RACHEL AND THE NIGHT CHILD

It grew hot. In the classroom the flies buzzed stickily against the dusty panes of glass, and now and then a wasp ventured threateningly close to the restless students. Rachel pushed the hair back from her damp forehead. She looked up the aisle. He was writing. Small, glistening beads stood out on his veined temples and streaked down in front of his ears. Rachel watched him as he wrote. He seemed more tired than she had ever seen him and finally his thin hand dropped to rest on the yellow paper and the pencil rolled out of his fingers. The teacher looked up. Then, rising quickly, she approached his desk and bent solicitously over his small frame, whispering something to him as he laboured to gather his books. The teacher seemed anxious and stood ineffectually as he fumbled in the scarred desk.

Finally he was ready. He stood for a moment and then, turning, he looked at Rachel. She froze, paralyzed in her seat, and waited for the words she knew he would say. Everyone was looking now. The classroom was deathly still and every child was watching. But the words did not come. Instead, he only looked for an infinite moment with dark and pleading eyes at the hypnotized girl and then walked slowly out of the room.

After school that day, the play yard buzzed with speculation. The chattering voices angered Rachel and she left quickly. The buses were waiting, lined and ready outside the door, but she passed them by. She walked slowly now, as she moved along the shoulder of the main road. She noticed little, only her red shoes moving rhythmically over the dirt. The bus went by. Rachel heard the children hooting and shouting at her from a distance but she didn't look up. Instead she looked into the woods beside which she walked, and up at the tips of the tall whispering pines as the voices trailed off in the wind.

She was late for dinner. The family had eaten and gone out to sit in the screened porch. Rachel ate alone. Then she went to her small room and lay on the soft bed. The window was open and mosquitoes droned persistently against the dark screen. One by one the fat stars appeared out over the trees, shining softly against the velvet sky like tiny crystal stepping stones across the darkness of the heavens. The voices from the porch faded softly into the evening until all that was left were Rachel and the black and sparkling secrets of the night.

The cool air swept in through the window. Rachel lay with her eyes closed, sensing the presence of the night as if from far, far away. Little by little, sense by sense, she came to herself until she realized with overwhelming suddenness that he was there. Her heart began to pound wildly. He stood at the foot of her bed, stiff and still; his thin arms hung simply from his bony shoulders and he gazed across the shadowy room and out at the starry night.

Rachel sat up suddenly and peered violently into the black at the foot of her bed. But he was gone. She lay back down, breathing hard. It was then that she realized she was still fully clothed. She smoothed her wrinkled dress and lay still for a few minutes. Then, rising quickly, she tiptoed out of the bedroom. Now she felt wide, wide awake. She unhooked the screened door and slipped silently out into the cool night. The frogs droned loudly from the ditches and the crickets rang out from the woods.

Rachel walked deliberately to the edge of the woods. She ran along the dry pine needle path carpeting the ground beneath her until she came to the far side of the pines where the swamp began. Then she sat down at the base of a tree and looked into the tangled trees from the dry safety of the ridge.

The moon hung low in the sky, spilling over the standing waters with a silver sheen and weaving among the creeping vines like neon shadows in the night. A small animal appeared, and scurried through the brush and into the pond, pulling a V of soft ripples over the still surface with his black nose. At the edge he disappeared among the great leafy elephant ears that massed in the swampy bottom. A large rotting log lay fallen across the earth at the far end of the pond and with a sudden secret courage Rachel rose and raced down the ridge, balancing her way lightly across the log.

RACHEL AND THE NIGHT CHILD

Now the ground was precarious: soft and wet. Rachel picked her way carefully. The cricket song was overpowering, rising in a great crescendo over the swamp and singing in the air. She slapped at a mosquito, and then at another. An owl called, and took wing, beating heavily against the darkness. Finally, she could go no further. She looked out into the swamp.

The water stood around the bases of the leafless trees in shining rings wedding them together like so many dark memories dying quietly in the water moonlight. And then she saw it. Nebulous and wispy, the specter-like form floated above the heart of the swamp, glowing with a light that only the night could reveal. Rachel stood staring, spellbound at the beauty of it all, while a mosquito gorged undisturbed on her leg. Then she called out over the swamp, over and over until the night echoed with the sound of her own name. And turning, she ran back through the spongy earth that sucked at her feet with every step: over the log and up the ridge where she stood triumphant. Facing the dark swamp one last time she called out, "Rachel . . . !", then ran quickly back to her home.

She rose at eight as usual, but this morning she hurried through her preparations, anxious to be free of the confining kitchen and out in the morning air. She slammed the screen door behind her and ran out to the drive. Now she walked quickly, passing the fence where the mourning dove always sat, but he was not there. The day was bright and sunny, and as she stood waiting for the bus she remembered the yesterday of no shadows. But today she had a shadow; everything had a shadow. The familiar black form at her feet seemed to make the sun brighter as it etched her carbon on the rough ground.

The bus came. Rachel rode in the front, laughing with the girls and shouting hordes of choice insults at the boys who crowded to the back of the bus in their own private coalition. They reached the school too quickly and poured through the doors, jostling and pushing their way into the rooms. The bell rang twice, and from each door the chant of the Pledge of Allegiance rang out into the halls.

KAREN PIETKIEWICZ

Rachel breezed through her assignments, anxious to be done and on to the next. It was not until the reading circle formed that she finally noticed the thin brown boy was gone.

* * *

The System

Friday. The sun began to filter through the large front window. It stretched its long fingers of light down the still wet roads and over the glistening lawns, and crept around and past the slumbering frame houses which lay unawakened beneath the diminishing shadow of the white frame church.

Marion had decided to attend mass on the first Friday of the next nine consecutive months. In regard to herself, there was little left of significance for her in the Roman Catholic Faith. She had no illusions that simply making the First Fridays, as the devotion was called, was going to eradicate the punishment due for her own sins. In fact, the biggest sin she could recognize within herself was the very hypocrisy of attending Mass at all. It was a well-disguised struggle, covered partially out of cowardice because of her teaching position within the Catholic system, and a not so insignificant dollop of pure lassitude at the thought of looking for another job. In regard to her decision to undertake the devotion, it came about after the theft, and after she met Katherine McCoy. It was a matter of pure curiosity.

For it was Katherine McCoy who had helped Marion retrieve her antique victrola, and it was the same little girl who had then announced her intention to undertake the religious devotion. Why a ten year old would feel the need to participate in such an archaism was very strange, but the child was more so. She was, in fact, almost mystical, and seemed to have evoked some lost sense of the mysterious within the older woman that now gripped her completely. Thus Marion latched onto the devotion as an excuse to resolve the mystery of Katherine McCoy.

And the child was odd.

Marion recalled having passed Katherine a number of times on the street, and seen her going to church, or coming home. She had noticed the child at school, navigating the crowded halls and chaotic cloakrooms before and after class. One day she met the girl on the bus, and sat politely down beside her through the hot dusty ride home.

It was a few days later that the girl appeared at the door, her dark blond hair neatly arranged in French braids from the temples, that joined the long braids down her back. She wore overalls and a plaid blouse and carried the jar which was to become her calling card. She was very polite, and asked if she could catch bumblebees in the adjoining garden.

It was only then Marion realized that she and the child were neighbours.

So it began: the child appeared at the door to ask about the flowers regularly until Marion suggested that she go right to the garden without stopping in. After that the child was a part of the garden, with her never-ending patience and her small glass jar.

Marion stood at the window remembering the weekend. She had worked all day - cleaned, washed, set everything right inside - even finished some of her gardening, and sprayed the apple tree for the first time that season.

Late in the afternoon she had made a cup of tea and savoured the fine, finished feeling the day had brought, along with its impending close. Through the window she had watched the girl catch bumblebees in a glass jar; watched her

THE SYSTEM

sit patiently beside the blue candidisma - bumblebee flowers, the girl called them - until the fat, pollen laden carrier sat upon the heart of the feathery blue flower to plumb its nectar. Only then would the child move. Slowly, carefully, the jar in one hand, the lid in the other, she would draw the two closer and closer together over the unsuspecting insect until, with a sudden snap, she enclosed the entire bloom, complete with the bee. Sometimes, if she were very careful, the bee would continue, undisturbed, dipping its shiny, threadlike tongue, combing and grooming the bulging pollen-laden limbs, oblivious of its captor. The child would then simply watch until the bee, its foraging completed, turned against the glass, only to suddenly fall back. Battering about, the uncomprehending and exhausted bee would stop to carefully explore the rim where the lid joined the jar, before resuming its self-defeating flight nowhere.

On the actual day of the theft, Marion had gone into the yard to where the child sat quietly waiting.
"Hello."
The girl looked up.
"Can I watch you?"
"Sure."
The child looked open, and friendly.
"Your name is Katherine, isn't it? Do you go by Kathy?"
"Katherine," the girl replied.
"Oh. All right then, Katherine it is ," said Marion, feeling unreasonably foolish.
The girl began to unscrew the lid of the jar.
"Are you letting him out?" Marion asked, stepping back a few feet.
"Oh, no, not yet. I'm putting in some other flowers."
"What if he gets out? He's going to be pretty mad."
The girl looked at Marion patiently. "You have to know *how*," she said, emphasizing `how'. "You have to wait until he is busy doing something else, when he is just crawling around. Then you open up the top and put in the new flow-

ers. Or some water. But not too much water, just a small drop. So he can drink."

As she spoke, she calmly unscrewed the lid and dropped in a sprig of yellow buttercups, then recapped the jar.

"How long will he live in that jar?" Marion asked.

"Live in the jar?" The child looked up, puzzled. "Bees don't live in jars. Bees live somewhere else, in nests."

"Well, you've got him in the jar," Marion replied, feeling again inappropriately foolish.

"I'm just looking at him!" The girl stood up. "See these holes in the top? Those are air holes. He has to have air or he will die. Even for a little while he has to have air. But even if there are air holes, he will die in a jar. He's supposed to live out there, in the air, not in a jar. You can only keep him for a little while, then you have to let him go or else he'll die. So you *have* to let him go."

"Oh!" Marion sat there. It occurred to her that it was getting toward supper.

"So do you want to watch me let him go?" Katherine spoke suddenly, and brightly.

"Sure. Yes. I'd like to watch you let him go." Marion got up.

"No, no, you don't have to move!" The child laughed benignly. "Now, watch this. You just loosen the lid like this and set the jar on its side, like this, and now watch 'till he starts crawling to the end. See? Now, you just take away the lid and out he comes. See?"

The bee crawled out, and into the grass. Then he flew away.

"So, see how easy it is? He likes the grass because it's like where he lives. He'd rather be in the grass than in the jar so he just crawls right out. Then he goes home."

"So, no problem!" Marion stood up.

"Yes. No problem," said the girl, looking straight at Marion, a strange, surprised look on her young face.

"Well, I'd better be going in to eat."

"I gotta get home too. G'bye." The girl raced off down the lawn.

THE SYSTEM

"Don't run with a glass jar!"

The girl stopped and began to walk

The old teacher instinct, thought Marion, upbraiding herself for her comment. She went into the house.

The evening that followed had been, like the day, particularly satisfying. After supper Marion sat and read, contemplating how at last she had time to sit and read: how the nagging trivialities of the past few years had one by one given way. John was out of town for a brief time - a fact she rather enjoyed, for it gave her time to herself and still the warm anticipation of his return at the week's end.

It was after nine; Marion was about to go upstairs when the bell rang. It was the old-fashioned kind of bell the visitor has to turn to make ring, and at the door stood James McCaffery. James was a non-descript sort of fellow and a non-descript sort of teacher who taught a split grade seven-eight at Marydale School, where Marion herself taught. Now James murmured something about having to find a room for his friend. Beside him, he had a rather sad looking fellow, a young man with pained, heavy eyes, and hair that was clean, but too long. Since Marion didn't relish having anyone else in the house and she didn't need the proffered extra money, she suggested another place. The whole conversation was laborious to the extreme, since James McCaffery seemed ever on the verge of falling back into his characteristic, shuffling silence. Marion felt sorry for him; he wasn't a bad sort of fellow, just rather nothing.

But the other man was an intense young man whose eyes now seemed to devour his surroundings. He walked straight past her, and went directly to the centre of the parlour like a somnambulist, mouth agape, his hands dangling limply at the ends of his thin wrists. It was as though only his eyes were alive and drew the rest of him along behind in a myopic trance. There he stood in the centre of the room, nodding and smiling, and repeating small phrases such as "how lovely" and "how beautiful". Now and then he reached out to stroke the velour of the sofa, which seemed to particularly please him, or to rest a finger on the rim of the crystal flower bowl that had been her mother's, and her grandmother's before that. He seemed so entranced that Marion could only stand and watch, bemused and somewhat flattered at such compulsive admiration. Finally, the young man, who had been introduced as Reginald McLaughlin, approached the old Victrola, where he stood entranced.

"Does it work?" he asked, without turning around.

"Yes, it does, as a matter of fact," Marion replied.

"Could I play something?" McLaughlin asked, again without taking his eyes off the machine.

Marion approached the machine. She had to step around McLaughlin, who remained entrenched before it. Laughing, she began to crank the machine by the wooden-knobbed handle that protruded from the side.

"See if you are familiar with this one," she said gently to the strange young man as she pushed the lever aside and the turntable began to spin. She set the huge arm with its steel needle on the whirling disc and at once the room filled with the sound of the music.

McLaughlin's face began to glow, and his hands clenched and unclenched spastically at his sides.

"Do you know it?" Marion asked once again. "It's called 'Roamin' in the Gloamin'.'" She began to sing, and sway from side to side:

> Roamin' in the Gloamin'
> on the bonnie banks of Clyde
> Roamin' in the Gloamin'
> wi' me lassie by mi side.

McLaughlin stood mesmerized, and then began to hum along softly, finally joining in with her in a quavering voice.

> When the sun ha' gone ta rrest
> that's the time th't I luv best.
> Oh! it's loovely rroamin' in
> the glooamin'."

As the refrain began again, Marion lifted the needle. McLaughlin started and looked up. Noticing his intense interest, she commented, as she closed the lid, "Who knows: maybe this old Victrola belonged to your family once, if you

THE SYSTEM

came from around here. It was up in the attic of this place for years, along with the old records. We found it last year when we were insulating."

McLaughlin spun and looked at her. Then he turned and walked straight out the door. James McCaffery, embarrassed, murmured something apologetic and hurried after McLaughlin, who by now was halfway up the street.

Marion stood, surprised, watching them go. 'Very strange,' she commented to herself, then turned off the lights and went upstairs to bed.

Sometime during that night the Victrola had disappeared.

Another early morning. Marion sighed, and headed for the bathroom. She ran the shower, hot, and stepped in. It was her favourite concession of all the changes she and John had made for the sake of convenience, when they restored the old house. Now the hot water beat upon her, melting away the stiffness that had begun to appear in her limbs. At least it was nice outside. The walk to the church and back would do her good, she noted cryptically, far better than any spiritual value she would get out of sitting through the dry and colourless ceremony the Mass had become. Since the conversion into English, and the accompanying new wave of burlap vestments that were all the ecclesiastical rage, the ceremony had lost the last remaining spark of appeal that it had held for her. Besides, she had grown to look forward to the walk with Katherine and had come to enjoy the child's strange, objective, bright patter, the odd, minute observations from which Katherine conjectured her daily philosophies. At least the child had an air of the mystical, which was more than the mass had managed to retain. Marion finished showering, dressed, and stepped out the door just as the small girl started up the walk. She closed and locked the door behind her, and smiled at her new found companion.

"Today is number seven," announced Katherine, as the two started down the walk. It was typical of the child to take up just where they had left off conversing a month before.

"So it is," Marion replied.
They headed for the church.
"How did you decide to make the First Fridays?" Marion asked, curious. "It's rather out of style."
"I read it in a book." The girl kept on walking.
"A Catechism? What kind of book?"
"An old book. It was in my grandmother's bookcase."
Marion was intrigued. "So you just read it in a book and decided to do it?"
"I sinned," said Katherine, matter-of-factly.
"You sinned?" Marion almost burst into laughter at the absurdity, but caught herself. Sinned. She hadn't even thought the word remained in the vocabulary.
The girl stopped. "Yes. I sinned," she replied, looking straight at Marion's face, "but it won't matter for long because I will soon be saved forever, so it will be all finished." Without another word, Katherine turned, crossed the street, and marched up the steps and into the church.
Marion was fascinated. All through the mass her mind conjectured as to the kind of sin the girl could have committed, her strange, archaic solution, and the even stranger conviction that permeated Katherine's every word. Perfunctorily, she followed the girl to the communion rail, and back. She watched, totally absorbed as Katherine took the Host and marched back to her pew.
After the mass was over, Marion had to suppress the urge to ask the child what sin she had committed. Her curiosity was maddening: how could she ask the girl such a question without intruding on her privacy? Her mind had become a lurid panoply of possibilities, from which she had selected and rejected according to age, character, and suitability. But she could not imagine a sin suitable to the nature of this child.
As they reached her walk, the girl spoke:
"Bye."
"Bye."
Marion went in.

Saturday was cleaning day. Marion started the laundry. The upstairs was done now; just the downstairs remained.

THE SYSTEM

She ran a bucket with warm water, poured in a dollop of Lysol and headed for the parlour. One of these days they would replace the old windows. The dust was getting to her.

She moved from the window sill to the stand where the Victrola sat, now returned. Marion lifted the lid. Not a single needle had been missing when it had been found. The record was intact; it was not even scratched. She had not bothered to pursue the matter further. It was evident to her who had taken it, and more evident still that he had a screw loose somewhere. What was odd was that he chose to leave it in the church. Lucky for her the church doors were never locked. However, hers were; from that night on, the doors were locked tight. It had been a matter of time, really, before someone broke in. She felt lucky to have gotten off so lightly. And again, the odd child had inserted herself into Marion's life, when she had found the Victrola.

Marion now recalled her surprise at finding the girl sitting on the porch steps that morning. She probably would not have noticed had she not been accustomed to looking out the window of the front door each day when she first came down the stairs. There sat the child in her plaid skirt and yellow sweater. Marion had opened the door, surprised. Katherine crossed the porch to the door.

"It's in the church."

"What's in the church?" Marion was bewildered.

"The *Victrola*," the child had said, a bit impatiently.

Marion had not even noticed it was gone. She had been shocked at first, then angry about the Victrola, and had gone straight to James McCaffery's small rented house, seeking McLaughlin, but he was gone. James McCaffery was useless in the presence of women, bumbling, and inarticulate; he mumbled only that McLaughlin, was some kind of student, and had "gone back". In the end, the struggle to make sense out of James McCaffery and his friend McLaughlin was more bother than it was worth, and, since the Victrola was safe and the half-wit had left town, Marion had let the matter drop.

KAREN PIETKIEWICZ

Afterwards, she had become friends withKatherine McCoy, as much as one could befriend the strange, compelling child.

Later that week, at school, her suspicions about Reginald McLaughlin had been confirmed. The few members of the staff who had met him were definitely unimpressed; it was rumoured that he was slow on the uptake, and there was strong conjecturing over coffee that he was some lost half-brother of James McCaffery -maybe even out on a pass from some home somewhere.

What had ended up being the biggest mystery of all was James McCaffery himself, and how he ever landed a job teaching with them. From there the staff had explored McCaffery's obvious inadequacies. This topic took up the rest of the lunch break and McLaughlin got lost in the shuffle.

Marion finished cleaning the windows. There was really nothing else to do. With John away, and no meals, there wasn't any mess. Even the bed was barely disturbed. All she had had to do was pull up the covers and reset the pillows.

She decided to go out to sunbathe and ended up sleeping half the day away in the backyard. Finally, she went in to shower and dress, planning on taking in a show by herself. She made a sandwich and took it out on the front porch to eat. The street was quiet. Katherine had not been around.

Now Marion thought again of the strange, small girl and her so-called sin. Abruptly it occurred to her: the dictionary. She went insideand pulled a book from the shelf. Page 1122, Webster's. It read, 'Plenary indulgence: in the Roman Catholic Church, an indulgence remitting in full the temporal punishment incurred by a sinner.'

It was hard to believe that at one time in her life she had believed that. Harder still to believe that, after years of trying and being thrust back into the maw of hell by the flu or a cold or whatever else conspired to interrupt her successful completion of the First Fridays, she was now on the verge of

THE SYSTEM

completing a devotion that meant nothing at all to her, anymore. She put the book back. It was time to leave.

    Marion walked both ways to the show. It was a beautiful night, with a fat full moon; too nice to go in. She headed to the backyard and sat on the step. The bugs would soon be out; she thought it would be nice if summer could be bug free like tonight. She got up and walked deeper into the yard to where her lone apple tree stood. She looked at the tree. It still bore the tattered remnants of the burlap bandage she had affixed to it. She had pruned one of the lower branches and was more than a little pleased that her amateur tree surgery had seemed to take. This year would tell the tale. As she stood staring up at the tree, she could see the dark profile of the next door house, and the slanted roof of the adjoining shed.
    Someone was sliding down the roof.
    She froze. Was it a thief? *The* thief? She stared through the black at the slight figure traversing the roof. Reaching the edge, the silhouette grabbed an overhanging branch of the apple tree and quickly shinnied to the ground. But it was Katherine. Marion could see her quite clearly in the bright moonlight. The child was carrying a large book under her arm. While Marion watched, silent, from the back of the yard, Katherine looked quickly around her, then ran across the yard and down the street.
    Marion stood stock still for a long moment, completely stunned. She looked at her watch. The hands read 11:45. Where on earth could the girl be going at this hour? Swiftly, she followed the small girl by moving along the dark side of the house. She reached the front just in time to see Katherine cross at the corner and head in the direction of the church. Marion crossed the street at an angle, cutting through two yards and down the alley, skirting the edge of the sidewalk, behind the shrubs and trees so as not to be seen. She followed the girl to the church, and watched to see the door close carefully behind her.
    Standing close to the hedge, Marion started across the moonlit street in front of the church, but just as she started to

move, the Church door began to open from the inside. Around the side of the building a small clutch of figures appeared; one by one, they ran around the corner of the building and up the steps into the church. The last two were apparently boys; they were struggling with some sort of box, which was draped in a large cloth. Again, the church door opened silently, and they disappeared inside.

A car appeared at the far end of the street, the lights peering down into the craters and potholes left by the departing winter, searching out every flaw. Marion stepped even further back into the shrubs until it passed, then crossed quickly to the other side of the street. She moved around to the side of the church where the small door was. It was open; she slipped inside and stood breathless and listening, pressed against the wall.

There was no one in the vestibule. Crossing the carpeted floor quietly, Marion moved toward the choir loft and crept up the stairs, peering into the black in case they were in the loft, but it was empty. Over the rail, dimly, she could perceive the faint glow of the votive candles from the front of the church. Red, yellow, green, the candles burned for intentions of the living, and for the sins of the dead. Now by the light of these candles, Marion could see a procession forming, hear the sounds of feet shuffling out a distinct rhythm, and the measured cadence of a single, unified voice.

"My God; they're chanting!" The realization exploded in Marion's head with a shock. But it seemed to be only the girls, their voices in unison above the sound of the feet.

> *"Some are black and some are white,*
> *and some are outside in the night.*
> *Some are black and some are white,*
> *and some are outside in the night."*

Now the hair began to rise on the woman's arms as she stared through the dark at the dim figures. They were all girls; there were no boys to be seen. Each girl was carrying a lighted votive candle. They were marching rigidly around a

THE SYSTEM

cloth draped box, which had been set in the centre aisle, on the floor directly in front of the altar. The altar gate was open to the steps beyond. There, Katherine stood at the pulpit, flanked by two candles. She appeared to be writing in a large black book.

Marion watched, spellbound, while the girls continued their ceremonial march with the rhythmic, sing-song chant. After a few minutes she heard low hurried voices punctuated by a boy's laugh. As she watched, the vestry door opened and the boys appeared in a cluster. The tallest of them was carrying a small flat dish or saucer. He held it above his head in the manner of an offering and walked slowly, with mock and solemnity, toward the girls, who now had separated to stand three on each side of the box. The rest of the boys stumbled after the lead boy, whispering and punctuating the air with snickers and suppressed laughter. As they came down the last step, the girls did an abrupt about-face and marched up to the altar while the boys gathered about the box. The tall boy with the dish stopped directly in front, stiffening his arms, which were still held up in front of him, carrying the saucer-like dish. A second boy approached the box and with a grand, sweeping gesture, snatched the covering from it, passing it to the outstretched arms of the next boy, who made an attempt to fold it, all the time breaking out in low bursts of laughter and whispered comments.

Marion stared through the dim light to see the box. It appeared to be an old crate with solid ends, the kind used to pack and ship fruit. The wooden end was toward her and she was unable to see what was in it, nor could she see through the top, upon which had been set some makeshift sort of lid. On the end of the box facing her, painted in a rough hand, was the face, or head, of a cat. It gave the appearance of a surrealist vision that alternately grew and diminished, pulsing ominously in the flickering light.

Suddenly, the girls raised their arms in salute, and together they sang out.

"Feed the Beast!"

The shock of the voiced chorus after the muffled silences startled the intruder that Marion had become. She felt her heart leap, and pound in her chest. Suddenly, there was a flurry of activity around the box. The boys now began to dance in place with wildly gesticulating arms. She could hear excited, muffled laughter.

"Feed 'im!"

"Yeah! Feed him!"

More muffled laughter.

"Feed the beast!"

"Shut up, you guys!" A boy's voice rose and fell, followed by more snickers and guffaws of laughter.

The tall boy approached the box, and as he did the nearest boy lifted the lid. The tall boy reached in, then withdrew his hand quickly as the lid dropped, amid mock snarls and growls, and muffled roars. For the boys by now had given up all sense of ceremony, and were bordering on hysterical laughter. Even the girls had begun to giggle, covering their mouths with their hands. As the lid dropped they resumed their chorus:

"Has the Beast been fed?"

"The Beast has been fed!" the boys roared out in unison. With that, boys and girls together rushed to the box, the boys jockeying for a hold while spreading the cover haphazardly over it. Convulsed with hysterical laughter, they jostled and bandied about it as they carried it down the aisle and disappeared under the loft into the foyer below.

Marion froze against the front of the pew; to her relief she heard the voices fade and the front door of the church clunk shut.

Except for one, they were gone. Marion raised her head in time to see Katherine close the gate to the altar, hurry down the aisle and head for the door, still carrying the large black book.

Marion awoke with a start and sat up in the bed. Her heart was pounding wildly; the moon spilled its splayed light over the rumpled bedcovers and across the room, to shimmer eerily against the far wall.

THE SYSTEM

Suddenly she was aware that she was speaking, that she was saying, over and over, "It's a dream. It's a dream," and shaking her head as if to jar herself awake. Switching on the small nightlight, she fell back against the pillow and lay staring at the ceiling, breathing deeply.

It had been a dream, and the dream was about the strange ceremony she had stumbled upon in the church that very evening. She lay now, trying to recall it.

But in the dream, she had been in the school, she and a couple of other women. They were looking for someone, but Marion did not know who it was supposed to be. She tried to recall the faces of the other two women, but they were always behind her or turned away: faceless, timid types of women. There had been something wrong; she was trying to keep the few young girls with them close by. And James McCaffery was there, somewhere in the school.

That was it; she could remember it now.

In the dream, Marion had left the young girls with the other two women while she went to look for James McCaffery. She had gone down the stairs to find him. But it wasn't a normal set of stairs. It went down to a landing, then turned and came back up the other side. It had started out like the stairwell leading down from the third floor of the original school, but this one only went halfway down.

Marion now remembered the first landing of the stairs in the school where she taught. The landing had once overlooked an old gymnasium that was used years ago when the nuns owned the building. The gymnasium was very small, and had fallen into disrepair. Eventually it had been boarded up, and the doors locked, thus the overlooking landing had been closed in as well. But in the dream there was a long narrow crack in the wall by the landing, and through this Marion had been able to once again see down into the closed off old gym.

It was almost like when she had followed Katherine to the Church. The same boys had been there, and the same box with the head of a cat painted on the end, such as Van Gogh would paint to pad about his Starry Night. But in the dream, the boys were prancing about the box, darting up to it and poking bits of something through narrow bars which had now appeared on either side of the wooden box.

And now, she could see in the box. It held an animal about the size of a cat. The thing had grey, wrinkled, hairless skin and a ratlike tail, and its head was almost non-existent except that it bore a great, elongated, outthrust mouth which the beast opened, exposing a lascivious, red, clotted lining surrounded by rows of sharp, tiny, white teeth which disappeared near a constricted red throat. As she watched, it opened its mouth again and again, as if to display an unlimited appetite. At its feet, in the bottom of the cage, hovered two more small grey shapes.

Marion had recoiled in horror.

A door then appeared to the left of the landing, which she rushed to, and opened. But Katherine had appeared behind the door and said, "Not this door." That had been it. Just, "Not this door." Marion, acquiescing, had turned and mounted the remaining set of stairs.

At the top, to the right of the last set of stairs, was another door. It was the door to the old chapel. She opened the door.

Inside the chapel were six girls, all with dark brown hair, and all wearing identical purple dresses. They were marching and chanting the same strange verse as the girls in the dark church, only this time they stopped, surprised and uncomfortable, as though caught in some forbidden act.

Katherine now reappeared in the chapel, her hair braided as always, but now she was wearing a royal blue dress. She stood to the left of the altar, observing. But Marion had withdrawn from the scene in shock and disgust, pulling the door closed quickly. She ran back to find the two women, but the girls the women were to have watched had slipped away. Marion had fled down the hall in anger and growing panic. She shouted at the empty walls:

"McCaffery!"

It was then she had awakened.

Sunday morning it rained. Marion slept in until almost eleven. The sodden drip-drop of the rain off the gutter onto

THE SYSTEM

the flagstones below measured out the last few minutes of her fading sleep. Looking out the curtained window at the grey day, it was almost impossible to recall the strange, mad, moon-drenched business that had occurred just a few hours before. She felt empty, drained.

On any other Sunday, John would be here. They would lie in bed and talk, and laze around, maybe go for donuts somewhere. Suddenly, she missed him intensely. She could talk to him about what had happened. If only he were here, had been here, she probably would not have happened on to things the way she had.

Marion lay quietly now, empty of thought. As she lay there, the strange events in the church began to run a shadowy replay through her mind. Katherine, the book, the girls in their purple dresses - or were they purple dresses in the dream? She could not recall, could not remember what they actually wore. But she remembered the boys snickering and laughing, and the tall boy with the plate. The cat's head rose before her in her mind's eye like the great Cheshire cat out of Alice in Wonderland; bits and pieces of the night before continued to pop up in her mind like flotsam from a lost ship.

Finally she arose, and dressed. There was still time to make the noon Mass if she drove. Today she actually wanted to go to church. She shivered, and shook her head. It was as though there was something to be found there, some unfinished part of last night's debauch waiting to fall into place. Perhaps Katherine would be there: Katherine, who up until last night had been warm, bright, young, and who now was a frozen enigma, a dark daguerreotype etched in the stained glass of the nave, her small frame rigid before the book.

But Katherine wasn't there. None of them were there. Only mothers with squirming children, young couples, and the usual assortment of teens who had stayed out until the wee hours of the morning. In the dull wash of daylight, nothing at all remained of the night before.

Exam week began, with the usual problems attendant upon the year's end. Parents who could not be roped into coming in for a conference, whose only participation had been an anxious exchange between themselves and their child over the poor report card, were suddenly showing great concern, as though an evening's attention could replace the tired disregard of the now past year and pluck a miracle out of the impending examination. And four of the grade eight girls had come to report that the Dwyer girl was crying in the girl's washroom because she had selected the same graduation dress as Marilyn Frazer and couldn't take it back because it was altered. This was, Marion thought, good reason to cry considering that Marilyn wore a C-Cup bra, which would leave poor Sheryl Dwyer looking as though her dress was still on the hanger.

As Marion headed for the girl's washroom, she all but collided with James McCaffery.

"Sorry, yes, sorry. I'm sorry, Mrs. Bailey," the young man stammered, as he bowed and tripped over himself in his embarrassed exit. He was hurrying down the hall, head down, mumbling something about windows, and he practically ran her down. Marion could hear his voice the rest of the way to his room, still apologizing.

Later in the day, on the way to the staff meeting, James McCaffery appeared again, and again apologized three or four more times. It seemed the only time he was ever secure was in regard to the subjects he taught. Now, James McCaffery made a brief report on Health and Hygiene: the course was completed and the examination was set for Tuesday morning.

James McCaffery had been selected by Sister Thecla for the Health and Hygiene course because there were more boys than girls in his split grade 7/8. He was also unmarried, and therefore unsullied, as Sister was prone to infer. Thus he was a prized example of elevated manhood to which she could point with pride. He was the perfect layman, in the ecclesiastical sense of the word; this in spite of the obvious fact that he had never been laid in his life, as Phillips, the staff rake, was often heard to comment.

And Sister, of course, "did" the girls when it came to health related feminine matters, leaving James McCaffery and

THE SYSTEM

the boys alone in the classroom with his fresh, long pieces of coloured chalk, used, rumour had it, to illustrate more specifically the masculine bodily parts. The staff, and for that matter the whole of the student body knew when the grade seven-eight's had been "done"; James McCaffery, whose palms sweated profusely, was habitually wiping them on his upper thighs which, in the course of the lectures, became streaked with the associative coloured chalks. This fact he had never come to recognize in the four years Marion had taught with him, and of course, no one was about to tell him.

Marion could recall her own sessions with Sister Thecla a number of years before. The body, the sacred vessel of motherhood, its biological clock ticking ever onward, was studied, swabbed, bathed and bound under the unrelenting eye of Sister Thecla and the Mother of God, who observed from her niche in the wall this preparation of her handmaidens for the great unknown. Never a word was said of the Babe in her arms; the benign smile on the face of the Child made the quantum leap from maiden to mother as nebulous as the sliver of moon and the silver stars upon which she rested her small pink feet. The biological details of sperm and egg efficiently accounted for, the only portent to be observed was the thrashing, lashing tail of the dominant sperm wriggling its milky way to the unsuspecting egg which drifted moonlike in its fallopian cosmogony awaiting the assault that would alter its destiny forever.

Throughout, the only voice to be heard in the inexorable silence of the hot, small room was that of Sister Thecla, who concluded the lecture by reading to the squirming girls the story of St. Maria Gioretti. A martyr to her virginity, her young life had been courageously given. Maria's piteous last prayers bubbled from blood-flecked lips while the knife in the soiled hands of the thwarted, lust-besotted field hand drove in again and again. At last, her young soul, still unremitting, still undefiled, broke free of its earthly bonds and wafted gloriously heavenward to the arms of her waiting Redeemer.

The story completed, the coup-de-grace delivered, Sister Thecla solemnly passed the book from hand to trembling hand to allow the girls to see for themselves the horror that was poor Maria's demise, the magnitude of her courage and virtue. There on the worn pages, the hulking, shirt-sleeved beast with the blood-spattered knife bent over the young Saint, who lay, arms folded over her punctured breasts, eyes upturned in her madonna-like face, while flights of cherubs pleaded above for her earthly release.

The lesson was remarkably effective.

As for the boys, Marion was not quite sure what was 'done', only that it was usually 'done' by a male staffer, or one of the priests. Following the lectures, words like 'purity' and 'spiritual temple' made their way around the classroom and showed up in essays, and phrases such as 'impure thoughts' were included in any discussion of the perfunctory examination of conscience before Confession and Communion. Chastity supplanted all other virtues in order of importance, the relegation of which was assumed by the girls, in accordance with some unspoken law, while 'self-abuse' had a particularly male correlation. Nothing more was ever said.

Marion recalled having reached grade nine before ever realizing the attendant implications of masculinity as experienced by some of her classmates. She could still recall Fred Brown's essay; how he stammered and stuttered; how the bulge in his tan khaki pants grew and grew, pressing out the entire length of his zippered fly. And then the ominous spot, wet and dark on the light fabric, and spreading even larger, while Freddy struggled on through the endless words, his face crimson before the hysterical class. She recalled the horror she felt as the spot appeared, and spread, and how embarrassed she felt for Freddy; how angry she felt at the cruel laughter that alienated both Freddy and her from the rest of the howling class.

And it had been Freddy, a year or two later, Fred, as he was then called, who told her about 'self-abuse'; how all the guys did it, unless they were queer, and even the priests did it. He was angry when he spoke, his voice bitter and resentful. He told how he had been inducted into the Order of the Arrow, and how, at Silverwood, the Scout camp, the youths

THE SYSTEM

had their own secret ceremonial place. At night when the staff was asleep, the Senior Girl Scouts from the camp across the lake regularly sneaked across in long, silent canoes. There the youths got drunk and made love; Freddy told how the boys without a date had ejaculated into the glowing coals that had been the campfire.

And nothing much had really changed in the years since she had gone to school, at least not with regard to the Church; to whet the sexual appetite through masturbation was to abuse the body by diverting it from its primary function of procreation, and to encourage the base, subliminal instincts to grow strong. The will, thus weakened by the encouraged onslaught, would allow the fetid instincts to arise. Thus racked with self-encouraged lust, the possessed practitioner would be driven to enact the ultimate outrage upon some innocent, unsuspecting girl.

James McCaffery was still delivering this same essential message to the boys, Marion suspected. She remembered waiting in the outer office while he and Sister Thecla finished reviewing the class outline for Health and Hygiene, in which she recalled hearing James McCaffery expound the necessity of instructing the boys inself-control. "Self-control is the basis for strengthening the will against the onslaughts of sexual appetite", he affirmed a number of times, while Sister Thecla pointed out the splendid example of St. Joseph, and the celibacy of Jesus Christ. Their voices rose and fell in crescendos of passionate conviction, and when James McCaffery left the office his eyes positively glowed. He seemed not even to notice Marion as he strode out, while Sister Thecla, whose cheeks were moist and flushed, was preoccupied to such an extent she hardly attended to what Marion was saying. Continuously interrupting, she flooded Marion with comments about James McCaffery and the valuable contribution he made as a member of the staff.

The bell rang for lunch. Marion locked the examination papers she had been preparing in the top drawer. She went down the back stairs to the courtyard. It was a nice place to eat, sheltered from the wind by the convent on one side and the old gymnasium on the other. Beside the gym was a worn concrete area, probably used for basketball or tennis years ago. It was small, and the sun reflected off it warmly. She headed for the cracked steps that led up to the recessed gym door and sat down, withdrawing a wrapped sandwich. She set her salad out before her on the cement stoop and began to pick at it with her fingers. Students milled about behind the school; those who smoked, gathered behind the far wing of the building where no one was supposed to know. Couples moved off in twos where the boys would press their attentions on the eager young women who fawned and gazed upon them. As she silently watched from her vantage point in the recessed doorway she found it hard to believe how precocious some of the older girls were now. She recalled a bright, attractive girl who had become pregnant the summer following her grade eight graduation, disappeared, returned in the fall to the adjoining high school no longer pregnant and an authority on abortion and obtaining the pill. But this was not what concerned her most about the girls and their would-be relationships; rather, it was the coldly calculated determination of some of the young girls she taught. There were a significant number of her female students that set upon the immature boys like swarming bees, their favours calculated to seduce, their stinging barbs flung out to deliberately humiliate when the short term flings were over. The tactical advantage of these aggressive young women, naturally ahead of the boys during the adolescent years, were now light years ahead of even the most sophisticated young males. What seemed to be entirely missing was the sense of relationship the young women used to bring into their escapades. One thing was obvious; the boys had more than met their match these days. In the strange reversal of the times, Marion now felt concerned, and in some cases actually afraid for some of the decent, naive, and unsophisticated young boys, just as she had always felt concern for the more immature young girls. She had come to dislike chaperoning the dances because of

THE SYSTEM

the girls alone. "I'm not dancing with you, you dick-head," announced the class valedictorian to a decent, amiable youth who approached her on the dance floor. Marion had seen the youth recoil as though he had been physically struck. "Fuck off, jerk," said Susan Forte to a nice looking Italian boy who was new in the school. Taking out her hair brush, the girl stroked at her expensive angora sweater while the gaggle of girls around her laughed aloud. "and by the way, buy yourself some mouthwash, why don't you?" Susan Forte shouted after the young boy.

Marion had watched the youth take his jacket and leave.

Things had become deeply out of balance somehow, she thought to herself.

With a sigh, she leaned back against the old door behind her and almost fell in.

It was open.

Marion Bailey dropped her empty salad bowl in her lunch bag and ducked into the old gymnasium. Once inside, it was warm, and dusty smelling. The lower windows were boarded, but there were others higher up through which the sun filtered in. She looked at the door; someone had splintered away a part of the jamb and the latch no longer held. The gym was cluttered with old desks and tables no longer used, and boxes and boxes of school books stored for whatever remote reason. Remnants of crepe paper trailed forlornly from the ceiling, left over from some past dance or party. On the end wall, near where the door had once opened into the school, hung a dozen or more class portraits, group pictures of the graduates in cap and gown, the girls carrying sprays of roses. Marion stood before the photographs, looking at the many faces. The beauties, the comics, the jocks, the losers; you could almost guess who among them had been destined for bigger things, and who had seen their moment pass and fade into oblivion when the rented gowns had been returned, the red roses wilted and thrown away. One of the pictures had been removed from the wall; the place where it hung stood out whitely. Curious, Marion looked around.

KAREN PIETKIEWICZ

The photo lay on an old desk. Oddly enough, it appeared to have been wiped clean of dust. Marion looked at the familiar grouping; to her surprise she recognized James McCaffery. She picked up the picture and carried it to the door. In the light she could see that it was indeed James McCaffery and behind him in the second row was another now familiar face; Reginald McLaughlin. In the front row, in the centre of the beaming capped and gowned girls was a beautiful, dark haired girl and upon this girl the frozen eyes of McLaughlin seemed permanently fixed.

Marion looked at the scrolled and embellished "Class of 46" that curved over the smiling faces like a proscenium arch. At the bottom of the photograph, in minuscule letters scripted to match the top, were the names of the graduates. She looked again at the dark, lovely girl, then followed her finger through the names until she found it; Madeleine Seward.

The first bell rang. Marion started, then carried the picture back to the table where she had found it. As she put it down she looked again at McLaughlin's strange, obsessed face. Little had changed about him. She could see even in the photograph the burning, feverish eyes, the defensive set of his shoulders. He had not even seemed to age; it was as though he were fixed in time and only his hair kept growing. It was rather an absurd thought.

Marion left the photo and went out of the dusty gym.

First period in the afternoon was abysmally long, as was always the case with study periods. The papers she intended to grade sat ungraded before her. Finally, she got up and left the room. Down the hall, at the end of the building, was the library. It was a lovely place, venerable, and appropriately musty, with fine old oak tables and paintings hung from a high moulded strip of wood. Had the library been only for the school, it would no doubt have been drab and practical, but it had been a common library for both church and convent originally, so many of the old books remained, impressive but unopened on the ancient shelves. Marion went to the far corner. There, in a long row, were the old yearbooks, pressed

THE SYSTEM

tightly together between the metal bookends so they wouldn't fall away. Marion withdrew a book from the center; 1938. She flipped the pages. All were girls; there had been no boys at that time since it was only a convent school. They looked prim and regulatory in their dark uniforms. The heavy fabric hung in a great box pleat from shoulder to waist, pulled in only slightly by a self-belt with two big buttons. At the neck was a large white collar, crisp and stiffly starched, with a dark, flat, grosgrain bow across the centre. At the ends of the long, dark sleeves were starched, wide cuffs held together with links. Some of the girls wore medals which hung between their camouflaged breasts on wide, flat ribbons. And of course the ever-present nuns with their black habits, their white, neatly starched and straight-pinned mantles. Looking at the stiff, posed pictures, the rows of expressionless faces over the identical uniforms, Marion felt the same odd sensation she had felt looking at the face of McLaughlin in the old gym.

She moved on down the aisle, pulled out a few more books until she found what she had been looking for, and returned to her restless, suffocating class. There she opened the book, and began to leaf through the pages until she came to the graduating class at the very end. Marydale, 1946. Beside each photograph was captioned the name and nickname of the owner. The lovely dark-haired girl was there, attired in a sweater set and a string of pearls. Madeleine Seward, 'Maddy', the caption read. There was James McCaffery - he had no nickname, only 'James', and there was the enigmatic McLaughlin: 'Reggie', as he had apparently been called. The activities photographs followed. Sports, clubs, dances, assemblies, and the Senior Prom, the girls afloat in lovely gowns, the boys also afloat, only in loose, ill fitting suits that made them look as though they were still waiting to be grown into.

In the centre of the gym, in a huge pink and white crepe paper constructed heart, stood the King and Queen, Reginald McLaughlin and Madeline Seward. Side by side they entwined, enclosed within the encircling heart, oblivious to the crowd of dress-clothes bedecked dancers, their eyes fixed solely upon each other, their hands clasped tightly together, fingers intertwined. On McLaughlin's right hand could be seen his class ring, gleaming; on Madeleine's wrist was affixed a spray of flowers.

Marion stared at the picture. Now she knew where it was she had seen the girl. It was in the church. Her photograph, tiny and enclosed in a gold case, was fixed on the wall beneath the statue of Our Lady of Sorrows: 'In Memory of Madeleine Seward'. She looked again at the bright, sparkling eyes of the lovely girl. Then she closed the book and picked up the first essay.

John Bailey called late that evening. Marion was in bed, dog-tired from grading, but he was lonely and he wanted to talk. Marion could always tell when he was lonely by his voice. His job was dragging on and on; parts that had been overdue for weeks still had not arrived on the site. But he promised to be home before the first, and she was glad. Suddenly tired of being alone, the evenings had begun to drag on endlessly. She missed him. She thought of McLaughlin and Madeleine in the flowered heart.

"John, did you ever hear of any Sewards?"

His voice was colourless through the line. "Sewards? Which Sewards?"

Marion was conscious of the mounting long distance charges. She replied, "Madeleine Seward. She died. There's a plaque and a picture in the church, under the statue of Mary."

"Oh. That Seward. I heard about her. She was in Harold's class, you know. Pat's husband. He said she ran in front of a train."

Marion thought of the beautiful, exuberant girl. "You mean she killed herself?"

The voice on the line crackled, and came back. "Yeah, something like that. She was pregnant; that's what Harold said. He knew her sister. Supposedly she got knocked up by her boyfriend after graduation. Her parents sent her away to have it. So while she was waiting for it to be born she ran out in front of a train. Anyways, that's what Harold said. Why?"

THE SYSTEM

Marion was thinking of the girl with McLaughlin. "I saw her picture in an old yearbook. Who was the father of the baby?"

"How would I know? Some kid in her class. Supposedly, he wanted to marry her, but it was her parents. They sent her away, and the next thing they knew she was dead. Apparently he tried to go to the funeral and her folks went nuts. Then the priest threw him out. I don't know what ever happened to him. I think he finally left town."

"It's hard to believe a scene like that." Marion was thinking again of the stiff, black uniformed girls.

"Yes it is. It's also hard to believe how much this call is going to cost. I better go. I'll call you Sunday."

"Do you love me?" Marion always asked, and he always answered, "Just your body."

"Bye, I love you."

"I love you too."

Marion Rose Bailey lay in her bed, the sound of her husband's voice still with her. She realized suddenly that she wanted him. She needed him. But he was not there.

No sooner had she thought this than the face of Madeleine Seward appeared before her, dark hair wafting, as though immersed in fathoms of deep, chilling water. As the face drifted helplessly by, the girl's dark eyes looked into her own and Marion saw the tragedy of her desire, her now hopeless longing for love.

What had the poor girl done that was worth the price she exacted of herself? She had made love, but not with the Holy Ghost. It was the very real Reginald McLaughlin who whispered in Madeleine Seward's ear. And because she loved him, she listened. Marion recalled the young man who had been mesmerized by her Victrola, but now it was in a very different light. No wonder he was so strange. Suddenly he became a sad, piteous, lonely young man who had paid dearly for his pathetic infraction.

The tragic, dark eyed face of Madeline Seward disappeared.

Now the events from the past weeks began to float back into Marion Bailey's sonambulant mind. She remembered the Church and the chanting girls. She remembered the sacrilegious youths and the disturbing dream she had had, and as she lay there drifting, she began to feel the full weight of it. She struggled to unravel its mystery, and the meaning of the ceremony she had witnessed in the Church as she drowsed in the comforting bed.

Suddenly the Virgin Mary appeared where Madeleine Seward's face had been. The Virgin looked pained, sad, exasperated, and tired. Why was her virginity her singular outstanding feature? she asked. Why the virgin birth her most radiant crown? Why was an untouched body the only integrity she was allowed all these centuries? By now there was an edge to her voice. The upset Virgin looked around as though to see if anyone else were listening, then suddenly leaned toward Marion Bailey and whispered rapidly, "I would trade all my spotless centuries for just one sin!" And with that, the isolated lady burst into tears. "I'm sorry," she sobbed, beginning to withdraw, "I'm not supposed to do any of these human types of things . . ." and wiping her eyes on a sleeve of her beautiful gown, she disappeared.

And now Marion could again see the dreaded box, with the creature still inside. The lasciviousness of the boys and the rigidity of the controlling girls Marion had always recognized.

The normal sexual relationship debased from its Divine construction, the female sexuality warped and reviled for centuries, the prescient light of women had often all but been extinguished. They had been reduced to mindless, constricting passages for centuries, to be bound, hidden, mantled, cloistered, and above all, controlled. Marion Bailey suddenly saw with blinding clarity the meaning of the beast in the box. The thwarted, primal female energy had finally been compressed into a smouldering rage. After millennia of being poked and prodded and then blamed for it all, no wonder the thing in the box was beginning to show its teeth.

THE SYSTEM

And what was its purpose, now?

Well, one thing was certain, thought Marion, troubled, and now very much awake. Times had certainly changed. She had witnessed a very different sort of ceremony in the Church. The girls were obviously in charge. Was this some cold projection of a new reality, risen like a spectre in her dreams?

Was she up to it? Was anyone? Was this why she had closed the door in her dream, and run?

By Wednesday the exams were done. It was hot and the few kids left were loud and unmanageable. Most of the staff were starting to unwind in anticipation of the summer; that is, all but James McCaffery. As a matter of fact, James McCaffery was acting progressively stranger, and by Wednesday had taken to avoiding the rest of them altogether. He hurried up and down the halls and disappeared into his room. He had even taken to pulling down the shade on his classroom door. Finally, on Thursday, everyone was commenting, and into the midst of one of the more speculative sessions walked Sister Thecla. The conversation ceased.

"Well, is everyone ready for the summer?"

Marion could barely resist a sing-song, "Yes, Sister Thecla." The nun had lately begun to weigh upon her unduly. Phillips, always one to save the day, replied, "You bet"

Thecla stood there. "I see Mr. McCaffery isn't here...?"

Marion could feel an unreasoning irritation growing within her. Somebody answered, "He's been working in his room all week."

Thecla replied absently, "Yes, yes." Then she looked at Marion. "Mrs. Bailey, could you stop by my office before you leave?"

Marion was taken by surprise. No one was asked to the office, nor did anyone go, except James McCaffery. The nun was inclined to make her announcements in the staff room. Since her announcements were for the most part perfunctory, thus duly ignored, no one had any interest in pursuing her. Except James McCaffery. Marion put on her classroom smile. "Certainly. I'll be down in just a few minutes."

KAREN PIETKIEWICZ

The nun left.

At three, Marion tapped on the office door, and went in. She had already decided how the conversation was going to go. Thecla would ask about James McCaffery. And Marion would ask about James McCaffery. And McLaughlin. The nun would know. She had been there for years. Play it by ear, Marion thought, as she nodded to the bobbing nun.

Thecla spoke first. "Mrs. Bailey. I'm concerned about Mr. McCaffery. Have you noticed, he has been keeping to himself almost all this week?"

"No I hadn't really noticed, Sister," Marion lied.

Well, I have noticed, and I wondered if you might have seen him. Perhaps he isn't well."

"He seems well enough to me..." Marion stared blandly at the nun, who had risen from her chair.

"I *really* think he may be ill," the nun pronounced.

Marion could see that it was working. Thecla was coming unstrung. She looked at the now pacing figure and became aware that she was taking a perverse pleasure in leading the nun out on a limb. She replied, "He looked fine to me, Sister," again in her brightest classroom voice.

"I *know* he must be ill!" Thecla leaned over the desk and delivered the word. Then she sat down. "Surely you must have noticed?" she confirmed, seating herself more comfortably and awaiting the now-to-come reply.

It was time. Marion spoke. "Well, I noticed he was acting strange, beginning last week when his visitor was here. Did you know about the visitor, Sister, a Reginald McLaughlin?"

That was all it took. Within minutes she had it all. McLaughlin was McCaffery's brother; half-brother, actually. Same mother, different fathers, and Reginald McLaughlin had been the one who compromised poor Madeleine, and caused her to kill herself. He had then burdened poor James with the shameful knowledge of his uncontrolled lust, and his sporadic visits to James were an unspeakable imposition. The long-suffering James, in keeping with his Christian compassion, had borne all of this, and now, because of it, he was most assuredly ill. With that conclusion so formidably drawn, Sister had no further need of Marion and dismissed her.

THE SYSTEM

Marion walked slowly down the hall. So that was how it was. Poor old James McCaffery and his skeletons. And Thecla. Obviously she had the hots for him. Not that she even knew what the hots were. If it wasn't for that sickening tragedy it could be almost amusing watching Thecla and James McCaffery go at it in their abstract, elevated way. Poor McLaughlin. No wonder he went nuts. Marion felt again the new compassion she had related for Reginald McLaughlin, whose tragic flaw, like Freddy Brown's, soiled the fabric of his life forever, while Thecla and James McCaffery pranced and gambolled like mincing fools for all the world to see.

That night the tension of the day grew and grew. Marion ate continuously from after school on, munching and snacking, hungering after God knows what. Finally, she threw the book she was attempting to read on the table and went out. She began to walk, briskly, non-thinking; she walked faster, determined only to walk and walk. She streetlights came on; still she walked. She walked to James McCaffery's house.

It was totally unplanned. Or was it. She stood on the edge of the sidewalk looking at the house. The lights were on but all the shades were pulled to the sill. As she watched she could see the profile of James McCaffery outlined now and then on the shade. She walked slowly by the house, watching furtively. At the corner she crossed the street and came back down the other side, still watching. The porch light blinked off. One by one the otherlights went out. Only the small one in the back corner of the house remained on. Marion perceived that it was probably his bedroom light.

That was a very odd thought, James McCaffery's bedroom. It was hard to conceive of him even going to bed; easier to imagine that he just stood in a corner, his eyes glazed like a fish, and shut himself off. Marion watched the window even as she walked. She was again at the corner.

As she crossed the street to James McCaffery's side she noticed some movement down the road. Kids. They ran across the street from the opposite alley to the one that ran behind James McCaffery's house. She quickened her pace. Reaching the fence adjoining his property, she stepped off the walk and crouched behind it. She could hear the youths creeping through McCaffery's yard. After a minute, they materialized beneath the window of his bedroom and moved in beside the wall. They had a box, *the* box, and placed it beneath the window. She could hear them whispering in the night air. She could also see that James McCaffery's carefully pulled blind had a tear through which beamed a sliver of light.

"Get up, get up," a voice urged in a whisper. One of the dark figures mounted the box. There was silence.

"What's he doing?"

More silence.

"Jesus, Bobby. What's he *doing*?" The voice was back.

"Shut up!" Another voice.

"Duck! Duck!" The figures fell to the ground as the shadow of James McCaffery swelled on the bright shade and then diminished. The dark figure again mounted the box. More silence.

"He's not gonna do it."

"Shut up!"

"Lemme watch.."

The dark figures changed places and resumed the patient vigil.

"Maybe he ran out!" Muffled laughter. The figure on the blind suddenly grew to a giant and the intruders scattered like frightened fish, then crept down the fence to where Marion crouched, unnoticed. They huddled together so close she could almost have touched them.

"He probably heard us." Voice number one.

"He can't see us from the bright room." Another voice.

"It doesn't matter. He's not gonna do it, I can tell." Third voice.

"Let's do it for him." Laughter. A girl could be heard snickering.

"Yeah! You guys do it!" More laughter. One of the boys threw himself down and pounded his fists in a fit of laughter while the girls jumped on him.

"Shut up! Shut up!" They were sitting on his back.

"Pull them off of me!" the boy whispered hoarsely.

THE SYSTEM

Two more boys joined the fray and in a minute the ground was writhing with giggling, whispering bodies, wrestling and rolling on the damp grass.

"Bob-by!" a girl's voice, in a muffled shriek.

"Bobby grabbed my tit!" The same high voice, followed by spasms of smothered laughter.

"Anyone for a box lunch?" A boy's voice, raucous beneath the squirming mass, followed by more shrieks and giggles. After a few minutes the mass began to break apart, the bodies rolling out to lie on the ground convulsing into their hands, wheezing, panting, and whispering lewd insults. Finally, one of the boys sat up.

"Let's feed the Beast."

"Yeah. Let's feed the Beast!"

Let's feed the Beast and give it to James McCaffery!"

The boys stood up, watching the window again. One of them whispered, "C'mon!", and they disappeared down the fence and behind the house. In a minute one of the figures crept along the wall to where the box still stood, and carried it off in the dark.

Marion watched, mesmerized. The girls crept up beneath the foundation of James McCaffery's porch, whispering, and huddling. They crouched there in the dark waiting; after a little while one of them moved out and along the side of the house, where she flattened herself against the siding and peered around the corner. Suddenly, she broke and ran back to the waiting girls.

"Come on! Come on!"

The girls got up and crept along the house to the still lighted window. After a few minutes the boys reappeared; the tall one was carrying the same white dish that he had carried in the church. They conferred, crouching low beneath the window, then they crept along the side of the house and onto the porch still carrying the dish. One boy remained at the edge of the porch and peeked around the corner at the girls who had stood up immediately beneath the window, facing the house. The other boys stood on the edge of the porch facing the door. On signal, the boy's arm raised as the girls yelled out into the night.

KAREN PIETKIEWICZ

"Feed the Beast!" and the dish went crashing and shattering into James McCaffery's door. In an instant the gang was gone, scattered into the night while the lights blazed on in James McCaffery's house and the front door burst open. There stood James McCaffery, dishevelled in his striped pyjamas, staring in horror at the shattered dish and the white ooze that dripped down his screen. From his mouth came a wail, and abruptly he fell back into the house and slammed the door. In less than a minute all his lights were out.

Marion was stunned. She remained motionless in the starlight; in the silence she could hear the lonely rustle of the leaves in the night air. A cat emerged from somewhere, crossing the lawn to take up a lonely vigil at James McCaffery's desecrated porch. Marion rose up suddenly and stepped out of the bush straight into the scurrying form of Katherine McCoy, carrying the great black book.

Saturday. A week from tomorrow John would be home. Marion was glad; the telephone call announcing the imminent completion of the job had set her back on track again. She took the lamb leg out of the freezer before going to the garden. It was fresh outside, fresh and cool, as is always the case after the early summer rains. The asparagus, erect against the mounded bed, drew her down to the warm earth. There was enough for a feast.

It had been a strange, wearing week: school and year end, and James McCaffery, and the kids, and, of course, Katherine. Marion looked across the yard into the apple tree that stood behind McCoy's. It was an ancient tree, a transparent, and the gnarled branches stood black against the newly blossoming tips. Katherine was in the tree again, as she had been ever since the night of the dish; hour after hour she lay in the outspread branches, as close to the top as she could climb, cradled in the limbs watching the clouds drift silently in the blue sky. Only when she was called, or when it grew cool, or dark did she climb out of the tree. Sometimes she had a

THE SYSTEM

book, sometimes she just lay there, rocking, and watching the clouds.

For after the debauch at McCaffery's house, Katherine had told all, simply and straightforwardly, walking home in the black night with Marion. She had told how she had broken the cherry tree; how she had climbed it at the insistence of the boys, to shake the cherries down. But the cherries would not fall, so Peter VanDann had come up the tree with her, and together they stood on either side of the crotched trunk and jumped up and down. The trunk had split in two. After that, there had been no end of trouble with Peter. Throughout the fall, and the long winter, the rambunctious boy had mercilessly threatened her until finally she had joined the gang.

Thus Katherine had come out into the night, but because she was too young for things of older girls, she was given the Book. She had written and written and written, to be free of his dreadful curse. Page after page, line after line, the young scribe had recorded the dark rituals of the secret summer nights. She had to write them; this was the price exacted of her.

Back in her yard, Marion asked Katherine for the book. For a long moment, the little girl had held it clutched to her chest with both arms. Then, looking directly at the older woman, she held out her hands and relinquished it. Turning, she walked away through the yard into the moonlight. As Marion watched, the child climbed the apple tree where she blended into the branches, scurried up the slanted roof, opened the window of her room, and disappeared.

And the great black book also disappeared, gone like the Victrola into the night: gone from the table upon which Marion had placed it, just a few hours before.

At seven-thirty that very same morning, the girl appeared on Marion's step for the last time. She rapped steadily at the door until Marion appeared, and said, calmly,

"It's time for confession."

KAREN PIETKIEWICZ

So Marion had gone with her to the church, walking the whole way in silence. But at the door of the church, Katherine stopped.

"I watched Reginald McLaughlin dance all by himself in the old gym," she announced.

"You what?" said Marion, stunned.

"I watched him dance. That's where he took the Victrola. He went there one night and danced all by himself. Then he brought it here and played it again." said the child, straining to open the huge door of the old church. "It used to belong to her before you got it." She pointed her finger inside to the small framed picture of Madeleine Seward.

"See that? That's why he did it. He wanted to play it once more for his girlfriend," Katherine said, closing the large green door. "After all, *that's* where the music belongs."

* * *

The Conversion of Terrence McPhee

Terrence watched the rain slide along the sodden branches and tremble on the tips. It was a dismal morning. The drops rolled slowly at first, then gathered momentum, twisting and merging into myriads of tiny rivulets on the scarred tree trunk until they disappeared in the grass like tears in an old man's beard.

A fly lay on the window sill, its stiff legs black against the glistening glass. Terrence lifted the brittle body by a thread-like limb. How still it was, how nothing. He balanced the simple form on its outspread legs but it would not stand. He tried again with diligence to place the dead fly on its dead feet but each time it fell, limbs upward in silent supplication.

The boy drew closer to the fly. He peered at its still form: the flat, veined wings, closed scissors-like over its back; the bristling, hairy body, scaly and blue-green in the dim morning light. He stared intently at the non-life and as he did so the memory of its buzzing yesterdays became as repellent to him as a broken promise. He dropped the fly suddenly and went downstairs.

The house was quiet. Only his grandparents went to the early mass and they were about to leave. The old blue car rumbled in the driveway, and as he watched, the aging couple emerged from the house next door and got into the warm car. Terrence ran outside and disappeared into the back seat just as the car started out of the driveway.

It was a short drive to the church. No one spoke. The small boy looked at the two grey heads in the front seat. His grandfather was still ringed with a haze of smoke from the pipe he had tapped and set on the dash. His hat sat close to his ears; it was a brown cap with ear flaps like the boy's own cap, only it was brown. His grandmother wore a black hat. It sat on her head like a fat feathered duck in a nest of grey speckled curls. Terrence looked at the many neat rolls of grey streaked hair, each pinned exactly in place on the tiny head. A pink gossamer scarf edged over the dark coat collar, then disappeared again, and the soft smell of his grandmother slowly filled the car.

The boy laid his head back on the seat of the car and watched the two old people. He closed one eye, then the other, and looked again at his grandparents. Then he placed his mittened hand over each eye, first the left one, then the right, but it was still the same. He could not see the one without the other.

The parking lot was only half-filled as the car stopped close to the front. The older couple got out and mounted the wet steps slowly. Terrence opened the door. Once inside, the church door creaked on its hinges and closed out the rain drenched greyness that hung on the dawn like an invisible shroud. Inside, the church was velvety and still. Terrence liked the quiet time before the mass, the shuffling feet and the flickering candles. The squares of the yellow glass windows were peculiarly opaque and resisted the struggling daylight like an unwelcome intruder. Only the door precluded the protective warm totality that enveloped the boy as he nestled in the corner of the warm oak pew.

Now, as the boy sat in the dim church he began to feel a strange heaviness, a peculiar, urging, and persistent foreboding. Suddenly, he started. "Catholics should confess their sins to a priest once a week." Terrence blinked his eyes. He had

THE CONVERSION OF TERRENCE MCPHEE

not made his weekly confession. What if he died? Gerald Sterling got polio, and died on a Tuesday. He could die too. He could die before next Saturday with sins on his soul, and he then he would go straight to hell. He would burn and burn, but he would never burn up. He would just keep on burning forever.

Terrence looked around at the scattering of people dotting the pews of the church. They could all die before next week. They could die with sins on their souls.

An altar boy now emerged from the sacristy and floated footless in his trailing cassock over the carpeted steps and up to the altar. He adjusted a flickering wick and strained to reach the six highest candles. Then he disappeared as silently as he had come.

The line at the confessional had began to lengthen. Soon Father Frankard emerged from the sacristy, opened the center door of the confessional box and slipped inside. The white light blinked on. A man entered the chamber on the left, and a young women slipped into the right side. The two red lights over the opposing chambers flicked on, one after the other.

Watching the line-up of people waiting to confess their sins, the boy again felt the strange heaviness, almost as though he had weights on his heart.

Now the boy envisioned his own heart. But it rose in his mind as a great slate upon which were enumerated all his sins, written over the erasures from last week's accumulation. He wanted to wash it off, to make it slick and shiny and fresh.

There were only three people left in line now. Terrence glanced quickly away. His eyes rested on the feet of the looming statue over the side altar. They were Mary's feet. Small and pink, they crushed a great green serpent which wound about a crescent moon and drooped over the incongruous plaster base. He followed the feet up the rippling blue gown to the folded hands and on past the compressed lips to the blank, expressionless eyes that stared fishlike over the gathering congregation. Terrence looked again at the serpent. He wondered if it was dead, or simply held in place by the small foot. Its forked tongue extended from the gaping mouth: it was not dead. Terrence knew it was alive and thrashing, awaiting the uplifted heel and freedom. He began to feel hot and uncomfortable. There was only one person left beside the confessional, and as he stared he rose automatically and took his place in line.

He felt strangely better now, safe almost, and for a moment his mind rested on the flickering votive candles. The creak of the kneeler revived him and he started.

He was next.

Now he began to think of his sins. Terrence had never forgotten the words of Sister Mary Blase as she stood before the religion class, a sharp pointer in her right hand. "You must examine your conscience before confession," she had said, in a sharp nasal voice, "You must find every sin, even the small, venial sins, and you must root out the Mortal Sin." Sister Mary Blase had now drawn up straight and stiff, while her mouth drew down at each corner. "The mortal sin is the deadliest of all sins. It is the serious sin you commit even when you know it is wrong. The minute you know that you have committed a mortal sin, you must confess it and do penance for it or it will cost you your eternal life with God."

Terrence's mind now began to reel: he had yet to prepare his list of sins. It must be a list. He pictured his heart again, the peculiar slate. It was strange how hard it was to dredge up the sins and write them there himself, so he would have them ready to recite. The peculiarity of it puzzled him; it was like an enigma, the existence of which he was aware but simply could not grasp. He began with the small sins. He never had trouble remembering the small sins. He could always come up with a good assortment. He now shuffled through his small sins, selecting an appropriate variety and listed them in his mind in descending order of wrong. The list always started with the second sin. The first place was reserved for the mortal sin. He pictured the slate on his heart. There, beside each Roman numeral except the first was a sin neatly listed. But the number-one sin had yet to be inscribed.

Now he began his examination of conscience. "I am the Lord Thy God." No one ever sinned against that one. Every-

THE CONVERSION OF TERRENCE MCPHEE

one knew there was only one God. Down the commandments he went. Time was running out. But he could not remember the number-one sin. He began to feel a creeping panic; his mind raced down the Precepts of the Church but there was still no sin for the first place. He chewed his lip and looked blankly at the rapidly filling church. Mrs. Munroe was just coming in.

Suddenly relief poured through his tense body. He stared, his eyes fixed on the woman's thin moving legs as they alternated up the aisle above the zippered boot tops. A hot burning sensation filled his being; he saw again the legs moving back and forth across the narrow lighted slit between the window and the sill, where he had stood, on that dark rainy night, watching the woman disrobe. And he remembered the Impure Thought as vividly as the night it had implanted itself in his heart.

Now his heart appeared again, but it was no longer a slate. It was a great white heart upon which was a great black spot. The heart began to beat, and as it did the black spot too throbbed and pulsed, becoming larger and smaller with each beat. It was an ugly black spot not simply affixed to the surface, but penetrating deep into the fibers through to the very core of the organ. That was the way of the Mortal Sins. He could vision the many small venial sins fluttering like bits of paper impaled by straight pins on the outside of his heart. But the mortal sin was a thing malignant whose presence seemed to Terrence inescapable, whose existence could not be purged, could not be crushed, but lay like the green serpent, alive and waiting to strike at the depths of his soul.

The dark red velveteen curtain parted before him at that instant and an old man passed by and into the accepting pews. Terrence slipped quickly inside the dark box. Now the list was complete. Beside the first number was chalked the impure thought, waiting and ready to be revealed.

The confessional was a strange place, almost like a tomb whose smothering darkness was broken only by the slivers of dim light that filtered through the small white curtain before his face. He waited, still and stiff on his knees, for the tiny, curtained door that separated him from the priest to slide open. It was time. He heard the soft scraping of the small door on the other side of the confessional. Then, slowly, the door before him opened, revealing a ghostlike apparition of the priest profiled in the dim light behind the rippling gauze.

He began. Down the list of sins he raced, breathless, exulting, as he checked them off one by one from the crowded slate. Selfishly, he gathered the list of prayers the priest gave him for his penance and then he reeled off the Act of Contrition. "Ego te absolve," said the whispering priest, but Terrence was on his feet. Stepping from the confessional into the now lighted church he dropped to his knees in the pew. Swiftly he ticked off the prayers, pouring the words forth in a flood that washed the sins from his heart until it was radiant, shining, and clean. He felt light and detached, floating and strangely remote. He waited for himself to return. But he did not. The bell tinkled, and the mass began.

Terrence watched the priest begin the prayers at the foot of the altar. But the peculiar detachment remained. He was there, but he was not there. He looked at his legs. They were still and stiff beneath him. His heart was beating. He wondered if it had stopped, but it had not. He could feel it now, steady and throbbing; drumlike and primitive within him. It filled his ears and swelled in his mind, and expanded into his whole body. The Kyrie began, the ephemeral voices assailing him in waves of strangely ringing words that bypassed his unknowing mind and rang in the chambers of his heart. The awareness of living people flooded in through his eyes and crowded his being until it became a tiny living point from which he could but observe. The pounding of his heart increased as it grew, absorbing all the hearts of the rows and rows of shuffling people who remained unaware as the boy appropriated their very beings unto himself until he became one great, throbbing heart. Then, like a spreading stain the spot appeared, growing and pulsing, black on the white heart that struggled heavily for release, twisting and writhing under its penetrating burden.

Now, the awareness of his own presence began to impinge itself on the boy's floating mind; there in the jungle of

THE CONVERSION OF TERRENCE MCPHEE

sound, in the myriad color and ringing bells and shuffling feet he became himself the priest and the great throbbing heart his victim. High before the congregation he bent, peering with eyes that were his but not his at a heart at once his but not his. Then, amidst the tinkling bells before the golden tabernacle, he seized the heart in his hands and raised it throbbing skyward before shattering it into the waiting chalice.

Now the heart began to bleed, red and profuse. When it filled the cup to the rim the boy seized the chalice and he drank, flooding his being with the living blood. And as he drank the heart appeared: triumphantly cleansed and radiantly white and floating within the open tabernacle, where it shimmered for a breathless moment until it burst like a skyrocket and fell sparkling amid the cup of pristine hosts.

It was over. Terrence shifted his weight from his aching limbs and leaned on the seat beside him. The congregation moved forward to the Communion rail but Terrence did not move. Instead, he put his hand over his left side. It was there. Quiet and steady, the reassuring beat soothed him into a strange and peaceful mood. He slipped into the aisle and tiptoed out through the large door where he stood for a minute on the top step, pensively, before he raced to the waiting car.

* * *

Maudie

The car crunched up the long drive and stopped beside the silvered wood of the sagging stoop at the rear of the house. A wispy trail of dust issued from the gravel and hung protestingly in the air, then, as if the effort were too great to sustain itself, disappeared thinly over the burdocks. The sunburned sky stretched stoically toward the horizon where a soothing ointment of cooling clouds had begun to gather. A solitary hawk arched like a knowing eyebrow over the silent barn.

A girl and a young child emerged from the white car. The child, a fair-haired boy of about eight, hung at her heels as they mounted the porch and edged toward the screened door. The boy could hear the menacing rumble from the coarse-haired sullen dog that was chained heavily to the shabby kennel beside the steps. The two disappeared into the house, and the door sprung closed with a snap.

"Maudie?" The girl set the sack of groceries on the table and began removing the items. A container of Mason jars steamed on the range and she remembered seeing a pail of freshly pulled beets soaking in the shed. The stairs creaked behind the basement door, so she opened it and peered in.

"Oh. There you are. I thought you were napping. You shouldn't be climbing the steps; what do you need?"

The old woman creaked through the door and eased herself onto a kitchen chair.

"Not a one. I ain't got a one."

"What's that you don't have, Maudie?"

"I was wanting to get these beets done up. I thought for sure I had some lids but I ain't got a one more'n what's there in the sink."

"Well, I can run in town and get you some if you like."

"No . . . no, it's just as well. My legs is done in for today anyway. Too much in the garden, it was. There's always tomorrow." She rubbed the heel of her hand in a circular movement over her brown stockinged knee.

The girl took an apron from behind the door and slipped it over her head.

"Why don't you go read the paper, Maudie; I'll get dinner."

"Well, the Lord bless you, maybe I just will." The old woman patted her thin grey-white hair and slipped a hairpin into the sparse knot at the nape of her wrinkled neck. Then, sighing, she placed her arms akimbo on her knees and levered herself up from the chair.

The girl busied herself about the kitchen while the old woman resolved herself to the leather recliner in the next room.

"What do you hear from your man?" The voice issued from the leather chair.

"Nothing yet, Maudie." The water splashed onto the dusty potatoes in the sink.

"A man can be a burden, that's the truth." The sonorous chime of the clock on the sideboard counted the half-hour. "I been a blessed woman in my day, Ruth, a blessed woman. Yes, my man Bill was awful good to me, awful good. He never done like the others. He never set in the tavern nor none of that, never once. He always wanted me near. Every night he come home, every night. There weren't a woman around didn't eye my Bill, but he always come home to me. Things ain't been straight since he got himself killed."

MAUDIE

"What happened to him, Maudie?" inquired Ruth, but the old woman cocked an eye at her, sharp and searching.

"It were a terrible accident, and that's all I'm gonna say. It happened, and I buried him right out back, right where I can see him every day, that's where he is right now."

"They let you bury him here?" asked Ruth, incredulous.

"Folks took care of their own in my day." the old woman announced, and rose from her chair. She looked at Ruth. "When's that man of yours comin' home?"

"He's in Vietnam, Maudie. How can I say when he'll be home?"

"You should have kept him when you had him. There ain't no difference. No difference at all," said the old woman. "Nothin' but war no more, nothin' but war."

The boy scuffed his feet under the wooden table. The meal steamed before him.

"Have him a spoonful of the creamed onions, here." The woman came back into the hot kitchen and her wrinkled hand wielded a wooden spoon which she now dipped into a pot on the wood range. "How's that, now, boy?" she asked. A white mass spread slowly over the child's plate. The boy murmured and dabbed the mass to the side of his plate.

"I don't like those, Mom."

"Have a bit now, boy. My Bill, he was a big eater!" The woman sat down at the table after dishing herself up. She ate, mopped her plate with a crust of bread and settled back in her chair to eye the boy while he ate.

After the meal was finished, the girl washed up the dishes while the older woman rocked in self-satisfaction. The boy stood silently near the parlour door and then drifted off up the bannistered stairway. The light in the sitting room began to fade and the girl finished her chores by hanging the worn apron back on its hook. She moved imperceptibly into the carpeted room where the old woman sat in her rocker, and reclined herself in the empty leather chair across from her. The clock ticked.

Now the woman began to rock. Soon, she said, "The boy been climbing the fence again."

The girl remained silent.

"I tell him, but he don't pay me no mind." The old woman leaned her head back on the doily covered rocker. "That there was built every stick by my Bill."

The clock struck six.

"He been kicking at the slats again too." Her black eyes flicked toward the west window. "He says he never but they're off just the same."

The girl looked out at the swaying fence, toothless with age and half hidden by the encroaching weeds.

"I'll talk to him, Maudie." The girl stared vacantly into the descending gloom.

"Won't do no good. The boy's headin' for bad times. I can tell. I can always tell." The silence was broken only by the rocker, protesting its burden.

"Did you feed the dog, did you?" The black eyes focussed on the girl.

"I gave him all the scraps that were left. He still had some in his pan from this morning."

"He's a mean one, that one. Makes a good watchdog for me. Don't never want to turn your back on him, though."

The girl straightened in the chair. "You know, Maudie, I think he's coming to like me a little. He doesn't snarl nearly as much as he used to anymore. Yesterday he let me come right up to feed him."

"Nope. They never change, not them kind. Been mean since he was a pup. Always was and always will be. I know the kind. I seen lots of 'em. Mean clear through. I can always tell."

The girl rose and stood looking out the window for a minute. Then, turning abruptly, she stated, "I'm going to bed now, Maudie," she said. "Do you need anything?"

"Nothing to need at an age like mine," said the old woman.

Ruth said nothing, and slowly disappeared from the room.

In the middle of the night, Ruth awoke to hear footsteps shuffling down the stairs. Shortly after, she heard the back

MAUDIE

door open and close quietly. From the driveway, she heard the gravel crunch beneath someone's feet.

Ruth Fischer rose from the sagging bed she had struggled to find sleep in for seven weeks. She had come to this small town to work, but the rents were still higher than she had anticipated, and good schools were scarce. Instead of a small apartment, she had taken up with this old woman as a companion in return for room and board for herself and her son. It was bearable, but that was all. Only the thought that her husband was on his final tour of duty and would soon be home, made her situation tolerable. She hoped to have some money saved by the time he arrived.

Now she found herself in the middle of an autumn night, pressed to the frame of a second floor window in this ancient house with an old woman who was completely mad.

And there was Maudie, standing in the drive in the cold moonlight, the shotgun in her hands, her gown hanging from her protruding bones, her long white hair down her back.

She was after the owl again, thought Ruth. For Ruth had seen the great bird where it sat each night, silent and all-knowing, on Maudie Williams' chimney. She was the one who had told Maudie about it, so it was her own fault. Who would have thought the sick old woman would want to kill the owl? But she did, thought Ruth, and peered out the glass from behind the curtain. The only saving grace was that the chimney was far enough removed from the window by where she and her son slept, to keep them out of the firing line. And, thought Ruth, with her eyes, it's not likely Maudie will ever hit the bird anyhow. But just as she had returned to her bed and begun to slide under the covers, she heard a tremendous blast. The glass in the window shook, and then, from the roof above her she heard the rolling thud of the owl that Maudie had finally hit. She rushed to the window as her small son sat up in bed.

"What is it, Mom? She shot the owl, didn't she?"

The boy began to cry.

"I hate it here, Mom. Why can't we move? I hate Maudie!"

Ruth had stayed at the window just long enough to see the bloodied body of the great white bird tumble lifeless to the ground.

She went immediately to her son.

"We will leave, Stevie," she said. "I promise. Mom will start looking right away, but don't tell Maudie. Promise."

"I won't tell, Mom," said the small boy, wiping his eyes and throwing his arms around his mother's shoulders. "Can we take Moser with us? Moser likes us, Mom, and he hates her."

Moser was Maudie Williams' dog; the dog she kicked at and abused constantly; the dog she teased and tormented; the dog she barely fed.

"I don't know, Stevie. We'll have to ask Maudie. Maybe we can buy old Moser off her. Okay? But for sure we'll get out of here as soon as we can."

She covered the boy, and tucked him in.

"Go to sleep, Stevie, it's late."

The sun squinted through the dusty window of the east bedroom as the alarm sounded another day. The girl and the child whispered softly as they dressed and tiptoed down the long stairway to the range-warmed kitchen. The beets bubbled on the flame already and the old woman hung in anticipation over a pot of cooked cereal.

"We didn't hear you get up ..."

"I been about for more'n an hour! You got to get up early to beat old Maudie." She smiled, and her eyes glittered and twinkled. "Sit down, there; have yourselves some breakfast."

"I thought I heard you up last night, Maudie," said the girl now, to the old woman. "Weren't you feeling well?"

"Nope. It warn't that. I got up and kilt that owl."

"Why did you kill the owl, Maudie. Owls don't hurt anyone."

"There's lots you don't know, girlie," said Maudie Williams now, her black eyes glittering, her head swaying back and forth.

MAUDIE

"An owl is a bad omen, my girl. Things you don't know about, girl, things you don't see. Like that boy, there, girl. A bad boy, girl. Things you don't see."

Ruth looked out the window to where Stevie was crouched beside the dog, Moser, pushing bits of bone and gristle at the cringing animal. She watched his small hand reach out, pet the huge shaggy head, watched the dog draw back, and then move carefully forward with his mouth to eat the scraps of roast.

"If I told him once, I told him a dozen times: keep away from thet dog. But the boy don't listen. Just don't listen."

The younger woman took her coat over her arm and opened the door.

"I have to go now, Maudie. I'll see you at four."

She went out.

The white car turned into the drive at precisely four, just as the orange school bus disappeared over the rise in the road. Stevie Fischer stepped onto the grass beside the driveway as his mother's car crept past him, then trailed lightly along behind it. He waited for his mother to alight and they walked toward the house together.

"I saved some of my sandwich for Moser, Mom," her son said.

At the back door of Maudie Williams' old farm house, the steps were freshly wet. A bucket sat overturned by the door, crowned with a worn scrub brush. The boy grabbed his mother's arm.

"Moser's gone, Mom. Where'd he go?"

Ruth leaned over the rail and called out at the top of Moser's old dog house, but Moser did not come out. Suddenly, she started.

On the ground beside the grey, insul-bricked dog house lay Moser's heavy chain, still attached to the kennel, and on the other end, his heavy leather collar. It was open, and empty.

The corners of her mouth began to twitch. Suddenly, she took her son by the hand. Maudie Williams was standing in the doorway, a cryptic smile on her thin, wrinkled lips.

"Lookin' fer old Moser, are you now?" she crackled. "Well, he ain't here no more, you can count on that. He were a mean one when he come up, and a mean one when he went down. Yup. Now get on in here to supper, I ain't got a mind to wait all day."

The old woman turned, and disappeared into the house.

The young mother and her son stood for a long minute by the door as the cry of a circling hawk echoed from his spiralling flight. Then, hand in hand, they went in.

* * *

The Boy Who Wished To Be God

Once upon a time, there was a rather small boy named George who wished that he were God. It was a secret wish; one that drifted through his heart like a twirling leaf on a summer stream, and peered wistfully from his clear blue eyes like a pup through a pet store window.

There are many kinds of wishes. Some are very big, like wishing to make your own wishes come true. Some are very small, like wishing for nothing; and some are quite silly, like wishing to be God. The big wishes are fun to wish, and George wished many of those. He would run from one corner of his heart's desire to another, gathering and exchanging, sorting and carrying, and packing his imagination with hundreds of good things, like a honeybee building a comb.

And there were small wishes too, that came at quiet times, like when he sat on the old log and threw pebbles in the still water, or when he lay deep in the swaying timothy grasses and looked at the cool blue sky. These were the times that he wished for nothing at all.

But it was, for George, the silly wishes that were the hardest to wish. They were spacious, but not large; pressing, but not heavy. They were, it seemed, like empty spaces in a picture puzzle, or tickly bubbles in soda pop, or a burp, waiting.

George did not have many silly wishes. As a matter of fact, he could recall only one other silly wish. He remembered when it had first come. He had found a clear, cool pond, off from the creek bed, and out in the sun. It was a spring-fed pond that bubbled up from a somewhere place deep beneath the ground.

That day, the day of the first silly wish, had been a magic day. George had sat on the banks of the slick brown stream watching his father fish. He could still hear the whip of the long line and the whir of the reel as the lengths spun out over the water. Then the fly would light: gently, precisely, on the surface of the stream. It was a beautiful time, then, an in-between time. And as the fly drifted over the dark, smooth-surfaced hole, George would watch only the water; watch and wait for the strike that would come, breaking the magical spell. It seemed not to matter after the strike; only the challenge between the man and the spreading telltale rings on the quiet surface captivated George.

It was after just such a strike that he had wandered off to the pond. He went alone, stepping softly through the grasses beneath the fluttering aspen that marked the way. He circled the pond halfway until he came to some low rocks that began on the banks, scattering over the gravel and down into the water. They were warm in the sun, and George lay down on his stomach with his hands under his chin and looked at the watery world.

It was strange how the bugs could skim over the water. The small jet beetles whirled and zagged an erratic course while the wide-spreading delicate legs of the mosquito catchers rested like spidery skeletons on the undented surface and drifted with the wind.

It was then that the silly wish came. George wished he could be under the water and see how the bugs looked from beneath the surface. He wondered how the beetles moved; whether beneath their shiny coats lay hidden many fast, flittering, tiny black feet paddling furiously, like so many row-

THE BOY WHO WISHED TO BE GOD

ers beneath a galleon. He wondered more at the spidery mosquito catcher as it moved dryly over the pond like an insect deity walking on the water.

George was engrossed. He looked down now, straight into the water with hungry eyes. The rocks were moss-covered and tiny fern-like plants waved gently on the bottom, softening into an undulating carpet of shiny green water grasses. It was a bright pond, the sun shone right to the bottom, and the waters teemed with tiny darting fish that schooled like flocks of tiny silver swallows over the watery landscape.

Now George watched the fish as they moved to the rocks beneath where he stared. They were each one, yet all one; they moved alone, yet together. George lowered his face to the water, closer and closer until the coldness nipped at his nose, scattering the fish like slivers of mercury spilled from a very great height.

George sat up, then, and removed his shoes. The water was very cold; he gingerly submerged his feet until they rested on the slippery bottom. His intrusion into the shiny waters offended the fish; they kept at a distance for a time before venturing in toward the rocks, but eventually they returned and began to nudge gently at his skin. George felt a curious exultation as the fish battered his feet with their velvet blows; he enjoyed a peculiar satisfaction at this intimacy and longed the more to take part in the watery world.

Abruptly, he removed his feet from the water and when the ripples cleared, the fish were gone. Then, leaning far over the water, he lowered his face toward it. His nose broke the surface of the cold water; slowly, slowly he dipped his whole face until it was all wet. Then, raising his head, he took a huge breath then submerged his head in the pond. He began to open his eyes, squinting in a controlled and deliberate fashion, allowing the water to seep between his lids a little at a time. Then, initiated, he opened his eyes wide and peered at last into the trespassed world.

But the magic was gone. There, amidst the beauties of the pond bottom, the small fish that slid between the round rocks and hung quivering in the green fronds were simply small, quivering fish. Their glassy, staring eyes seemed not to see the very beauty they were a part of.

Now George lifted his face, dripping from the water, and looked at the pond. A lonely breeze rippled the surface and he felt the soft wind lift his hair and tug gently at his shirt-sleeves as it passed by. He began to walk around the pond. When he reached the opposite side he stopped. He looked quietly at the place of the foolish wish, then turned and headed off to the stream.

His father was up on the bank now, crouching. George walked up silently; the great silvery-pink rainbow lay disembowelled, yet still staring, on the wet grass. George watched his father as he pulled up a tuft of grass and cleaned the blade of his knife. Then, flinging the innards back into the brown water, he hooked the great fish by the gills and moved toward the car. George watched the water swallow the remnants of the fish. Then he turned and followed his father.

That was the time of the first silly wish. George thought again of the first silly wish. But now it seemed far, far away and relevant to nothing.

It was different with the new wish.

George could feel the weight of it in his soul; it burned there like a filament of truth, scorching his heart with its burning desire. It seemed almost to implement his hopes and direct his dreams and George was, at times, all but overwhelmed by its existence within him.

Thus it was that on one warm, windy spring day, George decided to be God. He was eating at the time; it occurred to him as he sat there absently melting a marshmallow in his cocoa; and he was pleased.

Now he could change the world. He took a sip of his cocoa. There was no hurry. He smiled to himself. Of course James Cochrane was the first. George smiled again. Poor James. Wouldn't he be surprised? George almost laughed out loud. He felt a swelling within him, a full, bursting forth as he expanded with his new found power. He felt the strong beating of his heart and the idea made his mind swirl until he felt almost dizzy.

THE BOY WHO WISHED TO BE GOD

Finally, he shook his head sharply and the churning within him receded. He wiped his mouth and left for school.

On this very special day, George moved with new awareness. The leaves on the trees were just coming out, and George was struck by the definiteness of each unfolding green reality. Even the sidewalks were different; each fleck of silica glittered and winked amidst the lesser companion grains that were embedded forever in the mixture beneath his feet.

James was there as usual. George could see his sparse figure moving in and out among the passing groups of students that were streaming onto the schoolyard. George stood on the edge of the curb watching James with a new interest. Then, as he stepped off the curb, James saw him. Now the thin boy moved toward the place by which he knew George must pass, and he leaned smugly against the base of one of the old scarred elms that surrounded the school yard, waiting for George.

George studied the smirking boy with the glittering, defiant eyes. He could do this now. The frightened George of yesterday was gone; only his body remained to serve him in his new role. He approached the tree as James stepped out before him.

"Kick over, fink!"

George looked at the boy who stood blocking his way. He felt distant and inaccessible now, like when he ran softly out of snowball range during the winter, or in out of a summer storm. He began to smile: a small, compact little smile. James moved in until he was pressing against George. It was then that George began to laugh. And squinting his eyes, he focused all his new self on James's defiant face and said in a low, deliberate voice,

"I am Almighty God!"

James pulled back abruptly.

"You jerk!" he sneered, an indecisive look crossing his face.

Now George felt exultant; filled with the triumph of his first experience. He laughed again.

"I'll get you! Think about it, queer! I got nothin' but time." The boy hurled the words at George. George stopped laughing. He looked at the figure of James, who stood staring intensely, with his shoulders hunched, while his arms swung ridiculously at his sides. How strange he looked now, almost afraid, like a dog caught raiding the garbage, or a bug under an overturned rock.

George reached in his pocket and fished for a dime. He held it, rolling it between his fingers for a minute. Then he flipped it to James with a quick motion. The boy, surprised, reached instinctively, and retrieved the coin from the air.

"You just saved your neck!" He pocketed the dime. Then, he searched George with a quick, guarded look before he spat on the ground and walked away.

George watched the boy disappear among the forms that flooded the playground. He thought of the dime and smiled. A God could afford to be generous.

Now George began to walk. He wanted to think about being God. But now, at the moment of his triumph, he could feel the wish dissolving within him. Soon, all the plans he had made in his dreams had been swept from his mind as though an elusive genie had come and gone, called back to his lamp by some higher power, and all that remained for George was the glittering memory of his presence.

"George!"

George looked up. It was Buddie Taylor.

"Come on!"

Buddy was motioning excitedly to George from the near corner of the school. George stood for a minute. Then, pounding his chest with his fists, he emitted a triumphant Tarzan-like scream that rang out over the playground, and lowering his head, charged off across the yard toward the waiting child.

* * *

The Book House

The first day I opened the glass door of the library cabinet, it was raining. There were no scraps to sew up on the old treadle, no pie dough leftovers to twist, dip in cinnamon and bake, nothing at all to do on that long, dreary day, but read. I had often looked at the many dark brown books where they lined the two oak shelves; the back of each read, simply, "The Book House", beneath which were Roman numerals depicting the volume.

They were my grandmother's books; they must have once been very expensive. The pages were gold-emblazoned with multi-colored illustrations of Kings, Queens, and Knights, flaming dragons, green elves, witches, and beggar children. Of course my favourite character was there: Rapunzel, with her tumbling blond braids.

When I think about it now, I don't remember anyone else ever touching those books. I imagine that the only reason the books appealed to me in the first place was because they were kept behind glass, and locked with a gold key. My grandmother showed me where she kept it in the buffet drawer.

KAREN PIETKIEWICZ

From that day forward I began my forays into the worlds within the massive books. I tiptoed through dozens of stone castles. I crept behind field mice over damp, moss-covered steps. I read about maidens stolen by witches and locked up in high towers, or banished somewhere far away in the woods, separated forever from their one true love. I read about a virtuous princess, her golden hair dishevelled, her lovely face turned to the dungeon's cold wall in a desperate attempt to escape the lascivious desires of a Wicked Prince with his wart-covered, slathering lips. Once, when I had nothing to do, I sat for hours by the stone lip of the garden well waiting for an elusive frog to retrieve my golden ball.

Before that time, I had read little of such goings on. My experience with virtue was confined to the Mother of God, and the singular vice I had come in contact with was the one I held for my father while he clamped down his freshly glued wood.

But that was before the Robb family moved in to the small white house on Bingham Street.

Looking back now, I cannot recall who lived in that house to begin with, or when the bedeviled cherry tree was first planted in the small back yard. I only remember stooping beneath its growing branches to pick the occasional cherry from the green grass, and, occasionally, reaching up to snatch a bunch or two of the reddest, sweetest fruits to suck from their stoney pits.

The Robbs were a different breed of people; they painted and papered the little white house, they raked their lawn after they mowed it, and even carried the clippings away. Now, here was Mr. Robb, digging four holes through the grass to fence in the cherry tree that had never been fenced in before.

I imagine half the neighbourhood stood and watched Frederick Robb dig. It was like a ceremony. He would dig deep down into the earth, and carefully place each shovel-full of tan clay into the new wheelbarrow he had purchased for the occasion. During the time of digging, his wife stood there with her arms crossed and watched, making little, whispered comments occasionally, to which Frederick Robb would grunt,

THE BOOK HOUSE

or look up and frown. She was watching us as well, as we stood along the lot line dividing his house from the Laitonen's back yard. Our gang was all there: Phillip, Josephine, Peter and his sister, Twila, Bill, Ralphie Malport, - even Gerald from the other block, before his mother finally called him home. This was not before Josephine - we called her Josie - had sidled up to Gerald because he was new. I watched her rub herself up against him like a female cat, and give him that look before he left.

We found out the wife was called Glenda. In a neighbourhood of Madges, Friedas, Phoebes and Jeans, you could tell from the start that a Glenda would never fit in. Not a chance. Glenda Robb looked more like a girl than a housewife, and on top of that, she came from Detroit.

So that meant both of them were from somewhere else. They looked it, too. He wore bluejeans and a fake cowboy shirt he must have thought he was supposed to wear out digging, and she had on a soft blue skirt and a knitted sweater top with a scooped out neck and short sleeves. I remember that it was yellow.

The strangest thing about Glenda Robb was that she had thin arms. There was not a mother on the street whose arms were as thin on top as Glenda Robb's. I remember Mrs. Monroe's arms flattened out like two limp fish against the sides of her dress. Mrs. VanDaan's arms were so fat the flesh was dimpled and pockmarked. But not Glenda Robb's arms. Hers just hung there as round and perfect as a doll's, and almost as pale.

As if this weren't enough, she had freckles splattered all over the top of her body. There were freckles on her arms, freckles on her shoulders, and freckles even across the front of her chest, almost down to where the scoop-neck began. She must have had freckles underneath, too, because there was nothing much else showing. She had reddish blond hair, which she wore long, and in pin-curled waves like someone out of *Look* magazine. Glenda Robb said not one word to any of us, so we decided that very day that we would never like her, and we never did.

KAREN PIETKIEWICZ

We decided it must have been her idea to put up the fence. So there stood Glenda while her husband dug and dug. Finally, the holes were finished, and Frederick Robb got in his truck and left. He returned shortly with four long, unpeeled cedar posts from Lock City Hardware and Lumber, and by the end of the day, the fence was securely in place, complete with a padlocked gate.

It is a strange thing to think of now, but in that neighbourhood filled with apple trees, I cannot remember a single blossom from any one of them that Spring. Every other year, the entire neighbourhood turned white from the snow of scented blossoms, but in the Spring of 1948 only the cherry tree bloomed.

I used to stand across the lot line and look at the pristine blossoms; it seemed that not a petal fell on the carefully clipped grass within the fence.

Summer came. The hot, boring days gave way to cool, exciting evenings and the black, dark of the bushes around Laitonen's house, where we gathered every night after dark. There, we played Chase, the girls running, screaming, the boys whooping and yelling, and after us on the dead run as soon as we crossed the front yard. Ritually, we dived into the spirea bushes that sprawled against the grey stucco and trembled, waiting to be caught, to be wrestled down in the pickery black world beneath the shrubs, arms held tight, back pressed against the damp, black soil, only then to be let go, to chase, and run, and get caught again. There was an unspoken understanding; thus it was that Billy always chased me, and always let me go, while Peter VanDaan chased Josie and they stayed in the bushes for sometimes an hour.

It was just one of those nights when the rest of us were bored, tired of waiting for Peter to make his triumphant Tarzan call, tired of waiting for Josie to sway sullenly down the grass, that the boys decided to hit the cherry tree. Linda wasn't out that night and Josephine, as her mother called her, went home.

It was a perfect night with no moon, and the Frederick Robb residence was completely dark. I still remember how the small tree looked that night. The top, perfectly shaped and round like an air balloon, balanced in the basket-like fence. At first, the scene was an etching of dark upon dark, black forms against blacker forms, but as we stood beside the tree, the leaves began to shine. Each dark leaf seemed to have absorbed a stolen glitter from the long descended sun, which it hoarded for this darkest of all nights. Now the cherry tree glimmered ominously over the shapely profiles of the pendulous, hanging fruits.

Among us, not a word was said. Each stood silent, gazing up at the perfect tree while it stood perpetually waiting.

"So let's go for it!" Peter VanDaan vaulted the fence. It was always Peter. He was forever first.

Now his voice hissed out of the black beneath the waiting tree. "Put her up first! You! Get over the fence!" His voice was strange: hot, and excited, ablaze with the power that the words conveyed to his spellbound, silent companions.

I moved toward the fence, captivated by the spell of the glittering tree, and by the hissing power of Peter's voice. It called: singular, powerful and compelling.

I climbed the fence easily. The toes of my feet just fit into the octagonal holes of the chicken wire that stretched tautly between the cedar posts. Once inside, we crouched close to the ground and huddled against the trunk. Silent, and looking up, we could see the dark crotch of the tree. It was perfectly balanced, and symmetrical, the bark carefully pruned of each small twig or leaf. The crotch formed a perfect Y, thus the tree stood in absolute balance, its two main branches thrust upward on either side and joined together at the top in a great globe of fruitbearing oneness.

"Climb up and throw 'em down to us! Move! You should be able to get up to the top." Peter grasped my upper arm and thrust me at the tree; I scrambled for footing in his clasped, unsteady hands. The tree held without a tremor and I disappeared into the limbs, one foot on each part of the now divided trunk, my arms, as my legs, outstretched and grasping. The narrow, springing branches began to come to life within my hands, but once inside the tree I could not see the fruit. In the black, there appeared to be nothing, and not the smallest speck of light.

"I can't see!" My voice squeezed out between my rigid lips.

"For Christ's sake!" It was an unknown whisper.

"Tell her to jump up and down." Another whisper.

"Jump on it!" It was VanDaan.

Peter was now standing. The other three boys had swung over the fence and were somewhere in the dark beside him. I could see his white face like a moon as he looked up to see where I hung splayed in the protesting branches. I jumped for all I was worth, but no fruit fell.

Over and over, I pulled my feet up beneath me, hung suspended from my wrists, and landed full on the twin limbs, but no fruit fell.

"Put your feet farther apart!" It was VanDaan again.

Obedient, I balanced myself firmly over the splayed crotch and began again to spring up and down, trying to take the tree with my motion, but still no fruit fell.

"It's not working." I had begun to hiss.

"Jesus H. Christ! Move!" VanDaan was now scrambling up the tree. "Move, I said! Get over on your own half!" We struggled together in the center of the leaves, stomach to stomach, sliding past one another until we stood, balanced precariously, on either side of the small crotched tree.

"Now get a grip, and when I say, 'Jump!', jump!" VanDaan blew the words out of his compressed lips like bullets, and I waited, poised.

"Jump!"

Nothing.

"Harder!"

The cherries refused to budge. No matter how hard I jumped, the tree barely shook, and not one cherry fell to the ground.

"Lemmie up there, for Christ's sake!" VanDaan started higher up the tree.

"Move the hell over! Get up here on that side!" Peter was planted on the opposing limb, rustling through the leaves and branches for a death grip on the now trembling tree. We were close to the top. The leaves began to part and pale white shadows of dim light played over Peter's brow, and across the sharp bones of his cheeks.

"Now when I say jump, *jump*!"; his voice rang out the command.

It was as though the earth had split in two. The crack rang out like a rifle shot in the still of the black night as the tree began to split, writhing and twisting in mid-air, its cracked voice protesting all the way down. As it fell we jumped, and ran, and ran, and ran.

No one came out. The street was as quiet as before we had come. Now, one by one we returned, emerging out of the dark shadows of the yard, to reassemble by the corner of the house and stare in horror at the place where the cherry tree had stood.

It was finished. The small bright tree had split precisely in half. One side took the chicken wire almost to the ground, while the other half of the fence, pulled taut, displayed the white gash of the endless wound for everyone to see. Even the traitorous sky had opened. From between elongated slivers of ragged cloud, a non-descript moon plied its leftover light in a grey-white smear on the gaping and terminal slash as the cherry tree hung dying beneath it.

"We're fucked. . ." It was Phillip who now spoke. He was the timid, simple one and his voice had a ring of incredulity to it. He sounded as though he had just received a sentence of death from which there was no escape, and not even his mother would save him. Rising from his crouch, he walked straight across the yard and stood, dazed and staring, before the fallen tree.

No one said another word. While Phillip stood vigil beside the broken tree, the rest of us crept away in the dark.

A neighbourhood is a familiar place; it has a voice that speaks even when you do not wish to hear. That next morn-

KAREN PIETKIEWICZ

ing you could hear it before the clothes were hung. Too many words; women who would not cross the street until the evening meals were cooked were standing on the hard grey sidewalk, their arms folded, aprons still on. I could see them from the window of my room, just as I could smell the soap from the churning washer down the cement cellar steps, and hear it grinding away. Beneath the line, the first load sat abandoned in the wire-handled basket while the clothespins hung waiting on the line. No one was there. Never as long as I remember did my grandmother fail to hang the clothesbefore eight in the morning, but it was almost nine o'clock and there they sat.

I could smell the damp, fresh morning smell of that Monday and it seemed as though my waking had sullied the clean day. There was nothing to do but get up.

On the street, a blue and white car sat waiting. As I stepped out on the porch, I could see the officers talking to Mr. and Mrs. Robb, while the women stood at a distance and observed. Nothing would come of it. I knew that no one would speak. The police would make some small notes on their rolled- over pads and leave, like they always did. They would go back where they came from just like they did when old man Wilds slapped his wife. They would talk, and leave. Then the trouble would start.

And so they did. Now the street was silent. The women faded away, the washing got hung; traffic moved slowly up and down. I went in, made my toast, sat on the top step and ate it.

Things have a way of fading after awhile. They peak, fade, and fall away, given enough time. I went out.

At four o'clock the bus stopped on Young Street. Peter VanDaan stepped down from the wheezing vehicle, and crossed to the other side. He was wearing the baseball cap he always wore, and a red and white striped T-shirt. Even from the corner you could see the ring of stomach that hung above his belt. He was always fat; not huge fat, but fat. Fat enough to be noticed, and fat enough to be strong. We even called him Fathead.

THE BOOK HOUSE

I knew he saw me right away, and he spoke to me. Not in words; he spoke to me from half a block away but with his body. He held perfectly still, and stared. Then he turned down Young and headed for the alley.

Now I moved slowly out into the road. I crossed, moved up past Brown's, and edged down the fenceline to the back lane. I knew he would be waiting, and he was.

"Monroe got it good. I could hear him this morning." Peter looked tense and hard at the same time. I knew what he meant.

Phillip's mother was addicted to the strap. I had seen it once, hanging on a nail beside their bathroom sink. It was dark brown, almost black leather, shiny, and worn from use. He had felt it before. I had seen his mother press him to the garage wall and strap him while he screamed at the top of his lungs. Zelda Manning had a withered hand which she kept tucked between the bosom of her housedress and the top of her apron so no one could see it, but on that day she had used it to press Phillip to the wall. She whipped his legs, the thick strap flying in her good hand until she had raised welts on the backs of his calves and thighs. Along the edges of each swelling red band there ran a raised ridge where the belt cut deeper. Phillip had screamed and screamed. Some of the younger kids stayed to watch, but the rest of us finally left. It seemed no matter how often she strapped him, the next time up, Phillip never learned to lie. In some sad, perverse way he seemed to think he was caught in an inescapable world of which pain was an integral part. Thus he acquiesced to the inevitable immunization shots, ate fish on Fridays, carried out the trash, and submitted to the strap, all with the same bewildered look in his blue eyes. He even took the look with him to school where the teacher asked for answers Phillip didn't know, and from what I saw he never ever did.

Peter was a different case completely. He was coarse, he was boisterous, he was loud, and he was riddled with every toilet trick in the book, but he wasn't mean and he wasn't afraid. I think he passed all that because of his father.

Hans VanDaan was Dutch; a huge, heavy-set, fair-skinned man with red hair. He was mean, and he drank. Threasa, his wife, was Polish. She was a small woman, with a high-pitched voice, scatterbrained, but always smiling her ridiculous, inappropriate little smile. She trotted about the house washing walls, and cleaning windows, and scrubbing floors every minute of the day until the VanDaans had the cleanest floors in town. Threasa kneeled on the floor for hours and painted every other square tile blue, and waxed the floor until it shone like glass. Everything in the kitchen was blue and white but the wooden shoes filled with green plants. That was the way Hans wanted it, and that's what Hans got.

Each Saturday evening, Threasa VanDaan would make popcorn, and call everyone inside, then she left for church. It was rosary night; she prayed, and Hans drank. Only as I grew older did I understand what Hans had in mind with his popcorn parties, and his deck of dirty cards. I learned to avoid those Saturdays, as we all did, eventually, but not before I had had my turn to fend off his groping hands or push away from the reeking, whiskeyed kisses that he foisted off on the girls. Sometimes Peter would try to stop him, usually by swearing, or calling his father a name. Then Hans would turn on his own son and backhand him hard across the side of the head. Finally, he punched Peter full in the face, knocked him out cold, and broke his nose. After that, Threasa quit going to Rosary, and the kids quit going to popcorn.

So here stood Peter, staring at me.

"You did it, you know." He looked at me, and I could see a new look in his eyes. He was calculating; his mind ground out the plan behind the pupils of his eyes and I watched the primal flickerings of power.

"You owe me. You owe Billy and me."

One side of his mouth pulled up in the same half smile his father wore when he moved toward one of the girls.

"We'll be in the shack after supper. Be there." He turned and walked up the cinder lane behind Mannings', skirted the empty lot, cut across his back yard and disappeared through the door of his house.

THE BOOK HOUSE

At six o'clock I went to the shack. I would not have thought not to go; it was the way it was. Bill and Peter were already there when I stepped in. The two boys were sitting across from each other on the wooden floor.

Billy was now looking up at me with his green eyes. He had high, angular cheekbones, and his straight, fine cut nose seemed to sniff the air like a fox. He had eyes that saw beyond the other boys, and when he spoke he always looked straight into my own. I had known Billy first, and longest. He was older than the rest of us, and quiet, and he took great care of everything he owned. When we were young we used to play for hours in the sand of the construction sites, bulldozing roads, digging tunnels, and lining up row upon row of marbles in battalions, regiments, and squads. We ferried them across bridges made of leftover lumber from my father's shop, or loaded them into the dozens of small metal army trucks he collected in growing numbers and kept in stacks of shoe boxes in his room.

Billy Laitonen was Finnish, and he knew every star in the sky. He told me once that in Finland everyone looked at the stars, thus we came to lie on our backs on top of Cote's hill and watch them pop out of the sky while Billy named them one by one. I remember the names to this day. On afternoons when the sky was filled with fat, moving clouds, we would lie on our backs on the sweet smelling, fresh cut grass and find the shapes hidden in the cottony white blobs as they formed and reformed above our eyes.

Billy was like a visitor from somewhere else. Always looking up, or far away, he seemed as though he were looking for something that was lost to him. And like I said, he had a habit of looking right into a person as though he thought he might find it there, but all this came to an abrupt end. My grandmother found us lying on the grass and sent him away. He was strange, I was told. Not right in the head. After that, Billy just watched me from his yard, and I missed him. Only in the dark, in the chase, did he come to me again. In small, intense, groping sections torn out of the black night, he made hesitant, magic introductions, mystic, and unreal. Thus they were acceptable because I knew he came from a place beyond that which I knew, and retreated like the distant stars before dawn.

Now he just sat there, observing.

Peter VanDaan stood, hunched to accommodate the low pitched roof of the shack. He moved into the center where he could draw up to full height.

"This time you're not getting out of it."

I knew what he meant.

"The last time you ran. This time you're not running anywhere." He grinned a malevolent grin. Billy watched me with burning eyes.

It had been in the fall, shortly after school had begun. The days had been warm, and on one particular Saturday there was a full blown Indian Summer. It was hot, and bright, and beautiful, pungent with the smell of the piles of coloured leaves we rolled in and stuffed down each other's shirts, coughing in the leafy dust and itching from head to toe. Shirts were torn off, and shaken out; Josephine and I had pulled our blouses out from the belted jeans and shook them from the bottom.

"C'mon inside, I'll give you a look." Peter had said. He stood in the door of the shack, his shirt in his hand, his belt loosened, and his fly partially down. "What's the matter? 'Ya chicken? Wanna go first?"

"Try for a match!" roared Gerald, and rolled on the ground in a fit of laughter.

"You only have to show to her, Laity," VanDaan snickered at Bill, "you already seen your sister!" Peter leered at Josephine.

"We never seen hers," Gerald howled, prancing around Josephine with his two hands cupped and framing his eyes like binoculars. He darted in close to Josie, bent over, with his binoculared face lunging at her crotch.

"You sicko," Josephine hissed. "We're going in."

"Make us something to eat," Phillip chimed in, his blue eyes agog; "Bring it out."

"Go get your own lunch," Josephine snapped, and marched in the back door of her house.

THE BOOK HOUSE

I always trailed along. In those days homes were interchangeable; the doors were never locked, and even a kid was treated like a guest.

The Laitonen kitchen was spacious and airy. The sink beneath the window was always clean, and the sun shone in brightly. Eva Laitonen, thin, and bony, stood at the drain board. She was singeing the last few pinfeathers from one of the hens she and her husband raised in a coop in the far back yard. The long neck of the dead fowl stretched into the sink, still dripping an occasional drop of blood. Josephine took the mayonnaise out of the refrigerator, and some cheese, and we made two sandwiches. The telephone rang; Eva wiped her hands and left the room.

"We can get them, you know," Josephine said, smugly. "We'll take them out some lunch. Then we'll set them up." She started to laugh a strange, bitter laugh, more to herself than to me.

We made the lunch and went out to the shack.

The boys were sitting idly, bored. It was easy to make a deal, and like Josephine said, they fell for it. The lunch was the key to it all.

The boys had to go first.

Now, they trooped out of the singular door in the end of the shack, ecstatic, sandwiches in hand, mouths full, eyes bulging. and waited while we took our place. Josephine and I moved to the narrow bench at the far end of the shack.

"We're ready!" She called out to them.

"Who goes first?" A voice called back, and there was laughter behind it.

"Phillip!", Josephine called back, and with that Phillip stepped into the shack.

I remember sitting on the narrow board that served as the singular bench. The inside of the shack was semi-dark; the only light was that which came through the door, or squeezed through the cracks between the irregular grey boards that were nailed in parallel up the sides.

Now Phillip stood before us.

It was rather like show and tell at school, only Phillip didn't talk. He unzipped his jeans and lifted his penis from his printed shorts without saying a word, while we sat there staring. It was small, pale and insignificant, like Phillip was. He turned on his heel and left.

VanDaan was next, and he pranced through the door like a mincing satyr, his penis and testicles flopping in his two hands as he danced and thrust his pelvis to and fro. He was uncircumcised; I didn't know the name of the procedure at the time, but after that day I knew he was different from the other boys.

Billy was last. He walked straight in the door, showed himself, and walked out.

"All right!", VanDaan squealed with excitement, and followed that up with an ear-shattering chimpanzee howl. "Your turn, ladies," he evinced, sticking his head in under the door frame, and raising his eyebrows rapidly up and down.

Josie was in full control.

"Get in." She motioned with her head to the back of the shack where we were sitting. Peter and Phillip crowded through the door, struggling with each other to get in. "Move!", she hissed to me, and grabbing my shirt, yanked me toward her.

"Sit there!" She pointed the boys to the bench, while flattening herself against the wall of the shack. Peter dove for the grey board and stretched out with his knees bent in the middle. Phillip batted the legs down and plopped down beside him, his own legs apart, arms dangling from shoulders, hands dangling at the wrists, all between his outspread knees. Billy stood in the doorway and watched.

"Get in, Bill," his sister commanded. "All of you. On the bench."

Bill took a seat on the bench, and the three of them stared straight ahead.

This was it.

"We're going out, and then we're coming in dancing." Josie paused, hands on hips, to see if the message was clear. "No looking until we start to clap, understand?" Another pause. "Now close your eyes." The three boys closed their eyes. By this time VanDaan's left leg was bouncing up and down, drumming out a nervous patter on the floor.

THE BOOK HOUSE

"Now sit there and don't move, and don't look until the signal. We have to set up our dance, and if you look, we're gone, and so is the rest of the lunch." Josie shot out the orders like a drill sergeant as she ducked out the door, leaving the three boys pressed upright to the far wall of the shack.

"Now, don't move!" She hollered toward the shack door once again, and with that she tore at my arm and all but yanked me off my feet. We headed for the house, locked ourselves in her bedroom, fell on the bed, and regaled ourselves with successive fits of laughter.

The boys sat out there for what seemed like ages before we heard the back door open, and someone come in.

"Bitch!" I heard Billy's voice, a tight, low burst, outside the locked door of Josephine's room.

We hid out at home until the weekend. The only remnant of the flawed burlesque that remained sat on Josephine's lips in the form of a small, tight smile. On Saturday she left for camp; I watched her climb into her parents' car, watched it roll down the street, saw Josephine's cold face staring straight ahead as she passed by our house and disappeared.

Thing were different this time. This time it was me.

"*We*," said Peter, emphasizing the `we', "are going to play "House", he said, a wicked grin on his lips and his eyes sparkling with triumph, "and *You*," emphasizing the 'you', "are going to play *With* us, or *We* are going to *Tell* about the *Tree*!" And with that, even Bill began to smile.

The horror of Peter VanDaan hit me straight in the stomach. I felt it draw into a knot, as it has drawn into a knot ever since, in the face of unmitigated power. I felt as though I were not there; that only my feet were on the floor, my legs on top of my feet, my body balanced over the unmoving limbs, my arms hanging, my head, heavy on my neck. I had drawn up into a tiny ball to sit behind my eyes where I strained to see what I was confronting in the shape of the two boys.

But there was no one there. In the place where VanDaan had stood, there was, instead, a fat, red-headed boy with a stupid smirk, and strangely frightened eyes that his bold grin could not conceal. Behind him, Bill was no longer smiling. He looked straight into my eyes.

KAREN PIETKIEWICZ

I turned, ducked my head to clear the low door of the shack, and left.

There is something that calls to you when the dark comes; the twilight door to the night opens with soft, quiet sounds. The furtive shadow of the cat, the muffled bark of a restless dog awaken the animal heart of us, call us to secret things that beg to be explored. We watch the stalking cat with a different eye, listen for the sniffing dog, feel the damp, leftover heat diminish. We breathe deeply in the cooling air. If we remember to look up, we can watch the first star blink, and reappear, wait for Venus to rise above the treetops.

On that night I walked alone. Standing beneath the mountain ash on the segmented sidewalk that led to his house, I waited for Billy.

He came, as I knew he would, appeared behind the screened door, stood for a moment on the enamelled porch, walked down the steps to my side. Without a word, we moved up the yard to the waiting tree.

It was pitiful. Bound and taped, propped with two-by-fours and wrapped with pitch covered rags and sheets, the tree stood like a poorly embalmed corpse, its withering fruits no longer red, its leaves no longer green. In the fading light it wore a grey-brown pall over its drooping limbs as though it had wearied of the charade and longed for the mercy of the quick axe, the dissolution of the cleansing fire.

Now Billy walked directly across the shimmering grass and stood beside the berry-laden, tumbling bushes at the side of the house. The plethora of tiny white globes hung like a cosmos of miniature moons; in each was reflected the silver goddess of the night sky as she moved silently across the heavens.

As I watched him, he quietly turned to me, and with a deliberate gesture stretched out his arm toward where I stood, his hand, asking, palm up.

Who can remember the secrets of the summer nights? I recall only the dream, a sidewise glint of light on bone, awkward gropings in the nested dark. I could not see his eyes.

After that summer I read the entire Book House. Curled in the cracked leather chair beside the shelved glass doors, I

THE BOOK HOUSE

was elevated in stature in my grandmother's eyes. She brought me cake and cookies. Her eyes sparkled. I had grown up, she smiled to Clement Bednard; too old to play with the boys, she told my mother.

I don't know what happened to Peter VanDaan. I heard he grew up, married, lived well, died early. I suppose, for Phillip, the strappings went on until they called him Phil. He just disappeared.

I never spoke to Billy again. I often saw him watching me from his window, and now and then, when he was raking leaves, or working in the yard, he would look at me with that same look, before he turned away.

It has been a long time since I read about *Rapunzel* and her tumbling braids. All I remembered for ages was the tower, and Mother Gothel, who locked her up. I forgot about the Prince and eventually I forgot about Billy.

Years later, toward the end of the Korean war, he dropped me a line, right out of the blue. He had been stationed in Eniwitok, and married a native girl, but she died.

Those were the days when people came home for the holidays. In December Billy returned to town. We had agreed by mail to meet, but he forgot to call, and when he came to the house I was out. Later, I sat around the whole day waiting. I remember thinking about Rapunzel sitting around in her tumble down shack; I even thumbed through the Book House for Auld Lang Syne. That was when I remembered there had even been a Prince, and that he had finally come for his princess.

About Billy? I never knew for years he had even showed up. By the time I found out, I had forgotten all about him. But not my grandmother. Even in her seventies she could still see Billy and me lying together on the grass. When he showed up at the door that long ago day she had sent him packing a second time. I never saw him again.

* * *

Mr. Brown's Legacy

It was a sultry day. Katherine lay morosely on the old daybed in the sunporch while the sun filtered through the slits in the bamboo shade, seeking her hot sticky body.

Nothing would make the sun go away. Katherine thought back to the cold winter. But it was too cold, too long. In the spring, it was not yet warm, and it rained, In the fall it was nice, but summer was gone then. It was all stupid. Everything was stupid. Katherine hated herself and her stupid thoughts for an intense moment, then she jumped up and went into the house.

Everyone was gone. Even Carol. Carol was Katherine's aunt. She liked to dust things. It seemed to Katherine that Carol was always dusting: picking up lamps and doilies, and dusting. Sometimes Katherine would watch Carol dusting. The piano made funny sounds. Pudink . . . pudink . . . pudink . . . pudank . . . pudunk . . . pudonk. Then it was clean.

Aunt Carol was a careful, mindful person. She was like a butterfly caught in the tool shed. Katherine could always feel the funny sadness that hung about Aunt Carol when she dusted. It seemed to her that somewhere deep within, behind Aunt Carol's painful brown eyes lay a suffering thing that hated the dusty tables. But it never got out. And Aunt Carol always returned to dust the room again. Pudink . . . pudank . . . pudonk. It was all so stupid.

It was cooler in the kitchen. Katherine walked over to the Frigidaire and opened the heavy door. There were always the same things: milk, and juice, and eggs, and bits of leftover salad in odd bowls covered with saucers or wax paper. Katherine lifted the lids, searching for something to fill the annoying emptiness she felt. She found a bowl of fruit cocktail and took it to the table.

Katherine liked fruit cocktail. She looked at the chunks of fruit in the yellow bowl. There were two cherries. Halves of cherries. When you opened the can, the cherries were always near the top. Maybe they were lighter. And there were the gooseberries again. There were always more gooseberries than cherries. It was peculiar. Katherine stared at the fruits swimming in the heavy syrup. She knew vaguely what is was with the cherries. They were red and bright; prettier that the other fruits, and there were few to a can. She liked their taste.

It was different with the gooseberries. They were exotic fruits from far away. One day she had asked her grandmother about gooseberries. Gram knew everything. She said that the gooseberries grew in Oregon. Katherine tried to picture the gooseberries growing on a bush, but something about them escaped her. Only the feeling remained. She scooped a gooseberry out of the bowl. It looked like a pale, small green onion. But gooseberries had a nothing taste.

She put the gooseberry into her mouth. But now the peach flavour overwhelmed it. Katherine became annoyed. She sucked it gently, rolling it around between her tongue and the roof of her mouth to clean off the peachy syrup. Now she could feel its roundness. But she could not taste it. It was maddening.

She determined to taste the gooseberry; she pressed it close against the forward roof of her mouth, and began to squeeze: harder, and still harder, pressing slowly, deliberately, until it burst suddenly and she swallowed it.

MR. BROWN'S LEGACY

Katherine sat quite still. It had no taste. It was inside her now: just like all the gooseberries she had eaten before. And all of them had no taste.

Katherine went to bed early that night. The rain had finally come: hot, bursting torrents that softened to a soothing patter on the dormer roof beneath which she lay listening. She liked the rain. There were different kinds of rain: drippy, tired rain that fell from indifferent grey skies on long, nothing days; and cold driving rains that came and went quickly, splitting the summer into sections like an orange. Then there were the heavy, spattering sunshowers beating with fat black drops on the grey sidewalks, leaving the air charged with the scent of ozone.

But it was the bursting, flooding rains that Katherine loved. They came always after the hottest days, rumbling over the edge of the sky shooting out sharp, reaching bolts, and driving the remaining day over the darkening horizon.

It had been just such a rain: and now, Katherine felt relieved, as though an invisible burden had been lifted from her; one that she did not even know she carried until it was gone.

She fell into a dreamless sleep.

The next day was Monday. It was a vibrant day: washed and clean, and electric with promise. The radio blared out its early day jabber, punctuated with morning-type songs. Katherine sipped her milk slowly. She let it trickle down her throat. Across the kitchen, the baby batted his spoon on the metallic tray of his high chair. Katherine looked at the baby and loved him. Some day she would have a baby. She sipped again at her milk.

Now she concentrated intently on the milk. She could feel it travelling like a white river down her throat and into her chest. Then it branched, subtly, surely, as a forked stick, and slid silently to each waiting breast. She drank again. She must drink more milk now. She would need it soon.

KAREN PIETKIEWICZ

The mailman came. Katherine put her dishes absently in the sink. The obituary announcement program began to drone out its sudden music. The announcer came on, and said in a solemn voice, "There are no announcements today." It was stupid. All that music and no one dies. Katherine went out, disgusted.

There were no magazines in the mail. Katherine walked out to the sidewalk and stood examining the day. Across the street, Mrs. Greco was sweeping the walk. Katherine watched her. They said Mrs. Greco had a withered hand; Katherine looked intently. From the distance between herself and Mrs. Greco she could not observe any difference, but that was probably because Mrs. Greco was smart. In all her life she never let it show. When she shopped, she covered it with her purse. When she cooked, she covered it with her apron. It was always covered. Katherine had never seen the hand. Mrs. Greco had never made a mistake as long as Katherine could remember. For all the times Katherine had tried to see it, it had never once appeared.

Florie came out. Katherine began to walk toward her.

"Where're ya goin'?"

"Over to Gramma's."

The two girls walked in silence.

Old Mrs. Brown was in the side pantry baking pies. The side board was white with flour and bits of dough stuck to the glass roller.

Katherine liked to watch Gramma Brown bake. She used walnut shells and eggshells to measure out things. To Katherine, there was a lovely pleasantness about Gramma Brown, especially when she was in her kitchen. When she stood, her long arms hung out from her sides as though she was waiting for something to do next. She was always working.

Feet shuffled behind the girls. Katherine moved instinctively to one side. It was Mr. Brown. Now Mrs. Brown began to hurry back and forth to the table where the white-haired old man had taken his place. He unfolded his paper and began to read. Then, as an apparent afterthought, he set the

MR. BROWN'S LEGACY

paper aside and put on his glasses. The coffee was passed, and Gramma Brown returned to her pies as the old man began to eat.

Katherine was afraid of Mr. Brown, but not like she was when a strange dog chased out at her. Nor did she fear him in the same way that she feared Mrs. LaPlaunte at school. She knew Mr. Brown would never hurt her. For that matter, he hardly seemed to notice that she was around.

That was it: that was it exactly. He knew very well she was there, but he never let it show.

"Let's go swing." Florie moved toward the front room, which led out into the sunporch, and Katherine followed without reply.

The Browns' sunporch was a pleasant place. It had a particular smell: warm and comfortable, a bit old fashioned. By the door there was an old wooden chest with rope handles. It was painted brown, and was covered with an old linen scarf, upon which was stacked a pile of old magazines. They were mostly National Geographics and Reader's Digests, with an occasional Atlantic Monthly that had made its way from Mr. Brown's study out to the sunporch. The girls each selected a magazine and began to swing, reading, and pushing in unconscious unison against the old overstuffed chair that stood in front of them.

Katherine thumbed through the old magazine. The National Geographic was her favourite of all the magazines she knew. But this one was old: she had read it two, or even three times before. She got off the swing and went to the stack of magazines. They were all the same. She had read them all before.

Florie got up suddenly.

"I'm going home."

"Let's go down the basement and get some more." Katherine could picture the rows and rows of yellow magazines lined neatly on the three long shelves that ran across the end of Mr. Brown's basement.

"You go."

Florie left.

Katherine watched her disappear across the street, her long braids hanging neatly down her back. There was something perplexing about Florie, something cold and empty. She seemed at times almost cruel. Her father was like that too. Katherine thought back to the Sunday when Florie's father had deliberately showered her with water from the garden hose. It had made great spots of wet on her church dress, and he had laughed.

Now she thought of Florie's father. He had black, glittering eyes and long, heavy teeth that smiled cruelly. They were yellowed and stained from the cigarettes he forever smoked, and he seemed always to slink about in the darkest corners of the garage, doing nothing.

Florie's whole family was weird. Katherine thought of the old couple inside the house. They were peculiar too. But they were not cruel. Katherine became intrigued with the new thing that had come to occupy her mind. She wondered about the cruelness that she could see seeping out through the chinks in Florie's family.

One day she had been listening to her mother talk on the telephone. She had been talking about Bill. Bill was Florie's father. After she got off the phone, Katherine asked why *Bill* was so mean. Her mother had answered that *Mister* Titus was an orphan. Katherine thought again about old Mr. Brown. He was cold and distant too. Mr. Titus and Mr. Brown were very much alike in certain ways. Except for one thing. Mr. Brown was not cruel.

Katherine thought for a long minute. Then she decided: Florie's father was cruel because he wanted to be cruel. And furthermore, he liked it.

Katherine went out quietly from the porch and pulled the door closed behind her. It was warmer now; only the great spreading elm protected her from the mounting sun. She stood on the narrow, pitted walk that led off to the driveway. Great clusters of lavender and white phlox drooped over the cement, hanging their heads like disillusioned children grown old too soon. Katherine looked at the phlox. She thought of the great sweet phlox that clustered in her grandmother's garden, and how she loved to pick a tiny floret and suck the nectar from the tiny orifice.

But there would be no use in picking one of these. She had done so before: the nectar was there but it was never sweet.

Now the feeling was back. Katherine sighed. The great, persistent gnawing inside her, the restless, infinite hunger of yesterday had come again. Katherine began to walk toward the corner. The mailman had just collected the mail and was adjusting his leather work sack over his shoulder. Katherine looked at him as he started across the street. She thought of Mr. Brown again, and of Florie's father. It was all too much. It was like drowning in the unusual dream that had been recurring to her more and more often lately in the heavy sleep before waking.

She remembered it all: she remembered the overwhelming death-fear that had gripped her when the dreams first began to come; how she had fought desperately in an agonizing struggle against the suffocating waters, and how she would finally lose, and die. And when she awoke, she would be filled with a sick, crushing feeling that lingered for many long minutes, before she realized that it had been a dream. It was like dying to make the morning come. As she thought these things the horrifying feeling began to retreat from her, but it would return; it was waiting in abeyance for she knew not what.

It was hot. Katherine could feel the hair at her temple sticking wetly to her face. She turned into the alley. The barberry bushes that grew along the rear section of the cornerhouse were sparse and dusty, and on the other side of the alley the old picket fence that had once been white was now silvered and grey with age.

She walked slowly, feeling the dust stick to her warm legs. She crossed over to the other side of the drive where the shelter of the tall bushes behind the Brown's house offered her some shade.

KAREN PIETKIEWICZ

Raspberries were growing there; they poked their wandering branches through the old wire fence and Katherine was about to pick one when she first noticed Mr. Brown.

He was working in the flowerbeds. He wore the clothes that had become, to Katherine, a very part of him. His striped shirt was rolled neatly just above his elbows and the collar lay open at the neck. He wore the same brown pants he seemed always to wear, held by neat, wide suspenders that crossed beneath a leather patch in the centre of his back. Katherine watched the elderly man as he worked; he seemed gentler when he was alone, and she felt almost like an intruder as she stood quietly behind the bushes.

Yet she knew it was still there: the impenetrable distance that seemed to separate him from the world, as distinctly as the hoe he held in his hands separated him from the feel of the warm black earth in the flower beds.

Katherine looked at the hoe as it pushed and poked among the rooted flowers. She thought suddenly of her grandmother: how she knelt deep in the rich soil and dug with her small pointed trowel, scooping the earth aside to place a fat tuber in its black bed, or how she pulled the weeds with her hands, throwing them into the old wheelbarrow as she crept through the flower filled beds. Hers was a beautiful garden: bright, blooming flowers, each glorious and bursting. And when she would get up, she would groan and strain, and say to Katherine, in a matter of fact voice, "Gramma's getting old, Katherine, Gramma's getting old . . ." Then she would stand there for a minute with her brown stockings rolled in fat rings above her stiff old knees and look at the work she had done.

Katherine looked sadly at old Mr. Brown. His was not a pretty garden. It seemed to be forlornly waiting for something that would never come, like an old dog whose master moved away. And though the flowers bloomed, they came always late in the spring, and left with the first frost; having fulfilled their duty, they were glad to be gone.

Mr. Brown moved closer. It was time to leave. Katherine felt as though she had been watching far too long. She began to edge her way quickly across the sparse strip of grass bor-

MR. BROWN'S LEGACY

dering the alley until she reached the corner of Greco's garage. She looked one more time at the silent figure of the old man as he prodded beneath the flowers with his long hoe. Then she turned and ran away.

It was hot all week. Saturday passed quickly, filled with noise of lawnmowers and car doors closing. By Sunday noon the neighbourhood was deserted and Katherine was left alone. It was a picnic kind of Sunday, and Katherine's family was going too. Only it would have to be later; the baby was still napping.

Katherine walked over to Brown's. It was safe now. They were gone. Every Sunday they went for a ride. The garage door was open and empty of the familiar old car that waited with the rest of the Browns for Sunday to come.

A bed of blue bumblebee flowers stretched along the house to the side of the garage and Katherine walked back along the gravel drive toward the back of the house, looking for a bee. She came to the old cellar entrance just off the end if the drive.

It had always been there. It stood open to the outside, and if it had ever had a door, Katherine could not remember. It led downward by a narrow set of damp cement steps, and the cold, tunnel-like chamber was sticky with old spider webs. Katherine stood before the door. And as she looked down into the dim opening before her, she began to feel growing within her a pressing, pushing compulsion to go down into the musty coolness. The longer she stood, the more mysterious became the dank and mossy stairwell, and the more she desired to know what lay at the foot of it. She ducked her head and went in.

She was going. Now, all her thoughts were concentrated on her probing feet as she tapped them out before her in the darkening stairwell. She felt with her hands along the damp walls. There would be spiders. Katherine thought of the trembling daddy-long-

legs that spread their thread-like, reaching legs out beneath their perched round bodies. She dismissed the spiders from her mind.

She continued slowly down the steps until she stood at the last at the bottom. Now she looked back up the narrow steps, staring at the bright sun that could no longer reach her. Then she turned to face the wooden door that was set in the wall before which she stood: the door she had always known would be there, and she lifted the latch.

It was the workroom. But then she knew it would be. Through the dim light that filtered through the dusty side window she could see the metal shoe stand where old Mr. Brown had repaired half the neighbourhood shoes for many long years. There were tools here and there on the wooden bench, still lying where he had set them. The workshop was sectioned off from the rest of the basement by the shelved walls that were filled with more National Geographics than Katherine had ever seen. The three rows on the other side of the wall, she now realized, were simply later additions to the hundreds that filled the small workshop, and for which there was no more room. She felt at home in the small room, and the propriety of her being there was an issue over which she was quite unconcerned.

She began to pull out the magazines, selecting at random, and surveying the covers for interesting subjects. They were hard to reinsert; the bookshelves were filled to capacity. Finally, after trying unsuccessfully to replace one of the magazines, Katherine removed a stack of five, to which she added the other and was about to replace them all when she saw the box.

It sat on its side, flush against the back wall behind where she had removed the magazines. It was an old cigar box, and it was held shut by a small bent nail.

Katherine felt a thrill, as though the box was part of an immense other world and she was its discoverer. And although she knew she would look in the box, her hand still moved slowly back to the wall before it closed on the box and pulled it out.

It was quite light. Katherine took the box over to the workbench where she turned aside the finishing nail that was bent over the lid, and opened it.

MR. BROWN'S LEGACY

She stood looking at the opened box. On the bottom lay a carved wooden figure, and beside it lay a folded piece of paper, quite frayed, as though it had been folded and refolded many times. She reached in and picked up the figure.

It was a brown wooden form of a girl; she looked very poor, and she was very pregnant. Her hair hung in long tatters down her shoulders and her dress stretched tightly over the huge bulge that was her stomach, making creased lines that were carved in ripples on the wood. Her dress was shorter in the front, and she had her hands clasped childishly behind her back. She was barefoot, and stood on a small mound made out to look like grass. Katherine looked at the odd little figure, then she set it on the workbench and reached for the folded piece of paper.

She knew immediately what the paper meant. It was covered with ink drawings of pairs of feet. One set was bigger than the other, and they were Doing It.

Katherine laid the paper, open, on the bench beside the box. She looked at the form of the pregnant girl, and then on the paper covered with outlined feet. They were his. The carved figure and the footprinted paper belonged to Mr. Brown.

She refolded the paper carefully. Then, replacing the pregnant, wooden girl in the cigar box, she closed and hooked the lid. She set the box back in its hiding place, carefully replacing the magazines as they had been before. And opening the wooden door quickly, she went back out and into the daylight above.

It was almost two weeks before she saw Mr. Brown again. He was out by the side of the house watering the grass. He had been sick.

Mr. Brown got sick often now. Katherine knew that it was because of his age. He would probably die soon. As the summer passed, Katherine saw him outside less often; instead, he sat in the old armchair in the sunporch and stared out through the window.

It became a ritual with her: each morning she would watch the sunporch across the street until suddenly he was

KAREN PIETKIEWICZ

there. Now Katherine thought often of the box. She thought of Mr. Brown and Mrs. Brown. She thought of the small, bulging wooden figure, and the rows of feet. Mr. Brown Did It. And he Did It with Mrs. Brown. It was stupid. She knew they Did It. Everyone Did It when they were married. Or else you wouldn't have babies. Katherine was disgusted with herself. But still, the thought remained. Somehow, for all her knowing, something was eluding her.

Now she tried to picture Mr. Brown Doing It. But she could not.

One day in mid-August, Mr. Brown did not appear. Katherine felt sad and lonely as she looked at the empty sunporch. The familiar, white-haired figure had become a part of her during the long, slow summer, and it was surprising to see him gone.

Katherine crossed the street and cut through the Grecos' back yard. Then she walked up the alley to Mr. Brown's garage. She walked lightly alongside the sagging structure and up to the old cellar entrance. Then, looking around quickly, she slipped under the doorway and down the cellar steps.

It was still there. Katherine felt cold, and prickly. Upstairs, she could hear Mrs. Brown in the kitchen, walking back and forth. She opened the box quickly. Laying the statue aside on the cellar floor, she opened the paper again.

Now Katherine looked intently at the paper. She tried to imagine how Mr. Brown must have looked at the paper. She studied the rows of outlined feet. The paper was very worn. It must have been looked at many times. Mr. Brown liked to look at the paper.

Mr. Brown liked to Do. It.

It was almost funny. Now Katherine tried again to imagine Mr. Brown Doing It. She tried to picture him kissing Mrs. Brown. But all she could succeed in producing was the vivid image of him standing in the garden with his suspenders and striped shirt, in his brown suit, holding the long hoe.

MR. BROWN'S LEGACY

Katherine felt silly. She felt light-headed and it all seemed very, very funny. She looked at the paper again. Then she folded it and replaced it in the box. She picked up the captivating littlestatue and turned it in her hand. She ran her fingers over the bulging front of the wooden girl. Then, swiftly, she stuffed the statue in her pocket and put the box away.

No one was home when she got there, and Katherine was glad. She felt the queer lump pressing against her thigh as she went up the stairs to her room. She closed the door. Then, removing the statue from her pocket, she stood it on the window sill and lay down on her bed. Someday she would have a great bulge too. Katherine thought of Mr. Brown. Then she thought of Mrs. Brown. She tried to picture Mrs. Brown with a great bulge.

But now they were too old. Katherine wondered if you Did It when you were old. But suddenly, the idea no longer seemed important. She got up and took the statue off the sill. Then she placed it in the back corner of her clothes closet and went down the stairs.

Summer was almost over. Katherine forgot about the statue as the hot days of August crept by. She rarely looked for Mr. Brown, and on the few occasions that she saw him, he no longer seemed to interest her. Soon, she forgot him entirely.

Now she was busy preparing for school. She made trip after trip to the busy stores, and her dresser drawers were lined with new socks and underwear for school.

On the first day of September, Mr. Brown died.

Katherine had never been to a Protestant funeral. She dressed slowly. She would wear her new shoes. She knelt, and reached into the closet to retrieve the box, and as she did, she remembered once more the brown wooden girl.

Now she felt again the strange restless feeling that had been so long subdued. She reached into the corner and removed the statue. She knew it now: she was familiar with every crease and line around its stomach, every blade of grass carved around the small bare feet. She looked again at the pregnant girl. Then, dusting the wood with a corner of her bedspread, she put the statue into her new brown purse and snapped it shut.

The funeral was very sad. Poor old Mrs. Brown cried and cried, holding her white, laced-edged hanky in her large, veined hands, and wiping at her eyes until the hanky was a damp and wrinkled wad. Katherine had seen a dead person before. Mr. Brown was like the other one. It was the sameness about him that made Katherine sad. Dead people were dead people, no matter who they were. They were all the same. It was very sad.

After the funeral service, the cars lined up in a long procession and the people drove out to the great, rolling cemetery beside the river. Mr. Brown was in the large black hearse.

The ceremony did not take long. Katherine could not see: most of the adults slipped in front of her and she could only catch glimpses of the brown casket as it sat over the grave.

They lowered it into the ground. Now, one by one, the people walked around the grave, and as they did, each scooped a handful of soft earth and threw it gently into the dark, yawning hole.

Suddenly, Katherine was filled with horror, a great, welling horror. They were burying Mr. Brown. Mr. Brown of the workshop; Mr. Brown of the striped shirt; Mr. Brown of the sad, tired garden; Mr. Brown of the small wooden box.

And she knew what she must do.

People began to file toward the waiting line of cars. Katherine hung back further and further until the distance widened between her and the departing clusters. When she was finally alone, she took the wooden girl from her purse and looked at her one last time. Then she threw her into the grave and walked away.

* * *

Counting to Ten: Michael

She handed him a towel. A warmness came over her, a comfortableness. It was so nice, seemed so right, the easiness of them doing dishes. He made it seem nothing, the easy maleness about him a reassurance.

And afterwards they sang. He played her kind of stuff; the music came easy, naturally, and she felt the tensions and the dailyness drain out of her.

Threasa Bibby liked these evenings; such a change from the emptiness: a shower and cologne, the wet dew of roses, clean kids, drawn out sundowns, the clicketys of swaying bamboo chimes on the screened and candlelit sundeck, and him, there with her.

And Mike seemed glad to be with her. She would miss him when Sylvia and the kids came down. She enjoyed cooking for him if only because he was there. She could always count on him just after four, with his mirrored sunglasses and his drip-dry shirts, and always the cigar, but it never seemed quite so annoying with him. And she liked the way he bought food, so he wouldn't be sponging; liked the way he picked it out: a permanent-press, drip-dry hunter, but he still brought home the meat. There was something nice about it all.

KAREN PIETKIEWICZ

And Jack didn't care. It took the burden off him, made things easy for him. Lately he'd been just a blur anyhow: in and out, in and out. He looked like the world's most rising young man. But still, she could only picture him standing in the door, going out.

Mike finished the dishes while Threasa wiped up the counters. He went into the living room and lit up a cigar. Then he came back and stood in the doorway looking at her. He said, "I love you."

And now her days were fuzzy. Always the words, over and over, hanging between her and the laundry, her and the roses, her and the kids. "I love you". Just like that. No passion, no flowers, no dreams. Just, "I love you." A this-ness; an is-ness. Now Micheal had begun to call her every day, and Threasa began to look forward to the calls. They came in the afternoons, when the sun filtered through the drapes, and the icy-coolness of the air conditioner felt good after the hot outdoors. And she liked knowing he would come again at four.

For Michael was a reliable man. An engineer, he worked with Jack at the Boeing facilities; Threasa had first met him in Seattle when Michael Greenspan and his wife had dropped by, as scheduled, for a social visit on a Sunday afternoon.

It was a visit that inadvertently followed on the heels of the most horrendous debauch of Saturday night drunkenness Jack Bibby had ever indulged in. Returning in the wee hours of the night, he had demanded that Threasa prepare him a full meal. Enraged because there was no bread, he had pushed his wife out the door and down the steps of their mobile home, and into the November cold. Her hands and knees cut and scratched, her nightdress torn, Threasa had walked barefoot through the cold until she saw lights and signs of life. Knocking on the door, she had borrowed the necessary bread, fending off the inquiring look of the retired man who lived there, grateful only that he had stayed up watching TV.

She returned to chaos; her children were crying in their beds and the entire trailer had been trashed. Closets were

COUNTING TO TEN: MICHAEL

emptied, silverware strewn on the floor, her purse upended on the sofa. Jack had passed out face down on the living room floor. She had settled down the children and began the long chore of cleaning up, stepping over the inert body of her husband where he lay.

Three months later Jack was transferred. Threasa packed what belongings she was reluctant to ship with the mobile home, and she, Jack, and the children left for Louisiana. Jack had been among the first of his department to go.

Michael Greenspan followed six months later, but he came alone. And he had problems: his wife, Violet, like Threasa's husband Jack, drank inordinately. On one such day, Michael Greenspan had returned home to find her passed out, their two small children cold, crying, and trapped out on the third floor fire escape. The window through which the children had climbed had fallen, and had locked tight. It was a last straw for Mike, and as a result, he had placed his wife in an expensive clinic to dry out. The children were temporarily with his mother.

Now this had happened. Mike had said, "You take your kids, and I'll take my kids, and we'll take off out East and make a life together with our children." And there was no rush. He said, "Take your time". Each day he asked her, until she began to look forward to his asking her, until she began to feel that she *should* love him. He was worthy of loving.

At times like this, Threasa would imagine how he would react, how happy he would be. She could almost feel his joy. But at other times, regardless of his kindness, the consideration he showed her, his patient attentiveness to her children, she felt that things were not right. Something was missing. Something seemed to not to be there. Was it love? But what did that matter anymore. So what if it wasn't love: she already knew she didn't love him. Maybe it would come. Who was she to say it wouldn't, coming out of the mess she had made of her life, the total screw-up that was her own marriage? Back and forth she would go in her head between her marriage and the proposal Michael Greenspan had made to her. The fulcrum of her mind fixed on the welfare of her children, and then, on herself. Finally she decided. There would be plenty of time left for herself, after. The children needed a stable home. They needed a father, not a booze-bucket for a dad. She *should* love Mike Greenspan, and she *would*.

The phone rang. Now she would go to him. Try it out, like he said. See if things worked between them, before blowing everything up. She would meet him Tuesday, as he asked.

On Tuesday evening Threasa laid out her clothes on her bed, bathed slowly, carefully did her nails. She could not believe she was actually going to him. A peculiar feeling ran over her, a shiver of some primal energy at long last loosed. She felt the very being of it in her body as she put on her dress, felt it radiate as she combed her hair.

Now Threasa noticed how she looked in her dress. She looked sexy: sexy as she had made the dress to look, for the sexiness that was in her, and which now had a reason. Suddenly she became heavier, weighted with the knowledge of herself, of her sexiness, and conscious, oh so conscious, of how she walked, how she talked, of how she even breathed.

And as suddenly, all her casualness was gone. The self that she had known, which self moved easily and fluidly through the days, had been replaced by an awkward, self-conscious, heavy, and deliberate being who was trying casually to slip out for an evening of non-shopping while her sister, who had come to babysit, looked darkly upon her. And in spite of all her casualness, Threasa knew where she was going, and her sister knew where she was going and both of them knew that she was indeed, going.

He was there. God. What a relief. She could see his cigar winking and glowing, winking and glowing like a beacon. There was his white car with its drawn out and glassed over rear section waiting like a ship: waiting for her. She got in.

COUNTING TO TEN: MICHAEL

"Christ, it's nice to feel firm thighs!" Mike clamped his hand on her leg. She looked at his hand. It wasn't even lusty. It wasn't anything but a hand clamped onto a thigh. There was something clean about it, something honest. They drove in easy silence.

Threasa wasn't quite sure where they pulled off. It was over the bridge, by the river. And it was hot. Mike pulled in and parked beneath one of the big trees facing the water. He tried opening the windows but the bugs were wild. Then he climbed over the front seat and into the back section. It seemed rather cheap, but she followed. He pulled a pack of rubbers from his shirt pocket and set them where he could reach them, and then he took off his pants, and his shorts. But it was dark by then; Threasa noted that she couldn't see much, just something hanging. Mike reached for her wrist. "Come here, you!" She slid down beside him and he tucked a pillow under her head.

"God damn, you have a body!"

He reached up under her dress.

"I'd like to rip every shred of clothes right off you except it might be a little hard to explain when you got home," he snickered. That's what she liked about him. He was real, and he had that perverse wit about him.

"Christ, take those damn things off."

He snapped the leg of her underpants, then sat up and reached for the pack of rubbers. Threasa slipped out of her clothes, and suddenly felt tremendously bare and unprotected.

"Here, God-dammit, do something with this thing." Mike pressed a rolled prophylactic into her hand. He was talking rapidly now, and she thought oddly that if he were smoking, he'd really be puffing away.

There sat the thing in her hand. The moon had come out; Threasa held her hand up to the window, straining to see the condom. She had never really seen one before.

"I don't know how to work these things; we never use them." It came out so simply she wasn't even embarrassed.

"God damn Catholic women!" said Mike, sitting up, and shaking his head. Threasa didn't mind his chiding; there was something patient about it, and only the words were hard. He plopped himself down cross-legged in front of her, ripped open the foil, and handed her the slippery thing.

"Here. You do the honours and we'll kill two birds with one stone", he announced.

And then: why not? She reached for him.

"Plaaaay with it a minute, it won't go on like that," he announced, grimacing and drawing out all the a's.

She had noticed. Actually, it wasn't very big. Oh, well. Maybe it would get bigger. She hoped so. At least it was getting harder. She switched the rubber to her right hand, but it did not seem to want to go on.

"It won't work," she announced.

"Unroll it."

"What?"

"Unroll the god-damned thing. I hope you know you're driving me insane."

"I can't help it if it won't go on!" She started to laugh.

"Jesus, Jesus!"

He sat up.

"Gimmee the god-damned thing". He took it from her hand and unrolled it magically. It looked like a white rubber sombrero for an elf.

"There!" He stuck it in place, and lay back.

"*Now* unroll it!"

It still looked like a sombrero, only now it was stuck on an oversize clothespin. She started to laugh.

"God, but you're great for a guy's ego." Michael shook his head.

"I can't help it, it just strikes me funny. I told you, I never did this before."

"Jesus Christ, get down here!"

Suddenly he pulled her down and he was on her, kissing her face, her neck, gripping her breasts, her thighs, forcing his tongue between her teeth. And then he was saying it: open your legs, open your legs, and it wasn't a question and it wasn't a game. She circled her arms around his neck and buried her face in the side of the pillow and opened her legs

COUNTING TO TEN: MICHAEL

and he was there, jabbing and jabbing and jabbing, before he squealed and the jabbing stopped, and it was over.
   It never had gotten very big.

* * *

PRINTED BY
IMPRIMERIE D'ÉDITION MARQUIS
IN AUGUST 1995
MONTMAGNY (QUÉBEC)